MURDER MY NEIGHBOUR

MURDER MY NEIGHBOUR

An Ellie Quicke Mystery

Veronica Heley

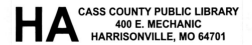

This first world edition published 2011
in Great Britain and in the USA by
SEVERN HOUSE PUBLISHERS LTD of
9–15 High Street, Sutton, Surrey, England, SM1 1DF.
Trade paperback edition first published
in Great Britain and the USA 2011 by
SEVERN HOUSE PUBLISHERS LTD

British Library Cataloguing in Publication Data

Heley, Veronica.
   Murder my neighbour. – (The Ellie Quicke mysteries)
   1. Quicke, Ellie (Fictitious character)–Fiction.
   2. Widows–Great Britain–Fiction. 3. Missing persons–
   Investigation–Fiction. 4. Detective and mystery stories.
   I. Title II. Series
   823.9'14-dc22

ISBN-13: 978-0-7278-8050-5   (cased)
ISBN-13: 978-1-84751-360-1   (trade paper)

All Severn House titles are printed on acid-free paper.

Severn House Publishers support The Forest Stewardship Council [FSC],
the leading international forest certification organisation. All our titles that
are printed on Greenpeace-approved FSC-certified paper carry the FSC logo.

MIX
Paper from
responsible sources
FSC
www.fsc.org   FSC® C018575

Typeset by Palimpsest Book Production Ltd.,
Falkirk, Stirlingshire, Scotland.
Printed and bound in Great Britain by
MPG Books Ltd., Bodmin, Cornwall.

ONE

It came naturally to Ellie Quicke to look after her family and friends, and she'd always thought, in her modest way, that she was rather good at it. But there were no easy answers to the problems of those around her, and one of these was about to get out of hand.

Monday morning

One shock followed another. Rose screamed and fell off the ladder.

Prompt on cue, the front doorbell rang.

First things first; Ellie rushed out into the garden only to find her dear friend and housekeeper lying on her back in a flower bed.

'Rose, what happened? Let me help you.'

Rose tried to get up and failed. 'Aargh! Just . . . minute.'

The doorbell rang again.

Ellie knew there was no one else around to answer the door, but Rose must be her first priority. 'Don't move.'

'I'm all right. Nothing broken.' Rose levered herself to a sitting position. 'Just . . . a minute.'

The doorbell rang again.

True, Rose didn't seem to have broken anything, but she was bleeding from some deep scratches, nursing one wrist and trembling. She held out her good hand for Ellie to help her to her feet.

'What on earth were you doing up the ladder? The gardener comes tomorrow.' It's natural to scold when you've been frightened.

'Tying back that rambling rose. Then I saw . . . and it gave me such a fright that I . . .' Rose gestured to where a neighbour's house could be glimpsed in the distance over the garden wall. 'A face . . . floating in mid-air at the top window.

Oh dear, I've wrecked some plants. I don't believe in ghosts, do you?'

No, Ellie didn't believe in ghosts, either. Of course she didn't. She helped Rose to the garden bench, and the doorbell rang again, this time with a longer, insistent peal.

'You see to the door. I'll be all right in a minute,' said Rose, who hated to make a fuss and would have said she was all right even if she'd broken her wrist – as looked likely.

Ellie dithered. If only her husband hadn't gone out early! But he had, and Ellie must decide what to do.

'Go on,' said Rose. 'Answer it.'

Ellie dashed back through the conservatory and into the hall to open the front door.

A strange young man pushed past her into the house. 'Took your time, didn't you? Mrs Quicke, please.'

Ellie put a hand to her throat to calm her breathing. 'I'm afraid this is a bad moment. Can you come back later?' Was that Rose crying out for help? From where she stood, Ellie could see the bench where she'd left Rose, but there was no little brown woman sitting on it. Did that mean Rose had got herself up off the seat and moved – where?

The newcomer danced around on his toes, eyes into everything. Hard eyes. A brutally short haircut, a single earring, piercings through lip and eyebrow which looked most uncomfortable. He was casually but expensively dressed.

'Done all right for herself now, eh? Change of fortune?'

Ellie blinked. 'Who are you and what do you want?'

'The name's Pryce. To see Mrs Quicke.'

'I'm Mrs Quicke, but I'm rather tied up at the moment. If you could call back later—'

Colour surged into his face. 'Don't waste my time!'

Ellie took half a step back. 'I'm not . . . Look; our housekeeper fell off a ladder just before you came and I'm afraid she may have broken something. I need to get her to the doctor's.'

He controlled himself with an effort. 'All right. Check her out if you must. I suppose I can wait a few minutes.'

Ellie looked back through the conservatory, but the garden was empty of all but sunshine and flowers – and their marauding cat Midge, stalking a butterfly. 'Rose, dear. Where are you?'

A faint voice came from inside the house. 'In the kitchen, Ellie.'

Ellie opened the door to the kitchen quarters. 'Rose, you shouldn't be—'

Down the corridor came Rose's voice, wobbling a bit, but not as faint as it had been when first she fell. 'I'm all right, having a little sit down. I'll make myself a cuppa in a minute.'

Ellie hovered. If Rose had got herself indoors and was convinced there was nothing broken, then she must be all right. Or almost all right. Perhaps she could be left to rest for a moment while Ellie got rid of the intruder . . . who had opened the door to the dining room and was looking in. How dare he!

Prioritize, Ellie. Get rid of the stranger. 'I can only give you a few minutes, Mr . . . er. I need to look after my friend. You wanted to speak to Mrs Quicke, and I'm Mrs Quicke. So how can I help you?'

'Don't give me that.' A sly twist to his lips. 'I know what Mrs Quicke looks like. My great-aunt told me. You're nothing like her.'

Ellie switched her eyes to the phone, because the man was clearly insane. She must call for help. Only, he was between her and the telephone, he was a lot bigger than her, and he projected an air of – well, almost of menace.

'I think you'd better go.' Oh dear, could he hear her voice tremble?

He barked out a laugh and moved along the hall to throw open the door to the sitting room. 'There's no point trying to hide her from me.'

If only Thomas hadn't had to go out today! If only it had been one of the days that the cleaning team came! Or their gardener. If only their sort-of adopted daughter hadn't gone out to meet a friend! Neither Ellie's part-time secretary nor any of her business colleagues were due to come in today.

Whatever was she to do? Had this horrible young man come to rob her? Incredibly, he walked into the sitting room and looked around him. Ellie had been about to tidy up in there when her difficult daughter Diana had arrived earlier that morning with news of her latest disaster . . . don't think about Diana now . . . and no sooner had Diana swept out than Rose had fallen off the ladder.

The young man said, 'All this must have cost a penny or two.'

Well, yes. Antique furniture, well polished. The summer breeze shifted the curtains at the French windows, stirring the petals of some peonies which had been placed in a cut-glass vase on an occasional table. There was a tasteful display of silver in the display cabinet, a square of Turkey carpet on polished floorboards, and gilt-framed paintings on the walls. The only modern notes were struck by Thomas's huge slimline television, stereo and La-Z-Boy chair.

The young man sat in Thomas's chair, swinging it around. 'I don't mind waiting but let me make myself clear: I'm not going till I've spoken to Mrs Quicke.'

Ellie told herself she wasn't prejudiced by young men who pierced their eyebrows and ears – though she wondered how he could manage to eat with a ring through his lower lip – but she did deplore his lack of manners. And it was quite unnecessary to be frightened. Wasn't it?

'As I said, I'm Mrs Quicke.'

He leant back in his chair, one leg crossed over the other. 'Oh, please! My great-aunt said she used to meet Mrs Quicke regularly, that she often picked her up from this house and gave her a lift to board meetings. She described her to me, so there really is no point your pretending to be her.'

'Ah.' Light dawned. 'You are referring to my aunt, Miss Quicke. She was indeed active in the world of finance. I'm sorry to say she died some months ago.'

That wiped the smile from his face. He sat upright, annoyed. 'But you are—'

'Her nephew's wife. Frank died some years ago and his aunt left me this house. I have remarried but I keep the Quicke family name.' She glanced at the clock – was that really the time? Was Rose coping all right? Even if she hadn't broken anything, it would be wise to get her checked out at the doctor's.

'But you know my great-aunt? Flavia Pryce with a "y". She lives over there.' He went to the French windows and pointed towards the multi-gabled mansion which could be glimpsed over Ellie's garden wall.

Ellie followed him. Yes, there was the attic window in which Rose swore she'd seen a face – which is why she'd fallen off the ladder. Although why she was on the ladder in the first place when they had a perfectly good gardener . . .

Ellie didn't believe in ghosts. Certainly not. Pure superstition. Whatever it was that had upset Rose, it had not been a ghost.

'I never knew the people in that house,' said Ellie, 'because it faces on to the next road. So far as I know, it's been empty for some time. I heard that the old lady who lived there—'

'My great-aunt, Flavia Pryce.'

'Left some time ago. I suppose I might well have seen her around but I can't put a face to her name. I only know she's gone because one of my cleaners used to work for her and told us about her cats being collected. At least, I think it was that house she was talking about, though I wasn't listening properly because I didn't know the lady. So I really must ask you to go.'

Why wouldn't this impertinent young man go away? Oh, if only Thomas hadn't had to go up to town today.

He couldn't seem to stand still for a minute. 'I suppose I shall have to ring the police.'

That caught her attention. 'Mm? Why?'

'I used to drop in to see her every now and then. All right, I missed a couple of months what with this and that, but when I last saw her she told me she was going to try out a retirement home. Naturally my dear Aunt Edwina was furious, because it was going to be expensive . . . Not that that matters, of course. It was Flavia's money to do what she liked with, wasn't it?'

He didn't sound impartial. Ellie wondered whether he'd visited Flavia because he'd liked her, or because he hoped for something from her will. 'Retirement homes can be costly, yes; but as you say, it was her money.'

'She told me she was putting the house on the market. She

said that when it was sold she'd let me have a little something to be going on with; I'm setting up in business with a friend—'

Ellie immediately found herself wondering if the 'friend' might be gay. She couldn't understand why that idea had popped into her head, and it wasn't at all like her to think such thoughts, but popped it had.

'And she gave me the address of the place she was moving to. So yesterday I went down to see her. It's not far away, very luxurious, all artificial flowers in the foyer and cleaners from Poland. They deny all knowledge of her.'

'I don't understand.'

'I made a fuss. Finally they trundled out the Paki who runs the place, and he said they had no one there by that name.'

Ellie was taken aback by his use of the word Paki. The sooner she got rid of this man, the better. 'So she didn't like it there and tried another one?'

'That's what I thought. But which one? I asked dear Edwina. She doesn't know. Bitter, she is, about it. Says she offered to have great-aunt live with her – which made me die laughing, to think of our grand lady Flavia slumming it with that sourpuss.'

'Well, someone must know.'

'That's it; but who? I went round to the house, and she's very much not there. I don't have a key but I've looked through all the windows downstairs at the front and the rooms are empty.'

Rose said she had seen someone – or something – at an upstairs window, which had caused her to fall off the ladder. Was that Flavia? But . . . why on earth should she be up in an attic? No, ridiculous.

'The house has been stripped of its furniture, the grounds are going to pot. So where is she?'

Ellie tried to think straight. 'At the home, of course. Only, for some reason, she told the people there that she didn't wish to see you.'

He kicked a low stool. 'If it had been Edwina, yes. Or anyone else from my ghastly family. But she doesn't mind me. I take her her favourite Liquorice Allsorts. She loves them. I've got the box in my car now.'

Ellie regarded him with disfavour. If she'd been his great-aunt, she wouldn't particularly have wished to see him either. He smelled rotten. Not dirty, but too much aftershave can be off-putting. And he was back to dancing around on his toes. Jittering. She seemed to remember her mother talking about 'jitterbugs'. Was that a kind of jive? Or had he – she tried not to smile at the thought – got 'ants in his pants'?

She said, 'Your aunt must be at the home. If for some reason she's moved on from there, they'll have a current address for her.'

'They said not.' He took out a pack of cigarettes and a disposable lighter.

'Please don't smoke in here.'

'Oh, keep your hair on.' He walked out through the French windows into the garden and lit up.

She followed him, seeing the garden ladder lying on the herbaceous border under the rambler which Rose had been trying to deal with. Catty-cornered to her garden were the spacious grounds of Flavia Pryce's multi-gabled house.

Her visitor was looking up at the big house, too. 'Great-aunt said Mrs Quicke hadn't a penny, was always asking her for lifts, but I see you've had this place done up nicely. Come into some money, have you?'

'Sort of.' It was too complicated to explain that Miss Quicke had been a miser who'd tried to make everyone believe she was a pauper, while sitting on a million or so of the readies and a lot of expensive rental property. It was only in the last couple of years of her life that Miss Quicke had had the house done up – and now it was Ellie's to maintain and enjoy.

He ground his half-smoked cigarettes into the lawn. 'The thing is that I'm in a bit of a fix. Flavia promised me some money, was going to let me have what she'd intended to leave me in her will. You see? And now, my sister's in a spot of bother, needs to leave her husband, but there's the kid and he's threatened her with everything if she leaves him. I said for her to go to the police, but she tried that once and they brushed her off, said she should go to some counselling service, you know? And then he beat her up . . .'

Ellie felt her eyes grow round. She was usually a sucker

for a sob story. Even her loving husband thought she was sometimes a trifle naive, taking everything people said at face value. But two sob stories were one too many, even for her. Besides which, this rigmarole sounded off-key. It was too pat, too easy. Too practised? Had he learned a case history off by heart, to trot out whenever he needed the sympathy vote?

He was still talking. 'So I said I'd rent a flat where we could all live together for a while, and I could look out for her.'

Except that he didn't look the selfless, caring type. He looked the type who'd kick a cat or a dog who got in his way, or laugh if an old woman fell off a ladder.

'But I must admit I can't at the moment lay my hands on enough money to make a down payment. I wouldn't ask if I weren't desperate . . .'

He was certainly desperate about something. There was a sheen of sweat on his forehead. The thought that he might be high on drugs came into her mind, which terrified her not a little. Everyone knew people on drugs were beyond reason.

She forced the words out. 'I'm sorry, I can't help you. Now, would you please go?'

'Oh, but you can. You have so much –' and here he swept his arm around to encompass the large garden and well-maintained house – 'and I have so little . . .'

'What, no job?'

He reddened. 'Well, of course. I'm deputy manager of the bedding department at a big department store, but I have outgoings, you know, the flat, the car. And the credit cards have been maxed out for months. I need a spot of help here.'

'Then go back to the retirement home and ask them nicely for your great-aunt's address.'

His eyes narrowed. 'I've tried that, and they won't play ball. Look, I'm sure you could write me a cheque for twenty thousand without turning a hair—'

'What!'

'Think of it as your charity for today. It would only be a loan, of course. Just till I can catch up with Flavia, and then I'd repay you. I could manage with a thousand for a starter, and the rest later.'

Ellie had inherited money and property both from her first husband and also from her aunt Drusilla, but she'd put the lot into a charitable trust which she administered for deserving cases. She didn't think her visitor qualified for assistance. 'Most certainly not!'

'You wouldn't even notice it. Five hundred? Surely you wouldn't condemn my sister to—'

Ellie realized she was trembling. 'I've asked you to leave once already. Will you please go. Now!'

He turned back to the French windows. 'No need to get your knickers in a twist. You attend to the ancient retainer and I'll see myself out.' He stood back to let her pass through the French windows in front of him.

'Yes. Well, thank you.' She felt limp with relief that he was going without harming her in any way.

The phone was ringing in the hall. They didn't have an extension in the sitting room, so she hurried through to take the call.

A pleasant man's voice, with undertones of anxiety. 'Ellie? Stewart here. I know I don't usually call in on a Monday, but—'

Oh, the relief. She was fond of her broad-shouldered, practical son-in-law, who managed her properties-to-let. Well, ex son-in-law, actually, but their relationship had survived her daughter Diana's dumping him for a series of dangerous liaisons. Don't think about Diana and her terrible news . . . or was that why he was ringing? Ah, but . . . Yes, he could well have heard what Diana wanted.

She said, 'Are you coming round, Stewart? I could do with—'

'If I may, yes. The thing is, I have little Frank with me. He hardly slept last night. Nightmares. We couldn't get him to go to school today.'

So Diana had spread the bad news around, had she? Oh dear. Frank was a lively little boy and perfectly happy living with his father, his sensible and loving stepmother, and the two little girls who adored their older half-brother.

Diana was supposed to have her son at weekends, and actually did so; occasionally. But she was not always wise in what

she said or did with him, and now and then he returned to his
father in a distressed state of mind.

Ellie said, 'Can you come straight away? The thing is, apart
from anything else – oh, not to worry, just a rather difficult
visitor, who is about to leave – no, it's not Diana, though I
suppose you'll have heard about . . . No, it's Rose. She fell
off a ladder in the garden and I need to get her to the doctor's.'

She lifted a hand to wave off the aforesaid difficult visitor
as he let himself out of the front door. He didn't close it
properly behind him – it needed a good strong pull in hot
weather – and it swung open again. Ellie edged forward, still
holding on to the phone as Stewart said he'd be with her in
less than ten.

As Ellie slammed the door shut, she caught a glimpse of
the Pryce boy driving off in a bright yellow car. Egg-yolk
yellow.

Oh well. At least he'd gone. She cradled the phone and
rushed out to check on Rose in the kitchen.

It was only much later in the day that Ellie discovered her
morning's visitor had helped himself to more than a few
minutes of her time.

Monday morning

*He parked the car in a quiet side road to inspect his haul.
The Kindle would fetch a penny or two, and if the diamonds
in the ring were genuine, it might be worth a couple of hundred.
The enamelled snuff box that he'd swiped from a side table
was pretty enough, probably eighteenth century, but very recognizable. Too recognizable to sell easily?*

*He almost wished he hadn't taken it, but there . . . He'd
picked it up and put it in his pocket without thinking clearly.*

*All in all, it might be enough to stave off the Leech for now.
And tomorrow he'd have another go at the retirement home.
They must know where she was!*

TWO

Rose was sitting at the big table, holding her elbow in a bowl of water. Midge the cat sat beside her, watching with interest as the water turned a gruesome pink. Rose had skinned her elbow and grazed her chin, but her eyes were bright enough, and she didn't seem sleepy so she probably hadn't suffered a concussion. Only, one wrist was swollen and the stocking on her right leg was in shreds, with bright stains on the skin beneath. She'd also lost one of her shoes.

'I ought never to have left you,' said Ellie, relieved that Rose hadn't gone off into a swoon but concerned about her swollen wrist. 'Stewart's on his way. We'll get you checked out at the doctor's. Did you make yourself a cup of tea?'

'Tell the truth, I didn't get as far as that. I could do with a cuppa, and no mistake. Who'd have thought I'd be so clumsy? But there, who'd have thought there'd be someone peeking down at me from that old house? I didn't imagine it, did I? Have I completely lost the plot, Ellie?'

'No, no,' said Ellie, running a clean cloth under the tap, wringing it out and placing it round Rose's wrist.

'Gave me such a fright! There ought to be a law.'

'Let me have a look at that elbow. And your leg? Ouch. Nasty. But we'll have you right as rain in a minute.'

The doorbell gave three short peals, and Stewart used his key to let himself into the house. Stewart was accustomed to report weekly – and sometimes oftener than that – to Ellie, so he had his own key to the house.

There was a rush of feet, and little Frank, all bony arms and legs, cannoned into Ellie and sent her flying back into a chair. He clung to her, burying his face in her shoulder, and wrapped his arms and legs around her. She folded her arms around him. 'There, there.'

Stewart followed his son into the kitchen, looking harassed. 'I'm sorry, Ellie. He's been in such a state that—'

'You did the right thing.' Ellie stroked Frank's hair, which was only now beginning to darken from the blonde of his father to the brunette – almost black – of his mother. 'There, there.'

Rose tried to get up. 'I'll just make us a pot of tea, shall I?' She collapsed back into her chair, ashen-faced.

Ellie said, 'Stewart, we have to get Rose to the doctor's. She fell off the ladder in the garden and I'm worried about her wrist.'

'We'll see to all that,' said Stewart, reliable as ever. 'Frank, you'll help us look after Rose, won't you? Once we've seen to her, we can talk about our other problem, right?'

Frank lifted his head from Ellie's shoulder. 'Mum can't just give me a new daddy, can she?'

'No,' said Stewart. 'I've told you already; she can't. Now, let's help Rose, shall we?'

Ellie managed to get Frank standing on his own two feet. 'That's the ticket, Frank. This is an emergency and we need you to help. First, can you find Rose's handbag for us, and then another pair of shoes for her to wear?'

He sniffed, but did as he was asked.

The doctor sent them to hospital for an X-ray. Rose didn't lose consciousness, but her colour was poor and she breathed as lightly as a bird. Ellie made a call on her mobile to Thomas only to find he wasn't picking up, so she left him a message to say they were having to wait at the hospital till Rose had been dealt with.

It transpired that nothing had been broken, thank God, but Rose had to have some stitches in the cut on her leg. Then they had to wait for a tetanus injection and painkillers from the pharmacy. Also for a sling. Rose was instructed to keep her wrist up for some days.

It was teatime before they got Rose back home, cleaned up and dosed with painkillers. Ellie helped her battered house-keeper to change her clothes and slip into bed for a rest with the television on and the sound turned down low. Rose had been dozing off every few minutes since leaving the hospital, and Ellie thought she'd probably fall asleep any minute. With any luck, there'd be no lasting ill effects from her tumble.

Frank put away four shortbread biscuits, a banana, two pieces of toast and butter, a chocolate bar and half a pint of milk, before declaring that he wanted to watch the telly with Rose. Curled up in an armchair beside her bed he, too, was fast asleep within minutes.

Ellie took stock of herself. There were smears of Rose's blood on her skirt, and she felt sticky and uncomfortable. She knew Stewart wanted to talk about Diana, but Ellie didn't feel up to it. 'Give me five minutes, Stewart. I need to wash and change. Then I'll make us some sandwiches and a cup of tea. All right?'

He nodded, big shoulders relaxing. 'Would you mind if I had a cup of coffee instead? I'll make it.'

'Make some for me while you're at it.'

Ellie hauled herself up the stairs to her bedroom and stepped out of the light summer dress she'd put on when she got up that morning before . . . before everything happened. She threw it into the laundry basket. The bloodstains might come out with a good soak, or she might have to have it cleaned, but for the moment she had more important things to think about.

She pulled on a pretty pink dress with a scalloped neckline and checked that it hung straight at the back. Nothing destroyed your poise quicker than finding the back of your skirt tucked up into your pants.

As she sought in vain for a lipstick – she did have one somewhere and it might give her morale a boost – she allowed herself to think about the forthcoming interview and what Stewart might have to say about Diana.

Ellie's daughter was not ageing well. Not as well as Ellie, who carried just a smidgeon too much weight to look fashionable, and who never bothered with make-up if she could help it, but whose prematurely silver hair curled prettily around her head, whose skin was still good, and who always looked as if she were on the point of smiling.

Diana, on the other hand, had lines of discontent and ambition etched into her skin, she wore her almost-black hair in a severe helmet and was so string bean thin that she could wear the most outrageous of today's fashions; provided they were in black, of course.

Diana had arrived early that morning, before Rose had fallen off the ladder and Ellie's life had become even more complicated than usual.

'Mother, I need you to help me out or I'll lose the agency and end up in the county court.'

'What?' Ellie had been on her way to the sitting room to tidy up, but this brought her up short. 'I can't believe . . . ! No, Diana. You're making it up.'

'I wish I were.'

'But . . . how?'

'The recession. Denis. Debts.'

Some time ago Diana had started an estate agency in partnership with a smarmy, steely-eyed estate agent called Denis. He had enthralled Diana, though Ellie had never liked him. He was now in prison awaiting trial for murdering a woman whose bank account he'd plundered.

Diana said, 'Since Denis left the agency –' and that was a neat way of putting it, wasn't it? – 'I've been struggling along on my own, trying to do the work of two. When we started, we signed an agreement saying that if one of us wants to leave the agency, the other has to buy them out. Denis needs the money to pay for his defence at the trial so he wants his pound of flesh.'

'You've got your own flat, and the house I made over to you. Take out a mortgage on them.'

A twitch of a black-clad shoulder. 'Been there, done that months ago. How else do you suppose I've been able to carry on for so long? I tell you, I'm going to lose the agency unless you can come up with the money to buy Denis out. And before you ask, all my credit cards are maxed out, and I haven't the wherewithal to pay them off.'

'Diana, you can't seriously think . . . ! How much?'

Diana told her, and Ellie sat down on the nearest chair with a bump. 'No way can I find you that sort of money.'

'But you will, mother dear; you will. Now, looking on the bright side, I've a new man in my life. He's prepared to absorb my little agency into his, provided I can pay Denis off. I suppose, if you're that grasping, you could make me a loan to be repaid some time in the future. I'll leave you to think over how you're going to find the money, and get back to you shortly.'

Diana left, slamming the front door behind her.

Troubles never came singly.

Rose screamed and fell off the ladder in the garden. The doorbell rang.

Ellie thought she might well be developing a headache. How on earth was she going to deal with Diana? And how much did Stewart know?

She brushed out her hair, abandoned the unsuccessful search for her lipstick and went downstairs to talk to Stewart. He had indeed made some excellent strong coffee, but seemed as little inclined to start talking about Diana as Ellie. While she busied herself making some sandwiches, he stirred the sugar round and round in its bowl.

He said, 'Rose said something about a ghost?'

Ellie handed him a bumper ham and tomato sandwich. 'She thought she saw a face at a window of an empty house. Some trick of the light, I suppose.'

Except that the Pryce boy had insisted something was wrong with his great-aunt, who had lived there.

Midge the cat appeared from nowhere and rubbed himself round her legs till she fed him. Midge believed in being fed on demand and usually got his own way. Like Diana. Ouch.

Stewart finished off the last bite of sandwich, replaced his empty mug on the table and took a deep, sighing breath. 'Diana.'

'Yes. She came round early this morning. What exactly did she tell you?'

He flexed his shoulders. 'She said I'd be glad to hear she had a new man in her life. Which I am. Especially after Denis dropped out, so to speak.' Stewart's lips twitched into a smile, and he felt the knuckles of one hand. He'd landed one heck of a wallop on Denis's jaw when he'd found out what that double-crossing slimeball had been up to. Good for Stewart.

His smile disappeared. 'She says her latest conquest will be a new "Daddy" for Frank. She's given notice to her tenants at the house you made over to her and says she plans to set

up home there with him and Frank. The last time she threatened Frank with a new "Daddy" it upset him terribly. He's
been getting on so well lately: gaining in confidence, school
work up to scratch, even trying out for the football team. Now
he's back to wetting the bed and having nightmares.'

Ellie was soothing. 'He's growing up. He can speak for
himself. The courts would never give him back to Diana against
his wishes.'

'Depends who the new man is. If he has money and can
offer Frank a private education, that might swing it.'

Well, it might at that. But Diana's record as a caring mother
was not impeccable. 'Did Diana say who her new man was?'

'She wouldn't give me a name. Did she tell you?'

Ellie shook her head. 'A man in the same line of business,
perhaps? But wouldn't he know her reputation? What would
he see in her?'

He'd see sex, of course. And if that's what he wanted from
Diana, then he wouldn't be the best possible stepfather for
Frank. He might even be younger than her. Oh dear. On the
other hand, an older man would surely have more sense than
to think he'd get companionship and loving care from Diana?

Ellie remembered something else Diana had said. 'She spoke
of a takeover by another, bigger estate agency. I wonder if the
new man is involved with that? Could you ask around?'

'There is a big estate agency in the Broadway which might
be interested in mopping up a small organization. I'll see what
I can discover.' He took their plates and mugs to the sink and
left them there while he looked out of the window. 'When she
brought Frank back last night, she asked me for a loan. A lot
of money. I was so surprised that I laughed, which made her
furious. She says she's in trouble at the agency, which I found
surprising. Despite the downturn in the economy the market
in London is buoyant, as there's never enough housing stock
to meet demand.'

He shook his head. 'She must be desperate to ask me for
money. Granted, I've never paid her alimony because she
wanted a clean break. She took half the proceeds from the
house we lived in when we divorced, while I had Frank.
She says I should take out a mortgage on my house now

and give her the money. I said, did she imagine we could have afforded to buy a three bedroom house in Ealing without taking out a mortgage in the first place? She says I should take out a second mortgage. I told her to get real. The thing is, having failed with me, Diana may try to hit on you instead.'

As indeed she had, and Ellie had absolutely no idea how she was going to deal with it. She rubbed her forehead. She was definitely getting a headache. 'Have you warned your dear wife about Diana's demand?'

'I tried, but one of the littlies had a tummy upset and that's partly why I brought Frank round. Do you think you could keep him here tonight? I'll have to tell her, of course, and I will as soon as I get back. We're – er – we're expecting another little one next spring. I expect you knew that?'

Ellie had guessed already, of course. 'I'm delighted, natur- ally. But how your dear wife can continue to work with two little ones round her knees, plus Frank and now another one to look after, I do not know.'

He laughed and sobered. 'She's a miracle, isn't she? She has some good staff now, thank goodness, and doesn't have to go in all day and every day. As for Diana, it's a constant surprise to me that one person can create so much havoc.' He looked at his watch. 'Where does the time go? I suppose that tomorrow it's back to the solicitor's and more interviews with Social Services, trying to persuade them it would be a disaster for Diana to have Frank to live with her again. You don't think she can get him, do you? I told him not, but she's so strong- willed that occasionally I . . . But talking to you makes it all so much clearer. Of course I'll fight to keep him. Thanks, Ellie.'

'I don't know what I've done to help, but I'm glad to hear you're not giving in. Of course Frank can stay tonight. His room's always ready for him here. Give your dear wife my love, and tell her I'll be over to see her and the babes again soon.'

She walked him to the front door. 'You don't know which estate agent is dealing with the Pryce house in the next road, do you? The big house, all turrets and gables?'

'Disneyland gone mad? I suspect some developer will demolish it and put up a block of flats instead. You wouldn't be interested in buying it, would you? It's not at all our kind of thing.'

She shook her head. 'No, no. Forget I asked. I'll be in touch, let you know how Frank is tomorrow morning.'

'And Rose. And is Thomas well? And the young girl you've been looking after? Is she feeling better now?'

'They're both fine. Mia is meeting an old school friend up in town today. They're planning a house share together.'

'That's good,' he said, looking at his watch, his mind moving ahead to what he had to do next. 'You've done wonders with her, but I expect it's time she moved away and got on with her life.'

Ellie shut the front door behind him and set her back to it.

Dear Lord, what a mess. Diana never looks where she's going, does she? All her life she's been showered with money that she hasn't earned, and it disappears like fairy gold as she handles it. I suppose Denis has the right to demand she buy him out. It would be quite wrong to ask my charity for money to help her out.

I want to run screaming away and never see her again, but I know I can't do that. I have to help her, somehow, don't I?

Dear Lord, you promised you wouldn't lay a burden on me that I can't bear. Tell me how to work this problem out. Please?

Ellie went back into the sitting room to finish the tidying-up she'd started early that morning. She picked up the newspapers which Thomas invariably spread around him on the floor and on any other surface to hand. She took an empty beer mug and a coffee cup out to the kitchen and put them in the dishwasher, together with the bits and pieces from the recent snacks. She filled the small watering can and took it back into the sitting room to fill up the vase in which the peonies stood and then . . .

And then she noticed that the pretty porcelain snuff box, which sat on the same table as the peonies, was no longer there.

Her ring! Her engagement ring, which was a trifle tight for her since she'd put on weight recently . . . She'd left it on the piecrust occasional table at the side of her chair by the fireplace. It wasn't there.

Thomas's much prized Kindle, which she'd bought him for

his birthday, and which he played with for hours. That wasn't where he'd left it, either.

In her mind's eye, she replayed the Pryce boy's visit. He'd held back to let her pass through the French windows into the house before him. She'd gone ahead of him into the hall because the phone had been ringing. She'd picked up the phone with her back to the boy. It had been Stewart, asking if he might come over.

She'd said yes. She hadn't been looking at her visitor as he left . . . picking up their valuables as he passed through the hall behind her. He'd not properly closed the front door behind him, which meant that she'd caught a glimpse of him driving off in a bright yellow car as she'd concluded her conversation with Stewart.

The boy had said he was desperate for money. She'd turned him down, and he'd taken his revenge on his way out. She felt for the arms of her chair and let herself down into it.

Dear Lord . . . this is all a bit much. I must ring the police.

Rose was always saying that worse things happen at sea. Well, yes. Possibly. But this was very bad.

There was a commotion in the hall.

'We're back!' That was Thomas, laughing, pleased to be home.

'We met at the station coming back, and it's great news! I'm moving out at the end of the month!' That was Mia's lighter voice. Mia had been so badly abused by her family that she'd thought she'd never laugh again, but some months of living with Ellie and Thomas, and of being cosseted by Rose, had worked a sea change in the girl, and she was now capable of leaving the house and even conducting business by herself. There were relapses, of course. But she was coming on a treat.

Thomas and Mia both sounded happy and fulfilled.

Ellie scolded herself to her feet. She even managed a smile as she threw open the door, only to be caught up in Mia's arms and waltzed around the hall. Mia's eyes were bright, there was a red rose in her dark curly hair, and altogether she looked ready to leave the nest – at last.

Giddy from being whirled around, Ellie ended up in Thomas's bear embrace. He was a big man who looked like a bearded sailor, but who had always been an academic – and

her own dear love. She clung to him, smiling. She could feel
laughter rumble through his chest as he picked her up off the
floor and gave her a socking great kiss.

'Oh, you!' She held on to his arms as he set her gently back
on to her feet.

Mia was on tiptoe, ready to fly off. 'I'm dying to tell Rose.'

'No!' said Ellie.

Thomas and Mia lost their smiles. 'What is it?'

Ellie hastened to explain. 'It's all right, not serious, but she
fell off the ladder in the garden this morning. Nothing broken,
but she's very shocked and she's resting now. Thomas, didn't
you pick up my message? I phoned from the hospital . . .'

He dived into his pockets. 'I must have left my mobile here.'

Oh, no. Had that been stolen as well?

Monday evening

*Curses on all thieving fences! Four hundred and fifty pounds
for the lot! He'd bet they were worth ten times that.*

Well, what was done, was done.

*Four fifty would go some way to keeping the Leech off his
back. A pity he hadn't lifted the old biddy's keys because he'd
go bail there were more trinkets lying around her house that
could do with a better home.*

*He hadn't left too many clues behind with her, had he? He'd
not given his first name. He hadn't told her where he lived, or
exactly where he worked. A pity he hadn't thought to park his
car outside in the road when he called on her, but he didn't think
she'd had a chance to see it, anyway. So he was quite safe.*

*Except that he still had to find some more money somehow
or other.*

*Which meant he was back to square one; where had Flavia
gone?*

THREE

Ellie needed to get rid of Mia, before she could tell Thomas what had happened.

'Mia, little Frank is in with Rose. He had a bad night. You'll want to make sure Rose is all right, but if she's asleep . . .'

'I won't disturb her.' Mia opened the door to the kitchen quarters and disappeared, closing it silently behind her.

Thomas put his arm around Ellie and urged her into the sitting room. 'Rose will be all right. She always bounces back.'

Thomas intended to reassure, but what he said wasn't quite true. Rose had become very frail after her beloved Miss Quicke died, and Ellie had feared they might lose her, too. However, Rose had rallied in the springtime and had been almost back to her old sprightly self recently . . . except for one mild eccentricity: she insisted she still occasionally saw and spoke with her previous employer.

Ellie wondered if Rose were now suffering from a more serious delusion. Someone spying on her from an attic window? The shock of falling off the ladder might easily have tipped her over the edge. But this was not the moment to explore that possibility.

'So, Thomas; how was your day?' She knew he'd been having problems with one of the contributors to the Christian magazine he edited.

'Better than yours, it seems.' He pulled her down on to the settee at his side. 'You can't fool me. Something's wrong. Why is Frank in with Rose, for a start?'

'Diana has a new man. She says he's going to be Frank's new daddy. Frank got upset, had nightmares. Stewart brought him over here, and he was a brave boy, helping us to look after Rose. Then he settled down to sleep beside her.'

That was the truth, but not the whole truth. Thomas knew her through and through. He knew that was not all she had to tell him, but she didn't know what she was going to say about the rest of Diana's news. If the girl owed so much money and also lost the agency, could she be forced into bankruptcy? Oh dear.

He teased her. 'You look like a little bird, a sparrow, all ruffled feathers.'

'I wish I felt like an eagle.'

'You want to kill someone?'

'Yes, I do. Rose was on a ladder in the garden, which she knows she shouldn't have been, and thought she saw something up at the top window of the house over the garden wall. She fell off the ladder, the doorbell rang and . . .' She told him about her caller's claim to be a great-nephew of Mrs Pryce's from the next road, his attempts to find her, his demand for money and Stewart's phone call – which had left the young man alone in the sitting room for a few all-important moments.

'I shouldn't have left him alone even for a second, but I did. Anyone with the sense of a peewit would have known he wasn't to be trusted. So it's all my fault.'

He looked around the room. 'He stole something? What?'

'Your Kindle. My birthday present to you.'

'What?' He half rose, then sank back into his seat. His eyes switched to and fro. She could see him brace himself. 'Well, that's not so terrible. It can be replaced. I had my favourite version of the Bible on it, but . . . don't look so tragic. Did he take my mobile, too? Now that really would be a nuisance, but—'

'I don't know. He might have done. I was just looking around, it's the first chance I've had to get in here all day. I noticed your Kindle was gone, and my engagement ring—'

He flushed with anger. 'Now that's more serious. I've been promising you I'd take it in to be altered for days. Serves me right for not doing it straight away. Well, it's insured. I suppose the Kindle is, too.'

'There's more. You know that pretty snuff box of Aunt Drusilla's that I found at the back of a drawer a couple of weeks ago? I'm sure it's worth a lot, but we've never had it valued. That's gone, too. It's as if he took the things which we love most: my ring, your Kindle, and Aunt's little box.'

'They're just things.' He put his arm around her and held her close. 'He didn't hurt you in any way?'

She tried to smile. 'Only in my pride.'

'Pride can be expensive. Lose it. And guilt. Have you phoned the police?'

'I've only just found out what he's done.'

'I'll ring them now, give them the details. They may need to speak to you, too, of course. What rotten luck.' He looked at the clock, hesitated. 'I'll have a search around here first, see if I can turn up my mobile. It may have dropped to the floor somewhere, or slipped behind a cushion.'

'Supper,' she said. 'Cold stuffs, I think. I was going to go out shopping but things happened. It's good about Mia finding a place of her own, isn't it?'

'Yes.' They both knew that Mia had been doing the bulk of the shopping and cooking lately, and that if Rose needed nursing and were to be out of the picture for a while, it would make things difficult for Ellie. He put his arm round Ellie's shoulders. 'We must see what we can do to help Mia move out.'

Ellie knew what he meant. She took a deep breath. 'We'll cope. Right?'

'Bless you, Ellie. Now, I'll have a hunt for my mobile and then ring the police.'

Ellie pushed thoughts of Diana to the back of her mind as she went to see about supper. Mia was nowhere to be seen; presumably she was phoning round her friends with news of her imminent removal. Rose and Frank were both still fast asleep.

Thomas brought some news to the supper table. 'The police say that your caller is probably a con artist, talking his way into big houses in order to steal what he can. If so, he's probably on their books already. They'll see if they can get someone to call round tomorrow to take some details.'

Ellie winced. 'I don't even know if Pryce is his real name, or where he lives.'

'The insurance people want me to send them a claim form. We'll do that in the morning, shall we?'

Mia came in just in time to hear Thomas's last words. 'What's up? You've lost something?' A look of anxiety replaced her former high spirits. That was the trouble with Mia; the slightest upset still had the power to make her fearful.

'Nothing for you to worry about.' Thomas managed a smile as he pulled out a chair for her to sit at the table. 'Have you been inviting all your friends to a house-warming party?'

The girl glowed with delight. 'Isn't it great? I rang Ursula, of course. She's my very best friend in all the world. Or she was till she got married. She was pleased, of course, but it's not the same when one of you is married and the other isn't. And yes, I did phone one or two others, of course.'

Ellie and Thomas tried not to exchange looks. Mia had a sort of follower, a roly-poly man whom she'd met at Ursula's wedding and seen regularly since. Mia had shied away from contact with men nowadays, but perhaps, some day . . . perhaps.

'Tell us all about it,' said Thomas. 'How many people are in the house, or is it a flat? And where is it?'

Mia talked, her enthusiasm making Thomas and Ellie forget their worries. But when the meal was over, Mia became serious. 'I'll keep an eye on Rose tonight, shall I? I'll leave my door open at the top of the stairs, so I can hear her if she wakes.'

'Are you sure?' said Ellie. 'I was wondering if you'd like me to sleep in your room so as to be near to her, and you can move into the spare room.'

'Certainly not!' A flash of her old spirit. 'She's been good to me, and we're used to one another now. Did they give her an anaesthetic at the hospital? Will she feel sick when she wakes up?'

'No. She can have some codeine when she wakes and perhaps some hot tea and a biscuit – whatever she fancies. If you don't mind, that is.'

'It will be a pleasure.' Mia seemed to mean it, too. It was a good sign that she was offering to help care for Rose. A short while ago she'd have shrunk into herself at the thought of having to take responsibility for someone else.

Mia started to clear the table. 'What about little Frank? He's still fast asleep in the chair next to Rose.'

'He's to sleep the night in his bedroom here and we'll see how he gets on tomorrow.'

'Leave him where he is for the moment,' said Thomas. 'Knowing the capacity of young boys for a regular supply of food, he'll wake up before long and demand sustenance. If not, I'll carry him upstairs and put him to bed.'

Mia offered to stack the dishwasher, so Ellie went along to her study to make a note of everything she could remember about the young con artist. It didn't take long. She wasn't feeling very bright.

The moment she stopped thinking about Rose and the thefts, Diana's problems leaped into Ellie's mind. It was ridiculous of Diana to say she wanted to reclaim Frank, but the courts did bend over backwards to allow the children to stay with their mothers if possible, and Diana could make out a good case – well, she might be able to, if she got married again – but little Frank was dead against it, and surely they'd take his feelings into account?

Oh, the hassle.

A nasty suspicious thought slid into Ellie's mind. Diana hadn't a good record of looking after Frank, even when she was supposed to do so. Diana was always saying how difficult it was for her to have him when she had to work at weekends, and surely that must be even more difficult now she was on her own at the agency. So, how serious was she about trying to reclaim him? Could she possibly be using the threat to remove Frank in order to put pressure on Stewart – and thus on Ellie – to meet her demand for money?

Ellie tried to laugh at herself. Diana wouldn't stoop so low. Would she?

The thought refused to be dismissed. Ellie's dealings with Diana had taught her not to take everything her daughter said at face value. It might be a good idea to check on what was really going on in the girl's life.

Who was Diana's new man, anyway? If he was reasonably solvent, then why wasn't Diana applying to him for help?

It might be that he was in no position to help her . . . which might mean that he'd be a liability rather than an asset. Oh dear.

As for Diana's debts . . . Ellie knew of a recent purchase of a top of the range car, extravagant clothes, the latest iPhone . . . Diana never stinted herself, did she?

Ellie put her head in her hands. She'd been brought up to fear bankruptcy. Her father had always been afraid of getting into debt, wouldn't even buy something on the never-never, had never held a credit card . . . though you didn't have them in those days, did you? Nowadays, of course, that was the way most people bought things. She'd heard that many businessmen regarded bankruptcy as a temporary embarrassment and somehow managed to get back on their feet again in next to no time.

But to bail Diana out by buying Denis off . . . and at such a cost! Ellie couldn't see how it was to be done.

When Ellie had decided to use her money for charitable purposes, she'd reserved an income for herself which had seemed ample to her at the time, though she knew Diana had sneered at it. Ellie wasn't extravagant, and though the upkeep of this big house was a drain on their finances, Thomas covered nearly all of their living expenses from his salary. True, they lived quietly, but they still enjoyed the little treats that made all the difference: meals out, trips to the theatre, a new television set, the occasional holiday; that sort of thing.

Of course, if Rose were going to need extra care, the cost of that must be taken into consideration . . . except that Miss Quicke had left Rose some money in her will, which might well cover it.

Ellie tried to work out how much she could manage to give Diana without going cap in hand to her charity for funds and decided there was no way she was going to be able to do it.

She would have to break the news to Thomas that Diana was in trouble again. Perhaps he'd have some sane and sensible advice to give her, to calm the turmoil in her head.

She abandoned her notes to go out into the garden to see what damage had been done to the plants by Rose's fall. In Miss Quicke's day, the garden had been a dull rectangle of lawn edged by various shrubs and small trees of the low-maintenance variety. Miss Quicke's gardener had approved as he could look after it without even breaking into a sweat, leaving ample time for gossip and cups of tea in the kitchen.

When Rose arrived to look after the elderly lady, she'd introduced colour with an enthusiasm which had sometimes outstripped her knowledge of what would or would not flourish in a clay soil. The gardener had disapproved, but Miss Quicke had enjoyed the result. Rose had managed to nibble away at the lawn to create wide flower beds filled with any plant bright enough to take her fancy. And roses; she loved roses. She'd introduced a curve here and a wooden seat there until the garden was a delight to the eye.

Ellie, who'd always loved gardening herself, had approved the changes Rose had made, and whenever the gardener complained about the extra work, she told him to stop grumbling and get on with it. He, of course, got back at her by neglecting to do all he should . . . hence the rambler rose left dangling from the wall.

Ellie considered the problem of the rose and decided to leave it as it was till a professional could deal with it.

Thomas came out to join her as she tried to lift the ladder off the border.

'Let me do that. No point having two of you ending up in casualty.' He took it off her to stow away in the garden shed. She gazed at the destruction Rose had wrought: some marguerites had been flattened, some petunias and a patch of alchemilla mollis had been crushed, a lupin decapitated. Not much damage, really. Their marauding cat Midge skittered across the lawn, pouncing on insects only he could see.

Thomas retrieved the secateurs and the lengths of wire which Rose had intended to use on the rambler rose. It was a prolific bloomer called American Pillar: spectacular in June and a nuisance for the rest of the year.

Ellie could feel Thomas studying her. As often happened with a happy marriage, each knew when the other was distressed or hiding something.

Thomas said, 'You're very quiet. Is something worrying you – apart from the con artist?'

She couldn't tell him yet. She bent to poke around in the

herbaceous border. 'Rose lost one of her shoes. It must be somewhere here.'

'Has Diana been around?'

'I'll tell you all about it later.'

He accepted that. 'You said Rose fell off the ladder. Why was she on it in the first place?'

'You might well ask. She said she was frightened by a face at the window of that house over there.' Ellie pointed to a small window under a gable of the Pryce house. The evening sunlight was reflected in the glass. 'A trick of the light. She's not getting any younger.'

Thomas stroked his beard. 'She insists she sees your aunt around the house now and then. When did she last have her eyes tested?'

'She reads the newspapers without glasses. Well, she doesn't read newspapers, but she does read the *Radio Times* to see what's on the telly, and she's got sharp enough eyesight to see if the cleaners have missed anything.' Ellie rooted around among some purple salvias and found Rose's missing shoe. 'Thank goodness it hasn't rained recently, or her shoe would have been fit for nothing but the dustbin. You think she's developing Alzheimer's?'

'It's a possibility, I suppose. Your visitor said the Pryce house has been stripped of furniture?'

'I'm so sorry about your Kindle. I ought to have realized he was up to no good.'

'I'm sorry about your ring, too, but both can be replaced. I found my mobile, by the way. It was on the desk in my study. Do you fancy a walk around the houses?'

Ellie stared. 'You mean, visit the scene of the crime? Not that there is a crime, of course.'

'Of course. I'll tell Mia what we're up to, and we'll be off, shall we? We can at least check to see if your light-fingered caller is living there or not. Right?'

Ellie couldn't think why they hadn't gone for a walk on a summer evening before, since they lived in a pleasant, quiet suburb with mature trees in the street. The houses were nearly all large with extensive gardens, built in the days when there'd been plenty of servants, who slept in the attics while labouring to keep the floors polished and meals on the tables.

Ellie had heard about those days from Miss Quicke: hampers of fresh vegetables were brought up weekly from country houses or delivered from Harrods; the butcher's boy came round daily with the meat; and the milk was delivered in the early hours of the morning.

No two houses in the road were alike, but nearly all had a coach house at the side. Nowadays, instead of live-in maids, there were contract cleaners to keep the dust down, and the coach houses had been converted into separate living quarters for live-in staff, with garage accommodation below. Or – as was the case with Ellie's domain – the coach building had been adapted and let out as separate living accommodation.

The upkeep of such large houses was steep; some had been well maintained and still looked prosperous, as did Ellie's. Some were sliding gently into decay, and one or two had already been demolished to make way for blocks of flats of indifferent design. As Stewart had said, there was never enough housing stock in London to satisfy demand.

As they walked along, Ellie thought that when God had made trees he'd been on a roll. What a variety there was to choose from: laburnum, viburnum, cherry, magnolia, dogwood . . . chestnut and plane . . . and those were just the ones she could see at a glance. She wondered if the huge old oak tree in a garden nearby had been there before the house behind it was built.

Not all the gardens had succumbed to the Victorian notion of covering the ground with shrubs such as laurel. Some front gardens were well worth looking at: bright with bedding plants, their driveways freshly tarred or paved.

'Is this the one?' Thomas stopped by a stone gatepost on which someone had carved the legend 'Pryce House' in the dim and distant. The green-painted gate to the drive had recently been shoved back into some overgrown privet. That was the trouble with privet; if you neglected to keep it trimmed, it put on a foot of growth in no time at all.

Pryce House was even larger than Ellie's; perhaps half as big again. As Stewart had said, it was reminiscent of Disneyland with turrets and gables galore. There was no other building quite so far over the top in the neighbourhood. Perhaps some Victorian ironmaster had made good and wanted to show off?

The drive hadn't seen attention for some time, and what had once been the front lawn was fast turning into a meadow. Overgrown shrubs shrouded the windows on the ground floor, but ivy hadn't yet taken hold of the brickwork.

There were curtains at some windows, but not at others. The windows hadn't been cleaned for a while, though the declining sun was reflected in the glass of the upper storeys from houses on the other side of the road.

'Dracula's Castle?' Thomas was enjoying this. 'Bats and spiders?'

'Do we dare explore?' Ellie considered the sandals she was wearing, which had a small heel. There were deep ruts in the clay and shingle of the driveway, but with care she wouldn't turn her ankle over. 'It certainly looks deserted.'

She took a few steps up the drive. 'The house itself isn't in bad condition. No tiles or pieces of fretwork missing. No windows broken.'

'Give it time.'

'Stewart wondered if the charity might like to buy it, but I can't see it myself. Too many turrets, which are a waste of space in my book.' She pushed her way between neglected bushes to peer into the ground-floor windows. Empty rooms, shadowy and dark. 'No one's living here.'

Thomas had his reading glasses out, inspecting the gate post. 'Somebody's drilled holes and nailed a piece of wood to this gatepost recently, and then broken it off. An estate agent's board? If it's still around, and I can find it . . .'

Ellie tried the front doorbell. It worked, but produced no response from inside the house. Naturally. The place was empty. Whatever had made her think otherwise? To the right the house bellied out into an extension with stained-glass windows rather high up – a billiard room, perhaps? Her progress after that was halted by a high wall with a door in it. The wall linked the house to what had once been a coach house, but which was probably now used as a garage. The double doors of the garage had windows above them which didn't look as if they were made to open. The doors themselves had been fitted with a bright, new padlock.

Ellie disregarded the garage and retraced her steps to the door which pierced the wall. She depressed the latch and pushed. To her surprise the door grated open.

She stepped into a shadowy glass-covered yard between the garage and the house, wide enough to be called a room in itself. On the house side there was a kitchen door. She tried the handle; locked.

On the right there was a door and a window which let on to the garage, then two other doors . . . Possibly an outside toilet, and a tool shed? All these doors were padlocked.

Somewhere nearby a machine purred into action, which made her jump.

Absurd. She smiled at herself. It was only a gardener starting up a lawnmower in one of the adjoining gardens. Of course.

A door at the end of the yard was neither locked nor padlocked, and led out into an extensive back garden and the heat of the evening sun.

'Wow!'

The garden was alive with roses. They were everywhere, in beds of their own, decorating the walls of the house and lining the brick walls of the garden. It took a lot of neglect before a rose stopped doing what came naturally.

The rose bushes in the beds near the house were mostly white and red: *Iceberg* and, probably, *Ena Harkness*. Over there she spotted *Peace*, pale peaches and cream. Smothering the wall on the right, and looking as if it would like to push it over, was that vigorous thug, *Kiftsgate*. On her left was *Compassion*, apricot and cream. *Paul's Scarlet* dropped crimson petals into a shallow ornamental pond, bright with algae. That was the problem with ponds; you had to keep cleaning them. No goldfish; she assumed that a heron or a crow would have had any that had been left behind when Mrs Pryce moved away.

The lawn beyond had been sadly neglected – the grass was over her ankles – but two large greenhouses looked intact, though a grape vine was trying to push through the roof of one. An outside tap dripped nearby. Hadn't the water been turned off at the mains?

Nearby was a rockery, which would be at its best in spring and now looked overgrown and unkempt. Beyond the greenhouses was a compost heap and a capacious shed with its door hanging open. Whatever had once been stored there had been removed. She smiled to see that ancient seed packets had been pinned to the door and left to fade and disintegrate in the sun. How many years had they been there? Forty, fifty? The gardener who had put them up must have died long ago.

A screen of fruit trees hid what had once been a vegetable garden, which looked as if it were producing a good crop of onions and broad beans.

How come?

The place was supposed to be deserted. Vegetables didn't flourish without input from a gardener. Someone had even planted some runner beans on a bamboo wigwam. And watered them.

The soil was not as full of weeds as might have been expected. Ah, perhaps the Pryce's gardener was still using the place to grow extra food for himself, treating it like an allotment for which he didn't have to pay rent? Well, if so . . .

She was being watched.

What!

She turned round to look up at the myriad of windows which overlooked the garden. Nothing. Nobody. Not even in the top window from which Rose said she'd seen a face looking down at her.

Naturally, there wasn't anyone there.

But . . .

She shivered, despite the warmth of the sun.

She looked round for Thomas, only to find that he hadn't followed her into the garden. Well, of course not. He was looking for an estate agent's board at the front, wasn't he? He was within shouting distance, though.

She'd seen what there was to be seen, and now she'd better get back to find out how Rose was doing. And Frank.

A trailing rose caught at her skirt and held her back, as if the garden were reluctant to let her go. A breeze rustled the leaves in the trees overhead. If she'd been a fanciful woman, she might have imagined they were discussing her intrusion into their territory. Ridiculous; of course they weren't.

Nevertheless, she had to fight down a desire to panic. The sooner she was out of this place the better. The light would be going soon.

She hastened back along the covered way, her footsteps sounding loud on the paving stones, and found the door to the front drive solidly shut. She pushed and kicked, but it wouldn't open. She told herself not to panic. This was ridiculous!

'Thomas!'

No reply. She closed her eyes, clenched her fists, breathed deeply. Was she still being watched? It felt like it, though of course she wasn't.

Dear Lord, help! Please!

Ah. The door opened towards her, not outwards.

She pulled it open. It grated on the stone flag and let her out into the front drive. Thomas was standing over an estate agent's board which he'd found in the bushes, taking a note of the name.

'Hoopers Estate Agency,' he said. 'Have you done snooping?'

She nodded. 'There's no one living here but someone's still looking after the vegetable garden. It's a big place, spooky. Must have cost something to keep up. Are we trespassing, do you think?'

He shut up his notebook. 'It's a moot point.'

She said, 'There's some wonderful roses in the back garden. If I'd brought my secateurs, I might have been tempted . . . but that would have been theft, wouldn't it?'

'The police can contact Hoopers tomorrow. They'll know where she's gone and have keys to the place.'

They turned back into the road. Walking along, she matched her pace to his, her arm within his elbow. 'Do you really think we'll get our things back?'

He patted her hand. 'Does it matter?'

Yes, it mattered. But she could tell he didn't want to make a song and dance of it.

Monday evening

Two frightened young people.
'Where have you been? I've been so scared. There was someone in the garden an hour ago.'
   'What? How could there have been?'
   'You promised me you'd put a padlock on the gate—'
   'I can't. The gardener wouldn't be able to come and go if I did that. Did they see you?'
   'No, I don't think so.'
   They peered out of the window. There was no one in the garden now. Despite the trees and shrubs which lined the walls of the gardens around them, they were so high up they had a good view of the neighbourhood.
   'There,' she said, pointing. 'She came from that house. I often see her there.'

FOUR

Monday evening

As Ellie and Thomas strolled back home, he said, 'I'm worried about Rose, aren't you? If she gets too . . . If you need help to look after her . . . ?'

Ellie was very definite. 'We are not going to put her into a home.'

He half smiled. 'I would have taken a bet that you'd say that, if I were a betting man, which I'm not. No, what I meant was . . . Didn't you say that your aunt left her some money? Well, would Rose want to be responsible for someone to come in and look after her, if she gets too frail to cope?'

Ellie had to think about this. Her instinct was to say that she'd look after Rose herself. Of course she would. The two of them went back a long way. Only, common sense reminded Ellie that she was no longer just a housewife, but had duties to fulfil.

She had to confer with Stewart and his team about what houses should have work done on them, and which could be let out straight away – and to whom. She had to make decisions about buying or selling certain properties. She had to sit on the committee of her charity and rule on what good causes should be helped and by how much. She had a number of people to help her make these decisions, but hers was the casting vote.

Besides which, she had friends to see and the house to run. She had to look after Thomas and Mia and Rose, and to babysit Frank at least once a week.

Suppose Rose needed help to get to the bathroom in the middle of a board meeting, or when she'd taken Frank on an outing? Suppose Rose needed assistance when Ellie had gone to church on Sunday, or had left the house with Thomas to visit friends?

Thomas shook her arm gently. 'I know you. You'd like to divide yourself into a hundred pieces and look after everyone. But you can't. Well; you could try, I suppose, and make yourself ill. Then what good would you be to man or beast?'

'Or to you.' She put her head against his shoulder for a moment. 'You hadn't forgotten I might like to spend time with you every now and then?'

He put his arm about her shoulder. 'It's a tough one, isn't it? While Mia is with us I don't think we need to worry too much about it, but she'll move on soon and then we'll have to think again.'

Tuesday morning

Ellie woke with a feeling of impending doom. Ah yes, Rose had fallen off the ladder after seeing a face floating in mid-air . . . as if! Rose must be watched with care . . . Little Frank was in his room down the corridor . . . and might have wet the bed and – Ouch! Diana!

No, don't think about Diana.

Then that dreadful young man had stolen Thomas's Kindle and her ring and oh dear! She was going to have to talk to the police about it. Talking to the police did not score highly on Ellie's pleasure chart. She knew she wasn't *Brain of Britain* material, but she felt that in some of her previous contacts with them she'd come across as next door to an idiot.

'Stupid housewife, sticking her nose in where she wasn't wanted' sort of thing. 'Too much imagination, and no common sense. Wouldn't know fact from fiction if you shoved it in her face.'

In this case, she had to admit that she'd been about as stupid as you could get. Fancy inviting a strange young man into the house and letting him walk off with their belongings!

It made her go hot and cold all over.

A thought. Perhaps Thomas could spare the time to be with her when the police came? They would never dare to treat him with the disdain – amounting to contempt – that they showed her. Particularly the policeman Ellie had most unfortunately referred to as 'Ears' after their first meeting, because he did have a pair of large, red ones. Well, that had gone down like a lead balloon. If only someone hadn't seen fit to report her gaffe to him . . . but they had. And she knew that they had. And he knew that . . .

Oh well. On with the day. It promised to be another fine, bright day, if perhaps a trifle on the warm side. A light summer dress would be in order.

Thomas's side of the bed was empty since he was an early riser. He had usually showered, dressed and made his way along the corridor to his Quiet Room before Ellie managed to open her eyes. He would spend time with his bible and God, and appear downstairs ready to cook breakfast for all of them if Rose were not up yet – and of late she hadn't been.

Mia was another slowcoach in the mornings. Ellie understood that completely. Sometimes, if Thomas were away on one of his lecture trips, Ellie and Mia would prepare and eat breakfast in complete silence.

Mia would soon be gone. Ellie was delighted that the girl felt able to move on, of course, but they would miss her.

Ellie sat on the edge of the bed, considered getting down on her knees to pray and decided against it.

Dear Lord, please forgive me for not kneeling. I'm feeling creaky this morning. I hope you don't mind. I could do with some courage today. You know what I'm up against. What am I going to do about Diana? Suppose I sold off part of this great house . . . ? But then it wouldn't be our home any more. I could mortgage it, I suppose, but how could I afford the repayments? I couldn't.

Then there's Rose . . .

And an interview with the police, which I can't see being pleasant. If you could see your way to prompting me, so that I don't make a complete fool of myself . . . ? Though I suppose that really doesn't matter, does it? I am what I am, and I can only do my best. Apologies. Feeling sorry for myself. Stupid. Take no notice.

It's a lovely day, I see. Thank you for that.

The roses in the Pryce garden yesterday – what a delight. I must get on with things, mustn't I? Thanks for listening.

There was a wail from Frank's room. He'd probably woken

in alarm, wondering where he was . . . and then remembered.

There was a snuffling at her bedroom door, and Frank shot in. He dived into bed with her, and clung. There, there! He was far too thin and anxious for his age. She held him tight. There, there. She checked, but he didn't seem to have wet the bed. Praise be.

If she kept the thought of Diana locked away at the back of her head, she might get through the day all right. One thing at a time. Soothe Frank off to school and give Stewart a progress report on how his son was doing . . .

Ellie tidied the sitting room. She cut and arranged some more flowers to replace the peonies, which were past their best. She darted into the kitchen to check on Rose and Mia, who said they were perfectly all right, thank you, and what was all the fuss about? Rose was developing some spectacular bruises, but said she'd had a good night.

The gardener came and complained about the mutilation of his flower bed. Ellie gave him a Look and said that if he'd tied the rambler rose back when it had first come loose, Rose wouldn't have had to put her life in danger by going up a ladder, so would he please see to it before he mowed the lawn that day. He said that that was all very well, but he wasn't Mr Whip-it-Quick, was he? And what did she expect when she was only paying him for four hours a week?

'I expect value for money, that's what,' said Ellie, folding her arms at him. He stumped off, muttering to himself. The cat Midge stalked past her to leap on to the staging in the conservatory, which the sun was heating up nicely.

The moment her hands were idle, Ellie found herself replaying yesterday's dramas in her head – which did her no good at all. Worrying didn't get you anywhere. She knew that. Of course she did. Which didn't stop her doing it.

She still hadn't told Thomas about Diana's visit, and she had to do so, didn't she? He had his own worries, something about a contributor to the magazine? She didn't want to disturb him.

The front doorbell rang. Ellie went to look through the

peephole in the door and recognized the policeman who was standing outside, fidgeting from one foot to the other. Of course, it would be 'Ears'.

Ellie told herself he couldn't kill her.

With him was a female detective constable, by the name of Milburn. Ellie recognized her, too. She'd proved quite human in the past.

Thomas had said he'd stop work to be with her if she really needed him, but he was expecting a difficult visitor that morning, so if she could manage . . . ? Ellie braced herself and opened the door to let the police in.

Ears looked round about him, much as the Pryce boy – if that was his name – had done the day before. 'A big place for a woman on her own.'

'There's four of us living here at present, five if you count my grandson who often stays overnight.'

Ellie led the way to the sitting room and offered tea or coffee. Both declined.

DC Milburn took out her notebook, but Ears strolled about, hands in pockets to emphasize his superior status. 'So you had a visit from a con artist? Weren't you aware that they're on the lookout for elderly women living alone in big houses?'

Ellie didn't like being called 'elderly' when she was only in her early sixties. 'I wasn't alone. Our housekeeper was in as well, but unfortunately she'd had a fall so wasn't feeling quite the thing.'

Ears had his usual chip on his shoulder. He probably thought anyone who employed live-in staff was a bloated capitalist and ought to be strung up from the nearest lamp-post. He wouldn't have believed Ellie if she'd told him Rose had not been asked to take on the job of housekeeper, but had insisted on staying on to do it after Ellie's ancient aunt had died.

Ears had a sneer on his face and in his voice. 'So what was this chap's spiel, then? He found out the name of some old dear in the neighbourhood and tried to pass himself off as a relative? He asked for money, of course.'

'Well, yes. But he did seem worried about his great-aunt. He'd called on the retirement home where she was supposed to be living, and they denied all knowledge of her.'

'Or so he said.' An unpleasant tone.

Ears thought she'd been taken in by a sob story, and perhaps she had. Ellie felt her colour rise. 'So he said. Yes.'

'Well, it's clear enough. I doubt if you'll see your valuables again. Been hocked before nightfall, I expect. To pay for drugs, of course.'

'I did wonder if he were into drugs. He certainly danced around a lot, but he also smoked. Do drug addicts smoke cigarettes as well as take drugs? I didn't think they did.'

'As you say, what do you know about it?' He really was a rude young man.

Ellie tried to keep calm. 'Of course, you know more about it than I do, and it's true that I wouldn't really know what a drug addict looks like. I thought at first he was on edge because he was worried about his great-aunt. Then I thought he was in a state because he was desperate for money. I'm pretty sure that's why he's after his great-aunt. I mean, she does seem to be missing, but . . . The only thing is, if he is on drugs he can't be very far gone because he's taken great care of his appearance.'

A condescending smile. 'As you say, you wouldn't really know what anyone on drugs looked like.' His mobile phone rang. He whipped it out, listened for a few seconds, and shut it off. 'Well, duty calls. Something more important, I'm afraid.' He was Mr Sarcasm himself. 'I'll leave DC Milburn here with you to take any details you can recall, and no doubt we'll be in touch when we've caught the man.'

He didn't really think they were going to catch him, that much was clear. As he would say, 'Another con job. End of.'

Ellie showed Ears out and returned to DC Milburn, who smiled at her in a completely normal, woman to woman, way. Ellie smiled back. 'Tea or coffee? And would you mind if I just popped in on Rose, who's not feeling too good today? Falling off a ladder at her age . . .'

'Climbing a ladder at any age,' said the DC. 'I get vertigo.'

Ellie smiled. 'I'm all right on ladders up to the fourth rung, then I cling on tight, close my eyes even tighter, and inch my way back down again.'

Rose had got herself dressed and moved as far as 'her'

armchair in the kitchen; or rather, Mia had helped get her there. Now they were sitting together happily going over some old recipe books, planning future meals and making a shopping list.

Ellie would have suggested she and the DC might sit outside, but the gardener was mowing the lawn so they returned to the sitting room, which was cool enough that early in the day.

'This is a lovely room.' The policewoman looked around her, relaxing.

'I am fortunate. But not lucky, yesterday. I know your superior officer has made up his mind that my caller was a con man. May I tell you exactly what happened and what makes me think he wasn't just that?'

DC Milburn eyed Ellie over the rim of her mug of coffee. 'Our chief super says you've a feeling for villainy. Of course, she doesn't like it when you report some ghastliness or other, but she has to admit you've a nose for crime.'

Ellie blushed. 'Why, thank you. I know I haven't got a trained mind or anything, and probably don't spot all sorts of things that professionals would, but I do notice this and that, and I made some notes you might like to see.'

She went through the notes she'd made the night before, concluding: 'The thing is, would your usual con man have such an outlandish appearance? Wouldn't he want to be unmemorable? I mean, this young man had brutally short hair but it had been cut by a good barber, it wasn't a home-made job. Also, he had rings in his ears, his eyebrow and his lip.'

'I must admit, I can't recall a con man looking like that. But an opportunist thief . . .' The DC shrugged.

'Well, what about his car? It was bright yellow. Not a lemon yellow, but a deep egg-yolk colour like custard powder.'

'You didn't get the licence number?'

'No.'

'What make was it?'

Ellie shook her head.

'You didn't notice.'

'I hardly know one make from another. When Thomas says, "Look at that Merc!" I don't know which car he means.'

'Well, was it a small car?'

'Not like a Mini, but yes; smallish. I only caught a glimpse as I closed the door, remember.'

'Was it built like a beetle?'

'Now I do know a Volkswagen when I see one. No, it wasn't. It had the normal up and down silhouette. Not an estate car. No sticky-out back.'

'Two door or four?'

Ellie concentrated. 'Four, I think; but I wouldn't like to swear to it. It had been recently cleaned, no dirt splashes. There was something hanging from the mirror at the front? I might be wrong about that.'

'You're doing well. Any stickers on the windows, or at the back?'

'You mean notices like Baby on Board, or those screens they put on windows to shield children from the sun? No, I don't think so. I'm a poor witness, I'm afraid.'

'If I got some pictures of different makes of car, would you look to see if you could identify this one?'

'I could try.' Both of them knew there was little likelihood of her succeeding.

The DC looked over her notes, frowning. 'He certainly doesn't sound like the usual run of con men, but I suppose . . . ?'

'He convinced me that his great-aunt did live at that big house and that he'd bought some Liquorice Allsorts for her.'

'Liquorice Allsorts?' The DC smiled. 'Yes, you'd think he'd talk about a box of Cadbury's Milk chocolates if he were a con man.'

'Or Thornton's, something expensive for an elderly relative you were hoping to tap for a loan. He rang true when he said he was desperate for money. I don't know whether I believed him or not about the sister and her partner and all the rest. He might even have been telling the truth about working in the bedding department of a big store.'

'We can't ring round every department store asking if they know him when we don't even know his name. He was probably lying, anyway.'

'But his appearance . . . ?'

The DC sighed. 'Perhaps it was his first venture into this

sort of crime? I sympathize, I really do, but we haven't the manpower to follow up every lead in this sort of case. The best we can do is to put his details and a note of what you've lost into circulation and see if anything turns up. If he tries again, we'll be sure to hear about it. I'll give you a police report number, which you'll need for the insurance people. I assume you are insured?'

Ellie let her visitor out. Ears had taken the car, of course, and the girl would have to walk back to the station. Not that it was all that far.

Thomas materialized from his office. 'Satisfactory?'

'The police think it was just another con artist.' Ellie wanted to hit something. Hard.

'Annoying. Are they going to follow up on the lost lady?'

'Did I even mention it? Yes, I did. In passing. But I'm not even a member of her family. In fact, I don't think I'd know her if I saw her in the street.' She shook her head. 'Honestly, I can see their point of view. I was very silly to let the boy into the house in the first place, and it's my own fault that he stole from us.'

'No, it isn't. What about Hoopers, the estate agency? Did they give you an address where Ms Pryce can be found?'

The doorbell rang. 'I'll take it,' he said. 'I'm expecting someone.' He didn't look happy about it, but went off to answer the door.

Ellie stormed off down the corridor to her office and banged the door behind her. There were times when . . . men could be so irritating . . . hadn't she got her hands full at the moment, what with Rose . . . and Mia must be encouraged to leave them, but it was going to be difficult to manage without her . . . and as for Diana . . . Don't think about Diana. That was one problem too far.

She must talk to Thomas about it soon.

Ellie sat down at her desk, pushing away the pile of paper-work which her part-time secretary had left for her to deal with. Well, if Thomas was too busy to help, and the police thought her an idiot, she would have to set about finding the thief herself. It shouldn't be too difficult.

First, she rang Stewart on his mobile phone. 'Stewart, it's

Ellie here . . . No, no problem with Frank. As I told you, he went off to school quite happy, said it was football this afternoon after school and he's looking forward to that. How the young can keep chasing a ball around a field in this heat, I don't know. Have you spoken to your solicitor yet about Diana?'

A sigh. 'I have. He needs all the paperwork from the time of the divorce. My darling wife took the news bravely. She reminded me that I'd put the deeds of this house in her name, which is true and means Diana can't force us to sell. How about you?'

'I'm going to have to talk to Thomas about it. I'm ringing about something different. We took a walk round by the Pryce house last night, and Thomas disinterred a rather battered estate agent's board from the undergrowth. Hoopers. I think I ought to know the name, but . . . You know everyone round here in that line. Do you know anything about them?'

'Doing well, branches all over West London. It makes sense that the Pryce house should have gone to them.'

'I'd like to find out more about it.'

'You said you weren't interested.'

'The vegetable garden's being worked for food; the house is empty but there's no attempt currently being made to sell it. An unsatisfactory situation, don't you think?'

'A messy situation, but I can't see—'

'What it's got to do with me? I know, Stewart. I know. We had a caller who said he was related to the old lady and went off with some of our valuables. I'll tell you all about it some time. If I disappear you'll find me floating in the pond in the deserted garden, chanting something from Shakespeare about never telling her love.'

She caught herself up and laughed. 'Sorry, Stewart. I don't know what's got into me today.'

A cautious tone. 'Is Rose all right?'

'So so. Mia's looking after her. But Mia really ought to be packing to leave, so that's another problem. I may have a word with your wife, see if she can find someone to come in to look after Rose for a few weeks till she's better.'

'My wife's not working today – it's the end-of-term nursery

show and the children are in it – but her assistant will be there, and I'm sure she'll be able to help.' Apart from looking after Stewart and the children, his wife owned the cleaning agency which looked after Ellie's house and many others in the area.

'Which reminds me,' said Ellie. 'Rose told me some gossip about the Pryce woman leaving, which I seem to recall she got from one of my cleaners. No, it's gone right out of my head. Sorry, I'm not quite myself today.'

Stewart was amused. 'It's the heat. It's getting to me, too.'

Ellie held back a sigh. 'I'd better ring the agency then.'

She rang off and phoned the agency. 'Ellie Quicke here. Can you spare a moment? It's Rose, our housekeeper. She fell and hurt her wrist, nothing serious, but she'll have to rest for a bit, and our dear little lodger, who's been so good to her, is supposed to be moving out to a place of her own. Do you have someone on your books who could come in every day for a while . . . ?'

They were sympathetic, of course. 'I can think of one person who would be suitable, but she may not be free. I'll ring you back, shall I? Is everything else all right, Mrs Quicke? You sound a bit fussed. Not like you.'

'Ah well. I did a silly thing.' Ellie repeated the story about the Pryce boy and his search for his great-aunt. 'Now am I dreaming it, or did one of my cleaners also work for Mrs Pryce in the past? Was there something about her cats being taken away?'

'Vera and Pet? They should have been with you by now. What's the time? Eleven, just gone?'

Ellie took the phone away from her ear and listened. A vacuum cleaner whined somewhere. 'Yes, they're here.'

'They used to go on to Mrs Pryce's when they finished with you on Tuesdays and Fridays, I think it was. The old lady was very particular who cleaned for her and liked those two, used to give them a nice bonus at Christmas. She paid us by cheque, on the nail. Hold on a minute, I'll access her account . . . Yes, here it is. All paid up, no problem.'

'Forwarding address? Did she ask for anyone to pop in and look after the house, or anything?'

'No, a clean break. No forwarding address. She was going

into a retirement home, I gather. They didn't allow pets, so she had the Cats Protection League come in to take her two. Vera said she'd have liked one of them, but I don't know what happened – maybe she came to an arrangement with the cat people.

'I only remember about the cats because I thought we might have a mouse here at the office, and Vera said Mrs Pryce was getting rid of hers. A something and a nothing, as you might say. I'm so sorry about Rose. I hope she gets better soon.'

Like Ellie, they knew that when older people had a fall, it could be the beginning of the end. Luckily Rose hadn't broken anything, but the shock might start off any number of problems: pneumonia being the one which occurred most frequently, often proving fatal.

'Thank you,' said Ellie, and she put the phone down.

She tried to collect her wits, which seemed to have gone gathering wool round the Wrekin, or wherever it was they went when they left her. How could she have been so stupid as not to remember the cleaners were due that day? How could she have been so criminally careless as to let the Pryce boy into the house and not keep an eye on him? How was she going to deal with Diana's challenge . . . for challenge it was?

Ellie heard herself groan.

Dear Lord, I suppose you want me to find the money for Diana somehow or other. We have to do this for our children, don't we? Please, tell me how?

She got to her feet, restless. What would the other trustees of her charitable trust say if she asked them to bail Diana out? They'd refuse. They must refuse. Their responsibility was to look after the money, and to disburse it to needy people.

She must talk to Thomas about it instead. Now.

Tuesday noon

In the garden of Pryce House.
The gardener parked his van by the garage, tucked away under the overgrown hedge. He unloaded his tools and the wheelbarrow, trundling the lot through the door into the yard, and from there on through the far door into the back garden. As

he made for his vegetable patch he was thinking there ought to be just one more picking from the broad beans, after which he'd cut them to the ground. Quite often they'd spring up new growth, and he might get another crop later on. Blackfly was the big problem with broad beans; with runner beans as well. He'd brought his spray gun, just in case.

One of these days he must put a new washer on the outside tap, as it tended to drip. Not that it mattered, as he didn't have to pay the water rates, did he?

He stooped to unload his tools and stared. There was the fresh imprint of a woman's shoe in the damp patch under the tap. It hadn't been there yesterday, and it was smaller than that made by the shoe of the girl living in the house.

He swung around. The breeze swayed a tendril from a rambler rose, which caught on his shirt. He shook it off. The breeze died away. The windows of the house looked blindly down at him. He looked back. He moved his shoulders uneasily.

'Is anyone there?'

The garden seemed to be listening to him. The girl was nowhere to be seen. She knew his times, wouldn't come down to the garden while he was around.

He looked at his watch. He was between jobs, had an hour on which to work his patch. He'd better get on with it. His wife would be wanting the beans for supper. Every little helped.

He scuffed out the telltale footprint. He wasn't going to panic; not he! After all, he had a better right to be in the garden than anyone else, didn't he?

FIVE

Ellie hurried along the corridor and tapped on the door of her husband's study. Too late she remembered that Thomas had a visitor . . . who turned out to be a bishop, no less. 'Sorry to interrupt. I was wondering . . .'

The bishop was plump, with a fat smile and rimless glasses. Ellie disliked him at sight, while telling herself she had no reason to do so.

'Ah, the little lady of the household. Yes, coffee would be much appreciated.'

She thought he was the type of man who avoided professional women and condescended to those who weren't. He probably thought of them as 'man's little helpmeets', had been vehemently against them being ordained, and believed the skies would fall if they ever became bishops.

Thomas sent her a look in which sympathy and irritation were nicely blended. Sympathy for her, and irritation for the bishop. She hoped. Half rising from his seat, he said, 'I'll make it, Ellie. I know you're busy.'

Ellie managed a smile, somehow. 'Not at all. It won't take a minute.'

She shut the door, considered kicking the wall, decided it would hurt too much as she was wearing open-toed sandals, and dutifully went away to fulfil the bishop's order.

She found her two cleaners in the kitchen having their elevenses with the gardener, as they always did on or about noon. On seeing her, the gardener lumbered to his feet, threw her a wounded look and disappeared – as well he might, considering he ought to have tied back that rambling rose himself, so that Rose didn't try to do it.

Ellie glanced around. The cleaners' first job on Tuesdays

was to deal with the kitchen quarters, which they had done. There was no sign of Rose or of Mia.

Ellie told herself to get her priorities straight. Coffee for the bishop. Check on Rose. Talk to the cleaners.

She said, 'Thomas's visitor would like some coffee, and so would he. Do you think you could you make some and take it into them? And let the rest of the cleaning wait, as I need to pick your brains about something.'

Ellie didn't usually have time to sit down and talk to the cleaners because she was always so busy, rushing around the place. Rose saw to it that they were appropriately deployed around the house and that they had their break at half time. Rose was interested in everybody and everything, and she often passed neighbourhood gossip on to Ellie, who sometimes listened with half an ear and sometimes didn't listen at all.

Ellie popped her head round the door into Rose's sitting-cum-bedroom and found her dozing in her big chair with the television on. Rose's colour was good. She started awake when she heard Ellie come in and said she was just having a little rest and was that all right?

Of course it was.

'And Mia?'

'Out shopping for food.'

Ellie nodded and returned to the kitchen, trying to recall what Rose had told her about their two cleaners.

Vera was the big, bony blonde. She had a long horse-like face, an amazing capacity for moving heavy furniture, and a son reputed to be autistic – or was it Attention Deficit Disorder that he had? A difficult child in some way. No husband or partner apparent.

Rose liked Vera; said she was reliable and thorough. Blue rosette for Vera.

Pet – short for Petula – was a Humpty Dumpty. She wore the kind of tracksuits which emphasized large hips. She had no children as yet, but was always hoping she'd get lucky one day. Was she saving up to try IVF? Ellie had heard that it was costly and didn't always work.

Pet's husband – who was even fatter than her, said Rose

– worked as a night porter in the local hospital and, as Pet got up early to clean, they didn't seem to spend much time together. Rose said you had to watch Pet or she'd scamp her work.

When coffee had been made and taken through to the men, Ellie seated herself at the table for a chat. 'Vera. Pet. I did a very silly thing yesterday. I let a young man into the house who said he wanted to find a Mrs Pryce who lived in the next road. He said he'd tried the retirement home and they'd given him the runaround, denied she was there. Anyway, when my back was turned, he made off with my engagement ring, Thomas's Kindle, and my aunt's little china snuffbox. Naturally I want to find him. Did you ever hear of or see a young man who might have been related to Mrs Pryce when you were working for her?'

The huge rings in Vera's ears caught the light as she whacked the table. 'Would that be her great-nephew, Terry Pryce? You remember, Pet? The one who brought her the turkey, the Christmas before last it would have been. Tell a lie; three Christmases ago.'

Pet looked bewildered.

'Ah,' said Vera. 'I forgot; it was before we teamed up, wasn't it?' She spurted into laughter. 'He brought her a turkey and it was off. We gave it to Fritz to bury in the garden, only he didn't. He took it home to his missus and she gave him a right rollicking. Dunno what he did with it in the end.'

'I'm enchanted,' said Ellie, with truth. 'Fritz is the gardener? Where could I find him?'

'Oh, him.' Pet fiddled with her nearly empty mug of coffee. 'Lives above the shops in the Lane at the far end, over the Co-op. Missus Pryce never minded if he took home some of the stuff he grew for her.'

A lightning glance passed between the two girls, and Ellie caught it. She remembered that the vegetable garden was still being worked by someone. By this Fritz, presumably? The girls knew and were not going to say. Well, well. It was no concern of Ellie's.

'You said her great-nephew Terry brought her a turkey and you think he might be the lad who stole from me?'

Vera furrowed her brow. 'Mrs Pryce always said she

wouldn't be surprised if he ended up in trouble. She never did think much of her husband's side of the family.'

Ellie looked a question, and Vera was happy to explain. 'Mrs Pryce used to sit down along of us when we was on our break sometimes, and she'd tell us such tales of her family, had us in stitches. The turkey tale was one, but some of the excuses they came up with to get money out of her! She used to say, "If I didn't have myself a laugh about that load of sharks, I'd cry."'

Pet stabbed the air with a pudgy forefinger. 'It could well be Terry that visited you yesterday. He must be, what, mid-twenties? She used to tell us how he'd come round now and then to make sure she was still in the land of the living. And then he'd touch her for a sub. A "smarmy git", she said.'

'What did he look like?'

'Dunno, really. Never saw him. What was it she used to say about him? I know; each time he come round he had another ring in his ear or his eyebrow, and she wondered where else he had them. She said it was a wonder he hadn't got blood poisoning because of all the piercings. She couldn't think how he'd got himself a job in a respectable shop.'

'Did he have a sister, by any chance?'

Both girls shook their heads. 'He was an only.'

So he'd lied about that. 'Did Mrs Pryce like Liquorice Allsorts, by any chance?'

A grin from Vera. 'She did, at that. We used to get her a box for Christmas and birthdays, didn't we, Pet?'

So maybe the Pryce boy had spoken the truth about some things.

Vera had gone all wistful. 'I liked Mrs Pryce. Sparky. Never let nothing get her down. No nonsense, tell us off if something weren't done right, but no side to her in spite of all her money. Her old man was in the hardware business, see; had five shops which she sold for a mint after he dropped off the twig on account of his liver. She was nobody's fool.'

'As she used to tell us, regular.' Pet's voice went fluting up. '"My Edgar left everything to me because he knew what his scumbag relatives were like, and I'm not letting them settle on me like a crowd of blowflies."'

Vera was enjoying this, squaring her elbows on the table. 'She promised him she'd go on looking after them, but they did get her down sometimes. She was his second wife, see. His first wife spoiled the children rotten and then ran off with a tennis player or football coach or something when his children were nineteen, twenty, maybe more. They'd never lifted a finger for themselves and spent money left, right and centre. The old man was subbing young Terry now and then, too. That's the one that come round with the turkey, remember?

'Then he, that's Mr Pryce, met our Flavia, who'd been doing all right for herself in a little boutique over in Maidenhead and they hit it off straight away. That's when Mr Pryce told his family that the good times were over; his children were to move out and fend for themselves, and there'd be no more handouts to Terry, either. They were furious, thought he ought to bankroll them all their lives, what a hoot!'

Ellie was both amused and appalled. 'They were old enough to earn their own living, I suppose. What did they do?'

'Oh, Mr Pryce's bark was worse than his bite. He helped them set up in business, and if they fell behind with the rent or couldn't pay the gas bill, he bailed them out. She, Mrs Pryce, carried on doing that all these years since. Apart from Terry-with-the-rings, there was a son and a daughter called Edwina. Now let me see; Pet, what was that she said about Edwina's wedding-that-wasn't?'

'Had a baby without bothering to get married, didn't she?'

'I remember now, it was broken off because there wasn't the money her fiancé imagined there ought to be, marrying into the Pryces, if you see what I mean. Anyway, when he went off and left Edwina with her little girl, the old man bought her a small flat and a partnership in a gift shop where she worked part-time for years—'

'Which Madam said was really beneath her dignity but they appreciated her style; or so she said, silly cow. That is, until it went bust last year some time and she started hanging around Mrs Pryce again with her hand out: give me more, give me more. Enough to make you sick.'

Vera nodded. 'Mr Pryce refused to stump up for private school fees for Edwina's child, even if she was his granddaughter. He said it wouldn't have done any good, as the girl wasn't that bright, and it would have given her a false idea of her expectations. I thought at the time it was rather hard, but maybe Mr Pryce was right, seeing how she turned out.'

'Lazy slut,' said Pet. 'If I'd had her opportunities . . .'

Vera was following another train of thought. 'Mrs Pryce put herself out if she thought it would do any good, though. When his schoolteacher told me my Mikey would do better in the private system, Mrs Pryce helped me get him to the right doctor, and it wasn't what the school said it was, but something that can be treated and on the whole he's doing all right in the primary school down the road and that's thanks to her, as I told her, the last time I saw her.'

Ellie asked, 'May I enquire if Mikey's father . . . ?'

Vera shook her head, making her earrings swing. 'A no good boy. My own fault. I drank too much at an end of term party and passed out. A boy I'd fancied had been there, and I'd hoped . . . Stupid of me. It was his friend that done it, and he didn't want to know. End of.'

Ellie thought it better not to follow that up. 'So, the Pryce daughter – Edwina? – that had the daughter, is she retired?'

Pet said, 'Shouldn't we be getting on with the cleaning, now?'

'No, no,' said Ellie. 'I'm interested. Go on.'

Vera shook her head. 'I don't think Edwina's capable of holding down a proper job any more . . . if she ever was. She must be in her early fifties and that frail-looking, but still gets her clothes at Harvey Nicholls and looks down on us, thinks we're common as muck and maybe we are, but at least we work for our living. And never a word of thanks to Mrs Pryce for bailing her out every time she got behind with her bills.'

'So that was Mr Pryce's daughter. What about his son?'

'What happened to him, Vera?' said Pet. 'Didn't she say he ended up as a dustman or something, working for the council?'

Vera snapped her fingers. 'School caretaker. The old man bought him a flat – same as he did for Edwina – and helped him start up some kind of business, but it didn't work out. His eyes was always bigger than his stomach, or so Mrs Pryce used to say. He lost the lot, including his flat. Lives in the caretaker's house in the school grounds somewhere. Married once, but it never took. Health problems. Sickly lot, that side of the family.'

Ellie asked, 'What school, do you know?'

Heads were shaken in unison. 'Nowhere near. Other side of the borough. Helping out with after-school clubs and that. He only came round Christmas and birthdays but, to give him his due, he didn't come begging like his sister.'

Pet wagged a finger. 'Mrs Pryce said she wished Edwina lived farther away too, because she used to come round three or four times a week, fetching stuff from the shops that Mrs Pryce couldn't eat, checking what was in the fridge and putting stuff in the deep freeze for her that she never touched. And always on at her, rabbit, rabbit, rabbit, never a moment's peace with her around. "Why don't you come and live with me, Mummy? There's a nice room in my flat you could have all to yourself." Called Mrs Pryce "Mummy" while trying to smile though you could see it hurt her face.'

Vera sighed. 'Tell the truth, I miss the old dear, but her knees were playing her up something chronic. We told her, put in a stairlift, but she wouldn't have it—'

Pet put on her fluting voice again. '"The day I can't climb the stairs is the day I move out. And not to Mrs Grabby-bags, either."'

Ellie caught on to this. 'That's what she called her stepdaughter?'

Both faces assumed the expression of someone who'd swallowed vinegar. 'Right old—'

'Now, now,' said Vera. 'Wash your mouth out with soap.'

'That one used to find fault with everything we done, said she coulda done it better herself and what was Mummy paying us for, she'd like to know?'

'And up hers, too! Pfah!' Vera gave a two-fingered salute.

Ellie said, 'You said Edwina popped in regularly. Do you know where she lives? Did she never marry? Was her name Pryce, too?'

'Edwina never got herself married,' said Pet, with the air of one delivering a pleasant item of gossip. 'Too sharp a tongue and too high an opinion of herself. Also, no boobs to speak of. Got a flat in that block after the shops, just before the Common.'

'And her daughter? The one the Pryces didn't pay private school fees for?'

'Typical teenager, no bra, big boots. Always sniffling, never has a tissue. Edwina used to drag the girl round with her sometimes. "Now you behave yourself and be nice to Granny." Fat chance. Evangeline, that's her name. Evangeline-no-knickers. When she sits down, her jeans ride so low you can see the divide at the back. Pardon me, but you can.'

Vera nodded. 'Evangeline-no-manners, either. We could always tell when she'd been round because we'd find chewing gum stuck to the tables and chairs. Left school hardly able to read and write. Parties all night but can't get up in the morning to save her life. Had a job in an off-licence for a while, pulls pints in a bar in the evenings now.'

'Lives with her mother?'

'She's got a room above the pub. Isn't that right, Pet?'

'Think so. I expect she'll get one up the spout any day and go on the social for the rest of her life, popping them out regular.'

Ellie took a couple of seconds to interpret that. Pet meant the girl would get pregnant time after time in order to avoid work. 'What about the lad Terry, who brought her the turkey? Where does he live? And his parents? Are they still alive and in contact?'

'All gone now. Mother and father divorced. She went to live up north somewhere, Manchester way, something like that. Lost touch, anyhow. Father drank himself to death, popped off last June, thereabouts, didn't he, Pet? She made a fuss about going to the funeral, down in Sussex somewhere, near Brighton. She wasn't driving long distances then and Fritz was going to drive her, but she didn't trust him, used a minicab firm instead. Edwina and her daughter wanted to go as well, expected to be given a lift because neither of them drive, but Madam said she couldn't stand being bored for that long. Besides, she'd made it known she was thinking of going into a home, and they'd all started to ask her for more money by then even though she'd promised to go on looking after them.'

Pet sighed, eased her back. 'Well, we ought to be getting on.'

Vera was still in full flow. 'Mrs Pryce kept her head up, put her make-up on, false eyelashes and all, to the last. But she was right to go where she could be looked after, keep her dignity, like. She give me these earrings when she went. Bought them at a shop in the Broadway. Gave me the receipt and all, in case I wanted to exchange them.'

Pet agreed. 'Gave me a necklace, too, with my lucky birth sign on it.'

Ellie looked, but Pet wasn't wearing the necklace that day.

Vera said, 'We're going down to see her next month for her birthday, aren't we, Pet?'

Ellie said, 'That's nice of you.'

Vera produced a twisted smile. 'Well, we would have done anyway, but she did say that when the house was sold, she might give us a little something to make our lives easier. I want to take Mikey to the seaside for a holiday. He's never seen the sea.'

Pet got to her feet. 'I dunno what's happening about the house. The "For Sale" board's gone. Perhaps she's changed her mind, taken it off the market.'

'You've got her new address?'

'Something Towers, Denham.' Vera scrabbled in her handbag and produced a dog-eared diary. 'Corfton Towers. Fritz is going to drive us there and back. It's all arranged.' She stood up. 'Well, this won't get the baby his bottle. You want us to turn out the big bedroom today, Mrs Quicke?'

'Hang on a moment.' Ellie reached for a pad of shopping lists and tore off a sheet to write on. 'Forget turning out today. Just do a top dust, clean the bathrooms, and then do the downstairs. Let me get this straight. There's Mrs Flavia Pryce, and her deceased husband. Then there's his brother, also deceased. What's the name of the brother's grandson with all the piercings?'

'That's Terry.'

Ellie drew a family tree, which sprawled all over the page

but would do. 'There was a son and daughter by Mr Pryce's first marriage. The son – what's his name? – works as a school caretaker.'

'That's Edgar. She sent him cheques for his birthday and Christmas which he did come round to thank her for. Tell the truth, I don't think he was as bad as his sister, never brought her his bills to pay that I know of.'

'Right; so the daughter is Edwina, and she lives in that dark block of flats just before you get to the Common, the ones that you can't see for the trees planted close in front. Fritz the gardener lives above the Co-op supermarket in the Lane. Right? Do you happen to know where Terry lives?'

Vera shrugged. 'Moved out to be with a "friend", if you know what I mean. He was always short for the rent and asking for a sub. Same as Evangeline. She got herself engaged a couple months back, and what a how-de-do that was. The missus wasn't best pleased to be asked for a present when she hadn't even been invited to their engagement party.'

Pet agreed. 'Didn't he break it off, soon after? Yes, because she come round weeping her eyes out, saying he'd gone off with the presents and that the ring he'd bought her was just glass. Just what you'd expect with her taste in men.'

'Poor girl.' Vera sighed. 'It must have been a shock, even if he did have an eye to the main chance. But at least she wasn't pregnant.'

'She thought she was, remember? Screaming and shouting all over the place. Mrs Pryce give us a blow by blow run-down. She didn't have all that many visitors, see, and she liked an audience.'

'It was a false alarm, and lucky for her that it was.' And Vera should know because Rose said her little Mikey was a right terror and no mistake.

'Hang on a minute.' Ellie turned her piece of paper over and scribbled on the back. 'Who was Mrs Pryce's solicitor?'

Vera shrugged. 'No idea. She didn't hold with them, nor with doctors. Keep out of their clutches and you'll live longer, she said.'

'She must have made a will.'

Pet said, 'They were always on at her about it. Dunno as she ever did, though.'

'Perhaps she will now,' said Vera, clearing away the coffee mugs.

'Who drove her off to the retirement home? Fritz?'

'He did offer, but she drove herself,' said Vera. 'We was a bit worried about her doing that, but she wanted to take this and that with her, precious things, you know? She said it would be all right, if she took it slow.'

'When did you see her last?'

'Coupla days before she left. We offered to come in after the Cats Protection people took the pussies, and the auctioneers and house clearance people took the furniture. To clean up, leave everything tidy. First she said yes, she'd like that, and then she left a message at the office for us not to bother. I'm glad, really. It's sad to see a house that's been a home pulled apart like that.'

'Vera, did you manage to get one of the cats for yourself?'

'I did think about it, but no; being out all day working, and then Mikey might not have handled it too well, so, no; it wasn't fair. They went to a good home.'

'Do you know which auction house she used? No?' Ellie took another sheet of paper off the pad. 'What about the keys you had?'

'Returned to the office.'

'We really must get on,' said Pet, picking up a box of cleaning materials. 'Shall I do your bathroom first?'

Ellie frowned at her jottings. She thought there were a lot more questions she ought to have asked but . . . another day, perhaps. She could hear Rose, weakly calling for her. First things first.

Rose was sitting in her chair, the television on but muted. Rose was crying.

Ellie was alarmed. 'You're in pain? I'll get you something.'

'No, no. Just a little throbbing, it will soon go, not to worry, I'm not made of paper, you know? But Ellie, we're such old friends and go back such a long way that – won't you sit down for a moment? There, always on the go, always thinking of other people, but as Miss Quicke said to me the other day, it's about time you took a little thought for yourself, so there's nothing for it, the time has come and I'm not complaining, I've had a good run for my money, haven't I? But all good things . . . You do understand, don't you?'

'Not really, my dear. Tell me.'

'You're far too soft-hearted to say it, so I'm saying it for you. It's time I went into a home.'

Ellie took one of Rose's frail, freckled hands in both of hers. 'If you're tired of living with us and think you'd get better care somewhere else, you must say so and of course we'll arrange it. But Rose, we'd much rather look after you here.'

Silvery trails ran down Rose's cheeks. 'It's no use, I'm losing the plot as they say. It was just little things at first, putting down onions instead of potatoes on the shopping list and forgetting to turn the oven on when I've put the pie in. I found the bread in the laundry basket the other day, and I've just realized I pulled up all those gladioli you planted, thinking they were montbretias, which are just like weeds and best be got rid of. There's no point saying I'm doing my job as a housekeeper when I haven't been able to manage the stairs for ever. And now I'm starting to see things.'

'Dear Rose. I've been round to look at the Pryce house and I, too, thought someone was watching me when I was in their garden.'

'I could see this face looking down at me, floating in mid-air. That's not right and you can't pretend that it is.'

'Maybe there was someone there, hiding in the attic.'

Rose closed her eyes and let her head fall to one side. 'It was all right when Mia was here to keep an eye on me. What a blessing that girl has been, picking up things after me, seeing to everything I forget, but it's only right and proper that she gets on with her own life now. I know you'd do your best to look after me, but it's too much to ask even of you, and unfair to Thomas, too. So I must go.'

Tuesday afternoon

'Vera! Have you finished with the hoover?'

'Coming. Fancy Terry Pryce ripping off Mrs Quicke like

that! When Mrs Pryce finds out, she'll do her nut, cut him out of her will and all.'

'Serve him right. He's got a job, hasn't he?'

'All that lot's short of the readies, Pet.'

'Not to mention us.'

'Mind that corner. She goes bonkers if you scratch her mahogany.' Vera straightened up from dusting the skirting board. 'I've got a funny feeling about Mrs Pryce. I wonder if she took sick driving down and is in hospital somewhere.'

Pet shrugged. 'She probably changed her mind about the retirement home and went off on a wild adventure to Spain or Monte Carlo.'

'I suppose.'

They finished their work in silence.

SIX

Tuesday afternoon

Ellie said, 'Now, Rose; you listen to me for a change. We've known one another for years and been through a lot together. You transformed my aunt's life for the good when you moved in with her, and you are part of our family now. What's more, you've had more to do with Mia's return to health than we have.

'We don't want you to leave us. Yes, you've had a shock, falling off the ladder and hurting yourself, and it may take a while for you to recover. Of course, we mustn't stand in Mia's way. It's only right and proper that she should move on. So I'm thinking about finding someone to come in every day to be with you when I have to go out. You can tell them what to do about the house, and they'll do it. Just until you're back on top of things again.'

'Suppose – suppose I don't ever get back to the way I used to be? Suppose I go on seeing things?'

It was true she'd been having imaginary conversations with her old employer recently. Thomas said this was because Rose had been so close to Miss Quicke that she could come out with whatever she thought her old employer might have had to say on any given situation. He said that if Rose chose to think she actually 'saw' Miss Quicke on these occasions, it was a harmless phenomenon and not to be confused with seeing a ghost.

Ellie had an inspiration. 'Have you asked my aunt about this? I don't think she'd want you to leave us – or her.'

'Oh.' Rose thought about that. 'No, I haven't seen her lately.' She struggled upright. 'I wonder . . . She was talking about the plants in the conservatory last time I saw her, said they weren't looking as good as when I was caring for them. I don't think that dratted gardener understands them. Perhaps I could get out there later on, have a look at the plants, see what she says.'

Miss Quicke had added the conservatory to the back of the house specifically for Rose to potter around in, and it seemed that that was where the old lady was usually to be found. Not that anyone apart from Rose had ever seen her.

'What a good idea,' said Ellie, looking at her watch. 'I'll get you some lunch and after you've had your little rest this afternoon, you can see if you feel up to it.'

Ellie left her old friend smiling. Back in the kitchen, Ellie inspected the contents of the fridge. As she put various items on the table for the meal, she noticed that her notes on the conversation with Vera and Pet had disappeared. Had they been disposed of by accident or design?

Come to think of it, hadn't there been a something and a nothing . . . a half-formed thought about . . . an uneasiness in her mind that had arisen during that apparently frank talk?

Ellie looked through the pile of newspapers put out ready for recycling, but the sheets from her shopping list were not there. The black bag that lined the bin in the kitchen was clean and fresh – and empty.

Ellie went outside the back door and found a rubbish bag which Vera or Pet had just filled and put there. She opened it, wincing as tiny vinegar flies stormed out. No notes. There was nothing in the green box used for recycled paper, either. How very odd.

'We're off now!' Vera put her head out of the kitchen door and waved goodbye. 'See you Friday.'

'Yes,' said Ellie. 'Have you seen . . . ?' She was talking to thin air. She went back indoors and down the corridor to her study, where she set about writing down again everything she could remember that Vera and Pet had told her.

She finished up by scrawling a couple of questions to herself. Why had her notes been removed? And which of the girls had done it?

She made soup and sandwiches for lunch and distributed them around the house. Thomas was on the phone and merely grunted to her when she took his tray in. At least the bishop had gone.

Ellie took her own tray into her study and, picking up the phone, asked Directory Enquiries to find her the number for the Corfton Towers Retirement home, which they did.

A bright-voiced woman answered the phone.

Ellie said, 'Is it possible to speak to Mrs Pryce? Mrs Flavia Pryce?'

'Who?' A pause. 'Sorry. We don't have anyone of that name here.'

'Are you sure? She told me she was moving into your place, oh, it must be nearly six weeks ago now. My friends had arranged to come out to see her on her birthday, but may have to change the date. My name is Quicke, Mrs Ellie Quicke, and I live in the next road to Mrs Pryce in Ealing.'

'One moment, please.' A tapping of keys. Using a computer? 'No, I'm sorry, we have no one of that name here.'

'How very odd. I mean; she's left her house here, all the furniture's gone, her cats have been collected, bills all paid up.' A gentle laugh. 'She can't have got married and changed her name again, can she?'

'Just a minute.' Ellie was put on hold. Some irritating music was played at her. Vivaldi. One of the Four Seasons? There's a muffled quality to sound played like that over the phone. Ellie grimaced.

'Mrs – er – Quicke? Is that right?' An educated man's voice, with a slight accent. Punjabi? Perhaps this was the man whom Terry Pryce had spoken to?

'Yes. Ellie Quicke. A neighbour of Mrs Pryce's. Our garden walls touch at one point, although the entrance to her house is on the next road.'

'My assistant tells me you and some friends have arranged to come over to visit Mrs Pryce. Do you know her well?'

'I don't understand. If she hasn't got a phone of her own in her room, then surely you can reach her through the switch-board, or send someone to tell her she's wanted on the phone?'

'That would be the position if we had a Mrs Pryce here. But we do not.'

'But – she said she was moving to—'

'That was the position as we understood it, too. Mrs Pryce paid six months rent in advance and booked our biggest room

with en suite and French doors leading on to the garden. She
was businesslike in all her dealings with us. She made it clear
that if she found our facilities not to her liking, she would be
moving on, in which case we agreed that she would give us
two months' notice.

'Although her furniture arrived here as arranged, she did
not. She phoned the day after she was due to arrive, saying
she'd changed her mind about moving in. She said she'd let
us have instructions as to what was to be done with her belongings. We have heard nothing since. We had no reason to suspect
that the balance of her mind was disturbed, but this is the only
explanation we have that fits the facts.'

'But . . . where has she gone?'

'We have no idea. We have repeatedly sent letters to her
old address, which remain unanswered. We are holding her
furniture until the six months that she paid for is up, although
naturally we have stored them in a back room as we can let
our best suite a dozen times over.'

Ellie rubbed her forehead. 'She gave you no hint as to where
she intended to go?'

'None. We did ask for a number on which we could reach
Mrs Pryce, and she gave us a mobile number which seems to
be out of service. We do not appreciate dealing with people
who can't make up their minds.'

'I'm sure you don't. What do her next of kin say?'

'She told us she had none.'

Oh. Mrs Pryce really didn't like her family, did she? 'I see.
Well, thank you.'

'My pleasure. Have a nice day.' He put the phone down,
and so did Ellie.

Thomas came into the room. He looked preoccupied, till
he saw Ellie's face. 'What's up, my love?'

'Mrs Pryce's furniture arrived at the retirement home, but
she didn't.'

'So, she changed her mind.'

'A woman doesn't carefully select what furniture she needs
to make herself comfortable in retirement and send it on to
her new home only to abandon it without explanation.
Something's happened to her.'

'Yes, that is odd. Tell me all about it.'

'In a minute.' Ellie keyed in the phone number for her ex son-in-law, Stewart. He picked up straight away. 'Listen, Stewart. I want to look round the Disneyland house in the next road. Can you get me an order to view?'

'Surely you don't want to buy it? It would be the devil and all to adapt it into flats, and it'd cost the earth. The house could be pulled down and the site developed, I suppose. That is, if you could get planning permission, which wouldn't be easy in that neighbourhood. You don't really want to go into that line, do you?'

Ellie felt her temper rise. 'I don't have time to explain at the moment. I could contact Hoopers myself, but they must know you deal with the property side of our business, and it would sound better coming from you. Will you arrange for me to have a look at it, the sooner the better, please?'

'Yes, of course. I'll ring you back.' He sounded hurt; was he going to be upset because she hadn't time to take him into her confidence? Well, tough.

She put the phone down and gave her attention to Thomas, saying, 'Have you got rid of your bishop?' And knew her tone was too sharp.

'As bishops go, he went.'

'You don't care for him? I thought bishops were in the habit of summoning you to their palaces, rather than finding their way out here to the wilds of West London.'

'Ah. Well. He's written a book and wants me to serialize it in the magazine, and I don't think it's, er, appropriate. He refuses to accept that it's not appropriate. He's tried writing and phoning me. No joy. Hence the state visit. Now, light of my life; what's worrying you? Diana?'

Ellie tried to switch her mind over to her daughter's problems and got there eventually. 'She says she's got a new man in her life.'

'Uh-huh.'

'She proposes to set up house with him and Frank in my old house, the one I made over to her.'

'Oh, but—'

'Stewart and I will resist with our last breath.'

'Quite right. That's all?'

'No. She wants me to bail her out of yet another financial difficulty. When she started the agency with Denis, they both signed a document saying that if one of them wanted to leave, the other would have to buy them out. Denis wants out, and she hasn't got the money to get rid of him. Plus, she's in debt all round. She says. I suggested she mortgage her flat and the house she'd rented out; she says she's done that already in order to keep the agency going.'

He stroked his beard. Sighed.

'She wants me to buy Denis off, so that the agency can be taken over by a larger concern. She even offered to repay the money as a loan later, which surprised me. I said I couldn't find the money. She doesn't believe me.'

Silence.

Ellie pushed back her chair. 'I'm at my wits' end. How can I find that much money for her, without taking it out of the charity – which I can't and won't do!'

'No.'

'But if I don't she'll go bankrupt. I can't bear the thought of that.'

'Ellie, I can understand your distress, but . . . may I gently point out that it's about time Diana took responsibility for her own actions?'

Ellie blinked. Was it? The relief, if it was. 'But . . .'

'See that Stewart has a good solicitor because I agree that there's no way Diana should have custody of Frank. Her life-style is not suitable.'

'Stewart's on to that already. Thomas, are you sure? I mean, the only way I could raise the money for her is to mortgage this house, but then we'd have difficulty repaying the instal-ments. We could sell it, but it's our home, and Rose's. Of course, we could live in a smaller place, but then you need an office and so do I, and I love this house, which is silly, I know it's only bricks and mortar, but I really don't want to move. Oh dear, hark at me. I'm babbling.'

'I don't see why you should have to move.'

She grimaced. 'A poor job I've made of bringing up Diana.'

'The responsibility for her upbringing was not entirely yours.'

'No.' She relaxed. Closed her eyes. Breathed deeply. Felt the burden roll off her. 'You're right. She's trying to push everything on to me as usual, and this is one too far for me.' The burden rolled back. 'And yet . . . No, I suppose you're right.'

'It's moral blackmail.'

Ellie nodded. 'Yes, I must try to think of it that way and not get into a tizzy about it.'

'You've prayed about it?'

She nodded. Oh. Actually, she hadn't. Not really.

'And the other problem? Mrs Pryce?'

'Could you bear to take another walk around there with me? I want to see if her car's still in the garage. Vera and Pet said Mrs Pryce was going to drive herself to her new home in her own car. There's a big padlock on the door, but perhaps we could take a torch and shine it through the window in the covered way to see if the car's gone.' She struck her forehead with her hand. 'I forgot. Mia's out and I can't leave Rose alone.'

'I'm expecting some more phone calls, so I can't come just yet. Mia was going to have lunch with her roly-poly boyfriend and said she wouldn't be late. Can you wait till she gets back and I've spoken to a couple of people? I'll come with you then.'

Ellie subsided into her chair and surveyed the paperwork her part-time secretary had left out for her to do. 'Yes, of course. That would be the sensible thing to do.'

Thomas nodded and left her to it.

Ellie wanted to sweep all the paperwork off her desk on to the floor. And maybe trample on it. She wanted to lie down on the floor and have a tantrum like a two year old.

Sensible? She didn't feel sensible. She felt . . . stressed.

She ought to pray about all sorts of things, but everything was going round and round in her head like a washing machine caught on a spin cycle.

Diana's finances.

Little Frank's bed-wetting.

Rose's failing health.

The missing Mrs Pryce. Find the lady.

Ellie couldn't concentrate on any one of them long enough to formulate a coherent appeal to the Almighty. After all, He knew all about it, didn't He? Oh yes. But she seemed to remember that He liked to be reminded. Well, the best she could do was . . . *Please, if you could spare a minute?*

So . . . be sensible? Deal with office work?

It was impossible to concentrate.

She went back to the kitchen to start a new shopping list. Mia had said she'd bring back something for supper, but they were nearly out of sugar and tea bags . . . spreadable butter . . . and they'd hardly any cereals left, or bread. They needed more eggs, of course. The freezer looked half empty; it was time to restock. There was an excellent greengrocery in the Lane. She needed more than she could carry in one go. She wondered if they would deliver if she made up a big enough order.

Mia had been doing most of the food shopping of late, but Mia would soon be gone.

Ellie bobbed around from cupboard to fridge to larder, her list growing. She'd been shown how to order online some time ago, but had forgotten how. Perhaps it was time to relearn a skill which would be useful when Mia left?

Rose slept a little and woke feeling more cheerful, much more like her old self. Her wrist was still swollen, though. They had tea at the kitchen table and ate the last of a sponge cake Mia had made. How did she manage to get her cakes so light?

Stewart rang to say that he'd arranged a viewing of Disneyland for the following morning. He said he was rather busy so did Ellie need him along? Oh dear, he was in a huff, wasn't he? She couldn't be bothered to explain, so said that would be perfectly all right, thank you.

Mia returned from her lengthy lunch date with glowing cheeks and eyes snapping with . . . temper? Or romance? Plus a rack of lamb chops which looked delicious.

She readily agreed to help Ellie put an order for food through online and stood over her while she did it, which made Ellie feel so inadequate that she fumbled every click of the mouse. Mia was patience itself. Ellie wanted to hit her. Finally the order was completed and Ellie pressed 'Send'.

'There, now,' said Mia. 'You can do it all by yourself next time, can't you?'

Ellie gritted her teeth and tried to smile. She didn't think she *could* do it all by herself next time. There were some things her brain wasn't well equipped for, and ordering things on the computer was one of them.

After supper, Ellie went out into the garden to do some watering. She tried to have a constructive think about all her problems, ended up soaking her skirt with a misdirected hose-pipe and had to stand there, flapping it about in order to get it to dry.

Action. That was the ticket. So she bearded Thomas in his den. 'Are you free now to take another walk round the block? I want to test a theory.'

'Sure. I need to get away for a while.' He abandoned his desk with alacrity.

This time Ellie didn't linger to admire God's creation of so many beautiful trees and flowers. This time she was anxious to get to the house.

Someone was already in the drive, standing by the garage. A woman, trying and failing to lift a young boy up to look through the windows above the garage doors.

It was Vera, with her brown-skinned son. 'Oh, Mrs Quicke, you'll say I'm daft, but I got to thinking after we talked this morning . . . and the more I thought, the more worried I got that maybe something had happened to Mrs Pryce, and I couldn't get her out of mind. I had to collect Mikey from the childminder's when I finished work, and I found myself walking back this way, just to look at the outside of her house. Say "hello" to Mrs Quicke, Mikey.'

The boy muttered something. He had lively brown eyes and curly black hair, quite a contrast to his fair-haired, grey-eyed mother. Ellie remembered that he was supposed to be difficult. Autistic? Badly-behaved? At a special school?

Vera stared up at the house. 'Do you think she might have had an accident on the way, driving herself, you know?'

'Have you tried ringing the hospitals, Vera?'

Vera shook her head, making her hoop earrings catch the light. 'It's only since you said something might be wrong today that I've been worried.'

'The same here. If we lifted Mikey up, do you think he could see if her car's still inside the garage? Only, that window over the double doors is rather small, and I doubt if anyone could see anything through it.'

'Don't you touch me!' Mikey kicked the door. And went on kicking it.

'Stop that now,' said his mother.

He didn't stop. She picked him up, and he went berserk, arms and legs all over the place. Vera staggered and would have fallen, but that Thomas took the boy off her and held him close. Mikey shrieked and struggled, but Thomas was able to control him. At last the boy went limp.

'Sorry about that,' said Vera, who was almost in tears. 'He gets so excited, and if he's crossed . . . Sometimes I'm afraid that . . .'

'Yes, of course,' said Thomas, and set Mikey on his feet while retaining one of the boy's hands in his.

Ellie felt limp, too. 'Do you want to take him home? Suppose we just have a quick look through the window in the covered way.' She pushed open the door in the wall and stepped through into the yard.

'Hang about,' said Vera. 'That door's always kept bolted.'

'Well, it isn't bolted now. I think your gardener is coming and going this way.'

Vera's eyes slid away from Ellie's. Vera knew the gardener was still coming, all right.

Thomas put on his reading glasses to inspect the door. 'See these screw holes? It looks as though a padlock has been screwed into the woodwork here, only to be removed later on.' He inspected the bolt on the inside of the door. It slid to and fro with ease. Had it been oiled recently? 'If I found the door padlocked and bolted I could easily unscrew the fitment that held the padlock in place. Then I'd stand on something to reach over the top of the door to knock the bolt back.'

Hm. Not brilliant security.

Once in the courtyard they surveyed doors and windows. Thomas tested the door into the kitchen quarters. 'Locked and possibly bolted as well.'

More padlocks were on the doors which led into the garage, and two further doors beyond that. There was just the one small window into the garage. Ellie went on tiptoe to look through it. It was very dark in the garage, but if there'd been a car inside, surely she would have been able to see a glint of metal here and there? The purr of machinery was soft but distinct. Someone mowing their lawn nearby?

Thomas lifted Mikey up to the window. 'Tell me what you can see, Mikey.'

Mikey announced: 'Nothing.'

'Can't you see the big car?' said Thomas.

Mikey shook his head. 'No car, stupid!' His colour had returned to normal, and when Thomas set him on his feet again, he didn't run off or misbehave.

'Of course the car's not there,' said Vera. 'Silly old me, thinking . . . I expect she had an accident, or ran out of petrol or something.' She looked to Thomas for confirmation that her fears had been ridiculous. Women always looked to Thomas to solve their problems. Some men, too.

Ellie said, 'I grant you that her car's not there, but it doesn't follow that she drove off in it.'

SEVEN

Tuesday evening

Mikey darted to the kitchen door and tried to open it. 'Can we go inside now? See the lady?'

'The lady's gone.' Vera pulled him away.

Thomas checked all the doors leading out of the covered area. All were locked and/or padlocked, except for the one they'd come in by and the one that led into the garden. 'Vera, oughtn't all these doors have been padlocked?'

Vera reddened. 'Bolted on the inside, usually. I suppose Fritz, the gardener, thought he might as well harvest the crops he'd sown, because he hasn't a garden of his own. I expect Mrs Pryce told him he could.'

Thomas fingered his beard. 'Fritz put the padlocks on when she left?'

'I think she asked the window cleaner. He did lots of odd jobs for her, because he had ladders to get up to the guttering if it needed attention, that sort of thing.'

'What's his name and where might we find him?'

A shrug. 'He comes when he feels like it. Jack; Jack the Lad. Likes the sun, goes to Spain for his holidays. Big man, gives me the shivers, but Mrs Pryce likes a man with muscles, if you see what I mean. No idea what his second name is.'

Ellie pushed the far door open into the garden. The sun had gone behind a cloud, but the scent of roses lay heavily around them. She walked down the path past the pond and the lawn to inspect the vegetable garden.

Thomas paced behind her. 'Fritz hasn't bothered to mow the lawn.'

Vera jumped to his defence. 'Mrs Pryce sold the mower and asked the estate agent to get a contractor in to cut the lawns. I don't know why they haven't done it.'

Mikey ran into the hayfield that had been the lawn, screamed with delight, dropped on to his stomach, and rolled around.

The adults ignored him to survey the vegetable garden.

'Fritz knows how to grow vegetables, doesn't he?' said Thomas. 'Where is he keeping his tools, or does he bring them in each time he comes?'

Vera shrugged. 'He has an old van that he takes his tools round in. He works all over the place.'

Thomas inspected the damp earth beside the still-dripping tap. 'Heavy boots. A man's, recent. Only one set. Fritz?'

Vera shrugged again.

Ellie was scanning the windows of the house. Was that one at the top slightly open? It was difficult to judge from where she stood. 'My housekeeper said she saw a face at that upstairs window.' She pointed.

Vera shook her head. 'Mrs Pryce hasn't been up to the top floor for months. Her knees, you know.'

Did Vera think . . . fear . . . hope . . . that Mrs Pryce was still in the house? 'Have you keys to the house, Vera?'

Vera shook her head. 'Mrs Pryce said to hand them in at the office, so we did. I must be getting back. If Mikey doesn't get his tea soon, he'll create something awful.'

Ellie said, 'I've arranged to look round the house tomorrow morning. Vera, if I fix it with the office and pay you for your time, do you think you could go round with me? You know the house better than anyone and can tell if . . . if anything's amiss.'

Vera blinked, taking in the subtext. 'OK. What about Pet?'

Ellie wasn't sure why she didn't want Pet, but knew she didn't. 'Just you and me. I'll see you're not out of pocket, and the office can fix someone else up to do your cleaning jobs with Pet.'

'You think . . . ?'

'I don't think. I want to check. By the way, did you happen to notice where I put the notes I made about the Pryce family?'

'Pet put them on one side for you. Are you going to ring the police, then?'

Ellie shuddered. She could imagine what Ears would say.

That silly woman, wasting our time. Of course Mrs Pryce changed her mind. That's what women do. 'I don't know, Vera. Thomas, what do you think?'

'If her car were still in the garage, I'd be inclined to think something had happened to her before she left. But if she drove away under her own steam . . . Perhaps she liked the look of a hotel en route and decided to stay there awhile? Vera, do you know what make of car she has, and the licence number?'

Vera shrugged. 'She changes her car every year, gets the latest, automatic, satnav and so on. I think she said it was a Toyota. Would that be right?'

Ellie was struck with a thought. 'It wasn't egg yellow, was it?'

'Toyotas are not egg yellow,' said Thomas, through his teeth.

'It was silver,' said Vera. 'With wide doors. It was easy to get in and out of which mattered to her because of her knees. I don't remember the licence number. She couldn't, either. She was cross with herself because she could have asked them to transfer her old number to her new car, only she forgot.'

Thomas gave Vera a look which meant he despaired of women who couldn't remember licence numbers and makes of car.

Ellie gave her a look, too, but hers was one of sympathy.

Thomas held back impatience with the pair of them. 'Well, it's not much use informing the police her car is missing, if we don't have the licence details and make. I agree, she ought to have let someone know where she is. Perhaps we should see if her daughter knows the licence number, before we send up alarm signals?'

Tuesday evening

Two frightened young people.
    'Why are you so late? I've been waiting for ever. We've got to leave, now!'
    'I'm only fifteen minutes late, stopped off to get us a pizza.'

'We'll have to eat it on the way. They're coming tomorrow to search the house!'

'Who? The gardener?'

'Of course not. He only comes at midday.'

'Calm down and tell me what's happened.'

The girl gulped, calmed her breathing. 'I heard a child scream. I had the window open just a crack, it's been so hot, I had to have some air. I crouched down below the sill. I could hear everything, as clear as if they were in the room with me. She was there, that woman from the house over the wall, a big man with a beard, and a blonde girl with a child. The boy was rolling around in the grass. They were looking for some woman who used to own the house—'

'Mrs Pryce? But she's long gone, and nobody's taken any interest in this house since. I'd have heard if they had.'

'I tell you they're coming tomorrow morning to search the place. We've got to get out of here tonight! Didn't you say your aunt might let me stay for a bit?'

'I'll ring her after we've eaten. It's all right; if they're not coming till tomorrow we've got time to clear up and get out.'

Tuesday evening

Ellie arranged to meet Vera next morning at ten, and they went their several ways: Thomas and Ellie to spend some time on the phone, and Vera to take her struggling, wriggling son back home for his tea.

The air was close, threatening a thunderstorm.

When Ellie got back home, she found that Rose had made no attempt to leave the kitchen, not even to visit the conservatory. Ah well.

Thomas said he'd do some investigating via the phone book, so Ellie took the opportunity to call the office of her cleaning company. It was after hours, but she left a message to say, with apologies for disrupting the system, that she'd arranged for Vera to work for her privately the following morning so could they get someone else to partner Pet.

There were no messages from Diana, for which Ellie was thankful.

Just as she was wondering what to do next, Stewart phoned to say he'd arranged for a Mr Abel from Hoopers to meet Ellie at Disneyland tomorrow at ten, if that was all right by her. She could tell Stewart was still annoyed with her, but it was too hot and too complicated to go into explanations.

'Thank you, Stewart. Do you know Mr Abel personally?'

'We've met.' Stewart was being very stiff and formal.

'What's he like?'

'Fine. He's keen to do business with us, as why wouldn't he be, but when I expressed surprise that the house hadn't already been snapped up by a developer, he hummed and hahed a bit, and then came clean. Mrs Pryce did put her house on the market with Hoopers, only to withdraw it later. They've heard nothing from her since, and it's not been put in any other estate agent's hands, so it's not at all clear what Mrs Pryce is playing at. Perhaps she's keeping all her options open, thinking she might wish to return there some day?

'Under the circumstances, Hoopers haven't advertised the house, but if you're interested they'll be happy to contact her to see what can be done. Houses which are left to their own devices tend to deteriorate, as you know very well. Mr Abel is enthusiastic, and he'll pull out all the stops for you. You aren't really interested in it, are you?'

'I need to see round it, that's all. What address do they have for her? They do have one, I assume?'

'Of course.' Very offhand. 'Well, if you could manage by yourself, I'm due to sign off the work on the block of flats by the river tomorrow morning.' He had taken umbrage, hadn't he? 'Are you sure you don't want me to cancel that, so that I can go round with you?'

'No, no. No need.'

Frost sharpened his tone. 'You'll let me know, if you decide you do want the house?'

'Of course.' Some day soon she'd explain and make it up to him, but not at the moment.

Several times she caught herself wondering why she hadn't wanted Pet to join her and Vera on the morrow. Well, Vera had said it was Pet who had tidied the notes on the Pryce family away. Had she put them where Ellie hadn't been able to find them by accident or design? But why would she do that?

Then again, Ellie only had Vera's word for it that it was Pet who had got rid of the notes. Perhaps it had been Vera instead, throwing the blame on Pet? But if so, why?

Thomas came in to say he'd tried Mrs Pryce's phone number at the Disneyland address, only to be informed by an irritating recorded voice that the number was no longer available. There were four other Pryces in the phone book; two were out, and he'd left messages on their answerphones. The other two had disclaimed any connection with the missing lady.

So far, so good.

In the middle of the night Ellie woke up, remembering something she'd seen. Or not seen, rather. Vera had been wearing the earrings Mrs Pryce had given her, but Pet – although she'd said her own gift had been just what she wanted – had not. Was there any significance in this? Perhaps Pet's necklet was too valuable to wear for work?

Mm. No. The earrings might have cost as much as twenty, possibly thirty pounds. If Mrs Pryce had been even-handed in her gifts, then Pet's would not have cost more than Vera's. Probably. Something else to think about.

Wednesday morning

Another hot day. Ellie rummaged around in her handbag, in the top drawers of her dressing table and in the stir fry on her desk before locating her sunglasses. They wrapped around her face nicely and had only cost a couple of quid from the charity shop. The downside was that the side pieces were straight, so if she looked down, they fell off. Well, never mind. She hadn't got another pair, and today was definitely a day for sunglasses.

She saw Thomas settled in his study – it was getting towards that time of the month when he had to email his copy off to the printers. Mia said she wasn't planning to go out in this heat, so she'd stay in with Rose. Perhaps they'd make some ice cream.

Pat, Ellie's part-time assistant and secretary, arrived to deal with the post and to sigh at her for not having attended to the correspondence which had been left out for her attention. Ellie dutifully spent an hour getting through the pile, and then set out for Disneyland with a clear conscience.

Would it have been sensible to ask Thomas or Stewart to come with her? No, not particularly. So long as Vera made it on time . . . which she had done. Ellie spotted her on the pavement outside the Pryce house, talking to a youngish, balding man in shirtsleeves and tailored trousers who was holding a clipboard of papers.

Although it wasn't yet noon, Mr Abel was perspiring. And oozing words in a stream.

'Ms Quicke? Are you Ms Quicke? I assumed this dear lady here was Ms Quicke, but she tells me she's not. What a pity, but now that we're all here, let me say what a pleasure it is to be meeting you, as I've heard . . .'

Etcetera.

Ellie and Vera whisked glances at one another and dutifully followed Mr Abel up the drive.

'Isn't this the most splendid example of Victorian Gothic? It must be the only one of its kind . . .'

'It reminds me of Disneyland, actually,' said Ellie, thinking that the next hour was going to be extremely trying if Mr Abel didn't dry up. Besides which, he was quite wrong if he thought this monstrosity had anything to do with Victorian Gothic, which had fallen out of favour fifty years before this particular house had been built.

'Disneyland? Oh, no!' said Mr Abel, and burst into inappropriate laughter.

Ellie refrained from rolling her eyes at Vera. Just.

Mr Abel patted his forehead and cheeks with a clean handkerchief. 'Well, as I was saying to this other dear lady, you can see what a majestic approach this drive makes to an imposing, original property. An hour with a strimmer and you can imagine how it would look, the bushes cut back, the lawn manicured.'

Vera turned her ankle on a rut in the driveway. 'Ouch.'

'Take care,' said Ellie. 'It's been so dry lately.' Under the overgrown bushes beyond the garage there were ruts which had been made when it last rained – which must be a couple of weeks back. The ruts were perhaps too wide apart for a car, but might have been made by a van. The gardener's?

The gravelled drive was too hard to take an impression, but the long grass on the wreck of a lawn had been crushed under wheels recently. Very recently.

Had the tracks been visible when they'd visited the previous evening? Would she have noticed if they had? Yes, she rather thought she would. Which meant they'd been made either last night after she left or early this morning.

She bent over to inspect the indentations in the grass, and her glasses slid forward on her nose. She caught them just in time and shoved them up again.

'As you can see,' Mr Abel burbled, 'the house is in excellent condition, having been beautifully maintained by the previous owner.' Reading from his clipboard: 'The whole house was rewired and replumbed, and a new kitchen and a wet room installed only two years ago . . .'

Ellie mounted the steps to the front door. 'You are in touch with her, of course? I heard she'd moved into a retirement home in the country.'

'Yes, yes.' With a quick glance at his notes. 'But you'll be going through us, won't you?'

So he thought Mrs Pryce was in the retirement home, too. Hm. Oh well, it would be a feather in Mr Abel's cap if he did manage to sell her this monstrosity . . . Not that she had any intention of buying it.

He unlocked the front door and pushed it open. There was a stack of letters, free papers and junk mail lying to one side on the floor within. But not, Ellie noticed, in a fan shape directly behind the door, which is where mail usually landed when pushed through the letterbox. The front door had been opened and shut recently, which had pushed the mail to one side. So who had done that?

Mr Abel bent to pick the letters up. 'I suppose she forgot to ask for her mail to be forwarded to her . . . Although junk mail, almost impossible to stop . . . As you can see . . . Phew, phew, a bit hard on the old heart, what? Should go to the gym more often, har, har! As you can see, a magnificent hall with original panelling, stained-glass windows and parquet floor.'

'Yes, it's like mine, only larger.' Ellie stepped around him, taking off her now redundant sunglasses.

'Just think what a splendid nursing home this would make,' said Mr Abel, clutching an armful of mail without knowing in the least what to do with it.

'Let me,' said Vera. She took the bundle from him and placed it on a wide ledge over a central heating radiator.

There was dust, everywhere. Of course.

Except . . . except for a cleared space on the floor between the front door and the imposing oak staircase.

Add it up. Someone had recently opened the front door, pushing the mail to one side. They had then swept a passage free of dust from the front door across the hall to the staircase. Ho, hum. 'Someone from the agency comes round regularly to check on the place?'

'Er, no. We have not been instructed to do so.' He was frowning at the dust-free track on the floor. No fool, Mr Abel. He knew as well as they did that someone beside themselves had recently been inside the house.

Had Vera noticed? She was looking at the floor, too.

Ellie decided that Mr Abel could be of no more assistance to her now that he'd got her into the house. How could she get rid of him? 'Would you like to sort through the mail, see what needs forwarding? Vera can show me around as she used to work here. And then I'll get back to you. Right?'

'Oh, but—'

Vera was quick to act on Ellie's hint and threw open the first door on the left. 'This room gets the morning sun. She used it as a study, big roll-top desk in the sticky-out round tower with windows all round. She attended to all her business affairs, paid her bills in here. Her computer and printer were on a side table, there. Velvet curtains to the floor.'

'Central heating, I see. Efficient?' There was a layer of dust everywhere.

Mr Abel couldn't bear to leave them and was now riffling through his notes to find the relevant page. 'She had a new boiler installed last year.'

'The heating cost a bomb to run,' said Vera, ignoring him, 'but she had money, didn't she? The library is next. As you can see the shelves were built in, so she had to leave them. And finally on this side of the house there's the sitting room that she liked best because it looked on to the garden . . .'

More dust. No footprints on the floor, except the ones they were making themselves. Mr Abel followed them round, struggling to sort the post as he did so. He went into a patter, eulogizing the height of the ceilings and the elaborate cornices.

These were huge rooms, which must have been difficult to furnish. There were marks on the floorboards where squares of carpet had once been, and squares of darker colour on the wallpapers where dozens of pictures had once hung . . . probably all with elaborate gold frames. There were French windows at the back looking on to the garden, overhung with climbing roses.

'Now, down this short corridor under the stairs is what she called the garden room,' said Vera. 'It gives on to the patio and lawn beyond.'

More dust. No footprints. An aged Belfast sink with straight sides, a wooden draining-board, lots of empty shelving and glass-fronted cabinets.

Vera was nostalgic. 'She kept her flower vases in here. She had dozens of them, mostly cut-glass and some of them valuable. She used to cut flowers from the garden and arrange them in here for the drawing room and her bedroom, right up to the end.

'The cats' baskets were kept here, too. You see the cat flap in the door? She fed them in here, and not in the kitchen. All their foodstuffs were kept in these cupboards so they couldn't get at them when they shouldn't, and of course the sink made it easy to wash out their dishes.'

Ellie spotted something. 'The tap's dripping. Wasn't the water turned off at the mains when she left?'

Vera was frowning. 'I believe so.'

'You weren't responsible?'

'I think the gardener, Fritz, was supposed to turn everything off.'

Mr Abel made a note, causing him to drop some of his bundle of post on to the floor. 'Water not turned off. I'd better see if I can stop that tap dripping.'

Ellie wondered if Fritz had turned the water off as instructed, but later turned it back on so that he could have water outside for his vegetables. In which case, how often had Fritz been coming back to visit the house, and what – if anything – did he know about Mrs Pryce's disappearance? If that, indeed, was what it was.

Vera led the way back to the hall and past the imposing stairs, leaving Mr Abel trying to turn off the dripping tap.

'Next we have the downstairs cloakroom, with a loo off it. She kept her outdoor clothes, wellies and brollies and shopping bags in here.'

All gone, now.

Vera threw open another door. 'This is the dining room, which Mrs Pryce said could seat twenty. The table had three leaves you could put in to extend it, and there was a set of matching chairs, which she said really belonged in a museum.'

Another huge room. More dust. No footprints. Vera said, 'She never used the dining room as long as I knew her. She had a tray on a table in her drawing room when she was by herself, though when she got a bit frail to carry trays, she used a trolley or ate in the kitchen.'

Mr Abel could be heard grunting with the effort to turn off the dripping tap as Vera led Ellie on to another room. 'The music room. It's been shut up for ever. She sold the grand piano way, way back.' Another huge, dusty room.

Vera turned back across the hall to a small, panelled reception room on the opposite side of the hall to the room Mrs Pryce had used as an office.

'This was a children's playroom once, she said. But of course she didn't have any children, and she used it only when she watched the telly, which wasn't often as she preferred to read a large-print book or listen to tapes. Her sight wasn't that good and she needed glasses for reading. She had a three-piece suite here and a small table, nothing much else.'

Vera crossed the room to throw open a door on the far side. 'This was the billiard room, which she never used. She managed to sell the table, and it took eight men to lift it, would you believe!'

It didn't look as if any of these rooms had been entered since Mrs Pryce left.

The two women returned to the hall to find Mr Abel with his sleeves rolled up and his shirt showing damp stains. He was trying to make notes while at the same time juggling with his mobile phone. And still perspiring. 'Ladies, I'll be with you in just a minute . . .' And into the phone: 'Yes, I'm out there now, but we've only just started.'

'Don't worry about us, Mr Abel,' said Ellie. 'You're being most helpful. Do you happen to know if your agency was asked to keep an eye on the property after Mrs Pryce left?'

'I'm not sure, I'll just check.' And into the phone: 'If could just hold on a minute.' He riffled through his paperwork, still holding his phone. And of course dropped everything again.

'Never mind for now,' said Ellie, graciously. 'I'll get right back to you when I've seen everything. What about the kitchens, Vera?'

Vera threw open an unobtrusive baize-lined door. The kitchen area wasn't as grand as the reception rooms. There was a back staircase – dusty. A sitting room set aside for the off-duty use of live-in staff – in the days when live-in staff were available. The kitchen itself was not all that large, though there was a pantry, a larder, a boiler room, a drying cupboard and a utility room leading off a corridor beyond.

'Everything,' said Vera, 'was updated a couple of years back: new wiring, new plumbing, new fitments.'

More dust. No footprints. No one had been this way recently.

'I did ask if I could buy her microwave,' said Vera, sorrowing as she looked at the gaps in the fitted units, 'but she sold it with the fridge, the washer, the drier and the oven. The whole lot went to a private buyer she found through an advert in the local paper. Even the big freezer from the garage.'

Ellie remembered that she'd thought she'd heard a motor purring into life when she'd been in the covered way. Would that have been the freezer? No, it couldn't be, because Vera said it had been sold.

Anyway, she couldn't have heard the freezer working because the electricity had long since been turned off. Hadn't it? She depressed the light switch by the door, and LED spot-lights came on in the ceiling above.

'Wasn't the electricity turned off when she left?'

Vera looked up, surprised. 'Yes, it was. She won't like it if her electricity bill is still being run up.'

'*You* didn't see Fritz turning off the water and electricity?'

'She was still using it, the last time I saw her. I thought she'd asked Fritz to do it but maybe he forgot.' Vera was puzzled. 'Do you want to bother with upstairs?'

Mr Abel was still on the phone as they passed him in the hall. The banister felt gritty under Ellie's hand, but someone had recently swept the treads. No, not swept. She'd be able to see brush marks if a broom had been used. The treads had been wiped clean with a cloth; but apparently it hadn't been necessary to clean the banister. Which argued that a young person, who didn't need to hold on to the banister, had been using the stairs recently . . . and wanted to hide the fact that he or she had done so.

Not Mrs Pryce, who'd had trouble with her knees and would have needed to hold on to the banister.

Was it possible that these young people – or perhaps just one of them – were still in the house?

EIGHT

E llie followed Vera upstairs, taking the path which had been cleaned through the dust. This path led across the landing and to a second flight of stairs, but Vera wanted to show off the first-floor bedrooms first. Lots of spacious bedrooms with big windows, most en suite. Lots of dust, no footprints. Again, there were darker patches on the walls showing where pictures and large pieces of furniture had once been. Unexpected additions bellied out from the larger bedrooms, which Ellie thought must be in the turrets that decorated the building.

Plenty of built-in cupboards. Linen room.

Vera threw open one last door. 'And this was her own bedroom, with its own wet-room en suite. She liked it because it overlooked the garden and caught the . . .' Her voice tailed away.

Ellie followed Vera's gaze. The room had been papered in a blue and white Chinese design of peonies. A handmade paper? A square of darker colour on the far wall showed where a large bed had once stood. The design of the wallpaper on either side was smudged.

Vera looked uneasy. Almost scared. 'I don't understand. Last winter she got bronchitis and had to stay in bed for a while. She was that rocky on her feet she upset her coffee over the wallpaper. I tried to clean it off, but the design was hand-painted, ever so old. Some of the colour came off and the pattern got smudged even though I tried my hardest not to spoil it.

'She was distressed because her husband had done the room out for her special. That was the only time I ever saw her cry, but she wasn't well, you know. I said she ought to have someone come in to look after her and what about her step-daughter, but that made Mrs Pryce have a choking fit because Edwina only ever looked out for herself and her granddaughter was even worse, which I should have known better than to suggest. Mrs Pryce asked Pet if she'd come round in the evenings to get her some food, but Pet couldn't as she had a second job in the evenings then, though it didn't work out, which was a pity because they were saving as much as they could.

'So I said I'd come like a shot if it weren't for Mikey, who can be a bit . . . well, you know. So she said to bring Mikey and let him watch telly or a video downstairs, which I did and he was fine for about half an hour but then he came looking for me and the next thing I know he was up on the bed with her, going through her bits and pieces of jewellery, happy as Larry, and he was trying on her necklaces, and then putting them on her head like a tiara. And she got better after that.' Vera scrubbed at her cheeks; removing tears?

'So the paper got stained on the far side of the bed last winter. And this side?'

Vera rung her hands. 'It was clean last I saw it, which was on the day before she left.'

Ellie bent down to the stain on the right. Something had been spilt on the paper all right, and someone had tried to clean it up. They hadn't done a very good job of it. So, had more coffee been thrown at the wall on Mrs Pryce's last night at home?

If it had been blood – which of course it hadn't been – then the police would be able to detect it.

Ellie straightened up. 'You mentioned her jewellery? Where did she keep it?'

'The best bits – his family pieces and hers that were mostly Victorian and ought to have been in the bank really – she told me were kept in the safe. She had some favourites which she wore every day, and they were kept in a locked brown leather box on her dressing table over there . . .' She pointed to the opposite wall. 'She also had a lot of costume jewellery in a big tin from Harrods that had once contained biscuits. That was what she had on the bed beside her for Mikey to play with.'

'So there's a safe in the house?'

'She didn't say where it was, mind, but I thought it must

be in the telly room downstairs, because that's the only room that's panelled and all the pictures have gone that used to hang on the walls and there's no safe to be seen anywhere, is there?'

Vera's face twisted. 'Mrs Quicke, nothing's happened to the old dear, has it? She dilly-dallied for ages about going into a home. I always thought – silly of me, maybe – that getting the wallpaper spoiled made up her mind for her.'

'You're probably right. Little things like that can be the last straw. I do think we ought to ring the police when we get back. This house needs searching properly from top to bottom, cupboards, cellar – if there is one – and all.'

'There is a cellar that they used as an air raid shelter in the war, but Mrs Pryce said it was damp and she didn't want anything put down there. The door to it leads off the boiler room.'

Vera led the way back to the landing. 'She paid double for me to come in extra last winter but I'd have come for nothing, she was so good with Mikey. He really liked her, you know; never played up with her.'

At that point Ellie decided that Vera really had been fond of Mrs Pryce, that Mrs Pryce had been a nice person, and that Ellie would have liked her, too, if they'd ever had the good fortune to meet. She also wondered if Vera might be the very person to come in and help look after Rose if . . . when . . . Think about it another day.

Ellie looked round the landing. 'While we're here, let's just check the top storey, shall we?'

'There's nothing up there. Oh, there was some junk, broken bits of furniture, that sort of thing; but she got rid of it all a couple of months ago, clearing out, ready to move . . .'

Vera's voice trailed away as she noted the cleaned path on the landing which led to another, narrower flight of stairs. Ellie led the way. On the top landing there were several closed doors and two half open. The cleared track encompassed almost half the landing. One of the half open doors gave on to a bathroom which gleamed from fresh scrubbing – and another to a separate loo, ditto.

Ellie went into the bathroom and turned on the taps. Water came out; clear water, which proved that someone had been using water up here recently. Water that's been standing in a tank or pipes for a long time usually comes out rusty, with lots of burps and gurgles. She depressed the light switch and an ancient bulb glowed into life.

She inspected the window frames. Frosted glass, so that no one outside could overlook the servants washing themselves. Someone had recently tacked cardboard over the glass with drawing pins and removed them in a hurry. Two pins winked brightly from the lino on the floor, together with a fragment of card.

'Can you smell shampoo?'

Vera sniffed and nodded. 'Not Mrs Pryce's. Will you look how clean the bath is? I couldn't have done it better myself.'

Two more doors on the landing were closed, and no cleared pathways led to them. The cleared patch included just one more door. Ellie opened it and went in. A fair-sized room, glowing with sunshine. The one window was shut fast.

Vera sniffed. 'Pizza?'

There was no furniture in the room, and it had been newly cleaned. No dust. No detritus, no drawing pins or scraps of paper.

Ellie clicked on the light switch. A bare lamp bulb glowed, and then shone brightly.

Vera was puzzled. 'That's one of those new long-life bulbs, isn't it? But no one's been living up here for years.'

Ellie inspected the window which, as she'd suspected, over-looked several gardens including her own. The window opened and shut easily. 'Ah. See this, Vera? It's the same in the bath-room and toilet. They took precautions not to be seen from outside at night but didn't make a good enough job of clearing up after themselves. Now we know why the electricity was turned on again.'

Someone had driven not drawing pins but nails into the top and one side of the window frame. A fragment of thick black cotton still clung to one nail.

Vera examined it. 'Was a curtain supposed to hang there?'

'They used card in the other rooms, but this is better. It's the sort of material which they used during the war in the blackout. My mother lined my bedroom curtains with it, because I couldn't get to sleep in the light summer nights. Doing this meant they could have lights on inside at night without being spotted. Unlike the bathroom and toilet, which must always have been kept dark, this curtain could be lifted to one side during the day to let air in. They tore the material away when they cleared up, but left enough for us to see what they'd been doing.'

Vera thought it through. 'Someone's been living up here but it's not the usual homeless man, who wouldn't have bothered to clear up after himself. Could it be squatters? Someone who knew the house was empty, moved in, turned on the electricity and used the water?'

'Squatters change the locks on the door, invite like-minded people to join them and spread themselves out over the best rooms downstairs. Why pick on one small room at the top of the house, unless they're hiding from somebody or something? Let's have a look at the back stairs. They go straight down to the kitchen area, don't they?'

The two women inspected the back stairs. More dust. No footprints. They could hear Mr Abel in the hall, still talking on his phone. 'Yes, yes. I'll attend to it directly I've finished here, but . . .'

Ellie kept her voice low. 'Whoever it was – possibly only one or two people – they must have had a key because there's no sign of a break-in anywhere. Plus, you can see they let themselves in through the front door and left the same way. We probably disturbed them yesterday, and instead of standing their ground as squatters do, they cleaned up after themselves and scarpered. I wonder how they got hold of a key to the front door?'

'Pet and I handed ours in to the office, who might have kept them, I suppose, hoping we'd get the contract to go on cleaning here when the house was sold.'

Ellie led the way downstairs. 'Does Pet's husband work in the cleaning line, too? No, wait a minute. You told me; he's a hospital porter, works nights.'

'I don't think he ever met Mrs Pryce.'

Ellie held Vera back when they reached the landing. '*You* liked Mrs Pryce. *I* like what I've heard about her. It's clear that Mr Abel knows less than we do, and lacking instructions from Mrs Pryce, he won't do anything about, well, anything. We've no proof that something's wrong, but . . . what do you think?'

Vera had been following a different line of thought. 'Whoever it was that was living here recently must have had a car to take away their stuff in last night.'

'Ah, right. This morning I spotted fresh car tracks at the front where someone reversed into the lawn.'

Vera grinned. 'I bet they didn't take all their trash away with them.'

'Where . . . ?'

'The dustbins are outside the back door in the covered way. Except that the dustbin men don't call on empty houses, do they?'

Mr Abel met them as they descended into the hall. He looked worried. 'At Hoopers we do most earnestly request our clients to turn off the gas, water and electricity at the mains before they leave. I don't know how it has come about that this has not been done, but I do not think it wise to leave this house with water dripping from taps and electricity connected. Now I've managed to locate the fuse boxes in the kitchen corridor and turned off the electricity, also the gas. I'm not sure where the water enters this house, but it must be in the kitchen quarters somewhere.'

'I'll show you,' said Vera, leading the way.

Ellie went into the panelled television room. Vera had said a safe might be concealed in this room. If so, there was nothing obvious to show where it might have been. Dust lay uniformly on every ledge. No one had been in this room since Mrs Pryce left. Disappointing. But what else had she expected?

There was a lot of banging and clattering going on. Footsteps backwards and forwards in the hall. Ellie walked along the panelling, rapping here and there. She couldn't detect any change in sound. If a safe was hidden there, it was not going to be found easily.

She drifted back to the hall as Mr Abel and Vera emerged from the kitchen quarters.

'So sorry to leave you,' said Mr Abel, who had transferred

a considerable amount of the dust in the house to his forehead and whose shirt was now very much the worse for wear. 'I had to fetch a wrench from my car to turn off the water, and then I tried to get the cellar door open, but it'll need an electric drill to break that down, it's rusted solid.'

Strike the cellar from a list of possible places to hide a body.

He attempted and failed to brush dirt from sodden shirt sleeves 'So, what are your first impressions, Mrs Quicke? A truly magnificent house, isn't it? Just waiting for someone like you to wake it from its sleep, har har. Now may I show you the grounds? Extensive, very. Greenhouses, pond, rose beds, vegetable garden.'

'Thank you, but I've seen enough for one day. I need to think about what you've shown me so far, and perhaps come back another time.'

'Ah. Right. Now, may I offer you a lift anywhere?'

Mr Abel collected the stack of post to be redirected and ushered them out of the house, still talking. Ellie smiled and said she didn't need a lift home, thank you, you've been most helpful. Mr Abel eeled his way into his car and drove off.

It was going to be another hot day. Ellie put her dark glasses on.

Vera said, 'While he was getting the water mains turned off, I popped into the backyard to check there'd been no rubbish left there. And there wasn't. On my way back I looked for the spare back door key that always hangs on a hook in the cupboard over where the fridge was, and it isn't there.'

'Really?' Ellie was amused. What did Vera think they were going to do – break into the house through the back quarters some moonlit night and search the house with torches? 'Well, I suppose Mrs Pryce took it when she left.'

Ellie walked out on to the pavement and looked up and down the road. 'Which day of the week do they collect the rubbish around here? What's today? Wednesday. Ours is collected today. Do you think this road's the same? We have to leave our rubbish just inside the drive for collection and not on the pavement, and not before seven in the mornings because if we leave it out overnight the foxes and the crows get at it. Now if our "squatters" wanted to get rid of their rubbish last night, would they dump it just anywhere and hope it's not ripped open by morning or . . . ?'

'Could that be theirs?' Vera pointed to where a couple of bulging black dustbin bags had been left under a tree two houses down from where they stood. The foxes or a cat had been at one of them, but not too badly.

Ellie went to have a closer look only to freeze, hearing the clang and clamour of the dustbin lorry somewhere close.

Vera pounced on the torn bag. 'Aha! A pizza box. That would attract the foxes all right.'

Ellie lifted the other. 'Heavy.'

'Wet rags would make it heavy, if they used them for wiping down the floorboards and cleaning the bathroom and toilet up top.'

'We should ring the police . . .'

The refuse lorry turned the corner into their road. 'They're coming!'

'If we leave them . . .'

The binmen were walking along the road in their Day-Glo jackets, collecting black plastic bags from the driveways, piling them into a heap in the road for collection by the lorry as it moved slowly along.

'Take those for you, missus?' A dustman, large, black and smiling.

'Oh, no. Thank you, but I've put something in the trash, something valuable. I shall have to go through . . . You understand?'

'Ah. Never mind, then. If you find it, just put the bags in the next road for us to collect, OK?'

'OK.'

Ellie and Vera picked up one bag each and started to walk down the road away from the binmen. Vera gave way to the giggles. Ellie did, too.

Vera said, 'What *do* we look like?'

'Bag ladies,' said Ellie as hers slipped from her grasp. She stooped to get a better hold on it, and her glasses fell off.

'Let me.' Vera took Ellie's bag from her.

'We're destroying fingerprints,' said Ellie. 'I'm sure we'll get into trouble about this.'

'You can talk us out of it,' said Vera.

How nice to be appreciated! What a splendid girl Vera was!

Ears shrieked down the phone at Ellie. 'You *stole* two bags of rubbish! Tell me this isn't happening!'

'Not *stole*. They were put out for the binmen to collect. They'd been out overnight and the foxes had torn one open but—'

'Give me strength. You picked up two bags off the street, without any idea where they might have come from—'

'The squatters – if that's what they were – had been eating pizza. We could smell it, and one of the bags had an empty pizza box in it.'

'And what, may I ask, makes you think that the police are going to waste their time chasing up squatters who exist only in your fertile imagination?'

'It's true that they've gone now, but don't you think it's worth investigating since Mrs Pryce never arrived where she said she would? And her car's missing.'

'So she changed her mind and booked herself into a luxury hotel somewhere. Have her family complained? No. Have you checked the hospitals to see if she had a traffic accident? No. Give me one piece of evidence—'

'We thought you'd find something in the bags. We've gloved up so we don't destroy any fingerprints.' Ellie was rather proud of the phrase 'gloved up', which she'd learned from watching crime programmes on television. The bags were on the kitchen table at that very moment, being investigated by Vera and Rose. Midge the cat was keeping an eye on everyone from his perch on top of the fridge.

Heavy breathing from Ears. 'No doubt you've found detonators and plastic jelly for making explosives, and this is a plot to blow up the Houses of Parliament. You'll be telling me next that you've seen little green men in the attic and unidentified flying objects circling round the chimneys. I am trying,' he said, enunciating each syllable, 'to work out how we can spare a detective to investigate this mythical plot of yours, but at the moment – if you'll forgive me – we have more important things to attend to.'

The phone crashed down.

Ellie winced.

Vera giggled. 'Prince Charming he is not, by the sound of it.'

Ellie held up her hands and let them drop. 'He's got reason, I suppose. I mean, what have we got that would convince the police there is a case to answer?'

'Apart from masses of J-cloths which have been wetted and used for wiping dust off from wherever it is they've been hiding?'

'We can't prove any of this came from the Pryce house.'

'Who else would leave their rubbish out on the pavement under a tree, instead of just inside their gates? And how about this?' Vera spread a fine black scarf with a frayed edge out on to the table. It had been much used and had a hole in it, which was probably why it had been discarded. 'Of course, lots of women wear scarves, though not in this hot weather. But Muslim women cover their hair all the time when they go out, don't they? Plus it stinks of cheap perfume. Yuk!'

Ho hum. Ellie considered a possible scenario. 'Rose, I wonder if that's who you saw at the window? Suppose a Muslim girl had been hiding up there – which someone certainly was – and she tied her head round with a black scarf as they do, and looked out of her window, wouldn't it have looked as if her face was floating in mid-air?'

'Another thing,' said Vera, 'they only wear scarves if they have to go outdoors, but if she had lots of very dark hair hanging down on either side of her face—'

'You mean I really didn't imagine it? Well, praise be!'

Wednesday morning

At Hoopers' estate agency.

'Hello, where's the keys to the Pryce house, then?'

'Mm? Oh, Mr Abel's gone out there with a customer, someone with money to burn.'

'You mean someone's actually taking an interest in the White Elephant? An Arab, maybe?'

'Nah. English. An old dear who made a fortune in the property market and might want it to turn into flats for sale and make another fortune. The boss is furious, has only just found out she's interested, says he should have taken her round himself. But he wasn't around yesterday when the appointment was made, so Mr Abel got the job. He says the place is in a right mess, our sign's been taken down, the lawns not cut.'

'Mr Abel had better get our "For Sale" sign back up, pronto. And who was supposed to be keeping the lawns cut?'

'The boss said not to bother with the lawns when the Pryce woman took the house off the market—'

'Use your head. If there's a potential buyer in sight, she won't be quibbling over that, will she?'

NINE

Vera held up an empty shampoo bottle. 'We smelled shampoo in the bathroom, didn't we? And here's some twists of black hair – from her hairbrush, I suppose, yuk!'

'Thirteen, fourteen.' Rose counted sets of plastic knives and forks. 'How long has she been living there?'

'Hello!' said Ellie. 'Here's a disposable razor. His or hers?'

Vera held up another, larger one. 'His AND hers. There were two people living there.'

Rose pried apart a stack of plastic food containers. 'Mostly salads. For two.'

'They didn't use the kitchen so they didn't cook anything.' Ellie set aside an empty box which had once contained paper tissues. 'The cheapest supermarket brand.'

Rose was back to counting again; this time flattened pizza boxes. 'Seven, eight, nine. All vegetarian, no meat dishes. I suppose he brought them in hot.'

He? A man and a woman? Perhaps she'd been a prisoner there, and he'd taken in food for her.

Midge the cat decided this was where he took part in the proceedings and leaped on to the table.

'Off!' yelled Ellie. Midge flattened his ears, but evaded Ellie's hand to sniff at the food containers. 'Rose, can you shove them back into the bag, or he'll have the lot on the floor.'

'Look what I've found.' Vera pulled out a stack of glossy magazines.

'Mm,' said Ellie. 'So the woman is young, possibly a Muslim, certainly a vegetarian. A prisoner, or a squatter?'

'Lots more cleaning rags,' said Vera.

Ellie pounced. 'Torn up receipts for credit card payments.'

She laid them out on the table and began to piece the scraps together. 'Someone's been buying petrol and foodstuffs at the big Tesco's on the A40. Bottled water and toiletries. They also bought cleaning materials, toilet rolls, foodstuffs, mostly salads. We must keep these. If we can get the police interested, the man can be traced by his credit card number.'

'He definitely had a car, because he bought petrol for it.' Vera liked this game.

Ellie smoothed out another torn-up bill. 'Now here's something different; he – or possibly she – visited a hardware store, but it's in Hayes, further away, and the date is . . . over a month ago.' She thought about it. 'The hammer and nails were to fix up curtains over the windows. I wonder where he got the black material from? Perhaps it was a cheap skirt she had. At the same time he bought an electric kettle and two long-life lamp bulbs. Luckily the paperwork wasn't in with the wet cloths for long, or it would be unreadable.'

'They expected the rubbish to be removed by the binmen this morning.'

The front doorbell rang, and they all looked round. Mia had gone out as soon as Ellie and Vera returned. Thomas didn't answer the doorbell unless he was expecting someone.

Vera glanced at the clock and yelped. 'I ought to be . . . where ought I to be by now? Pet will kill me if I'm late, especially after taking the morning off. And remember, Mrs Quicke, if you want me to go round with you again, this evening, say, then I'm game, provided I can bring Mikey, too.'

Rose got up on spindly legs, balanced herself and made for the door. 'I'll answer the door, Ellie. You clear up.'

The Lord be praised, Rose was looking far more like herself today. Ellie flourished two new black plastic bin liners. 'Thanks, Vera. I do think someone ought to search that place properly, but it's out of our hands at the moment. I'll stow everything away till we can get the police interested.'

'Thanks for letting me in on this, Mrs Quicke.'

'Call me Ellie.'

Vera smiled and nodded, but probably wouldn't.

Rose reappeared, frowning. 'A woman. Says her name is

Pryce, but she's not old enough to be our neighbour that was. I didn't let her in the house, said I'd see if you were in.'

Vera snapped her fingers. 'Edwina, her stepdaughter?'

'Vera; leave your telephone number, will you?'

'My mobile do? No landline.' She scribbled on the shopping list.

'Fine. Now you be off, and I'll see to the visitor. Rose; please don't let Midge get at anything while I'm gone, will you?'

'As if he would.' Rose picked Midge up and stroked him – which he permitted for all of five seconds before jumping out of her arms and disappearing under the table.

Edwina Pryce was dressed as if for a garden party at Buckingham Palace in a silk designer suit complete with a cute little hat which she'd perched high up on tightly curled, sparse, ginger hair. Freckled hands clutched a Louis Vuitton handbag, which must have cost a fortune. High-heeled shoes. A couple of thousand pounds on the hoof?

No boobs, Pet had said. Pet had been right about that. Ms Pryce looked as if someone had ironed her flat, and the process had removed all kindliness from her personality.

Ellie remembered Pet's mimicry of this woman and tried not to smile as she ushered her into the house.

Edwina looked about her. 'I need to speak to the man who phoned me last night about my stepmother, Flavia Pryce. Stupidly, he omitted to leave his address, but there's only one Quicke in the phone book, so here I am. Are you his cleaner? I do not appreciate being left on the doorstep like that.' Her tone of voice was even sharper than her nose.

'It was my husband who rang you. I'm Mrs Quicke.'

Edwina's eyes darted around, pricing everything in sight, and Ellie was unpleasantly reminded of Terry Pryce . . . Edwina's nephew? He'd had the same trick of calculation, hadn't he?

Edwina wore a gold wedding ring on the fourth finger of her right hand, not her left. She'd had a daughter, but kept her maiden name. Divorced? No, never married. Hadn't there been some tale of the man abandoning her when she got pregnant?

'These big houses,' stated Edwina, 'cost a fortune to run, as I should know since I was brought up in one.'

Ellie didn't respond, but led the way to the sitting room and asked her guest to sit. Ought she to offer tea or coffee? No. Ellie didn't like the woman enough to do that. 'I'm afraid my husband's busy, but I know what it was about, so—'

'I prefer to deal with him, as it was he who phoned me.'

'In a minute I'll see if he's available to speak to you, but in the meantime, may I explain why he called?'

A hard stare. 'I don't care to deal with hired help.'

Ellie was wearing one of her everyday outfits: a good white T-shirt and well-cut denim skirt. Did that make her look like hired help? No. Ellie wasn't sure whether to laugh or scream.

Edwina fidgeted. 'All right, then. What is it?'

'My name is Mrs Quicke. My aunt knew your stepmother. On Monday evening I received a visit from a young man who claimed to be searching for his great-aunt, Flavia Pryce. He had failed to find her at her old house, and the retirement home people said she wasn't there, either.'

A compression of lips. 'He's no favourite of Mummy's. I expect she told the people at the home she didn't want to see him.' Yet her eyes failed to meet Ellie's, and she seemed to be feeling the heat. She produced a lace-edged hankie and dabbed at beads of sweat on her forehead.

'I'd like to be sure we're talking about the same person. May I describe my visitor to you? Not much taller than me, casually but expensively dressed, his hair cut very short, rings in his ears, nose and lip.'

A thin-lipped smile. 'Terry Pryce. My uncle's grandson. Nothing but trouble from the day he was born. Wanting money, I suppose.'

'Yes. I refused, but when my back was turned, he made off with my engagement ring, my husband's Kindle, and a valuable snuff box.'

'I hope you informed the police.'

'I did, but I couldn't tell them where to find him.'

'If that's all, I can give you his address.' She scrabbled in her handbag, found a blank page in a diary, wrote out an address and tore the page out for Ellie. 'He may have moved on, though. That sort does.'

'Do you know where he works? He said in a bedding department of a big store.'

A sniff. 'Not in Oxford Street, if that's what he was trying to make out. Some place in West Ealing, I believe. Well, if that's all you wanted . . . ?' But she made no move to depart, and her clutch on her handbag was so tight that her fingers turned white. Why was she so anxious?

'Not quite,' said Ellie. 'After Terry's visit, we wondered what had happened to Mrs Pryce, so we went round by the house and found it locked up. I phoned the retirement home; she never arrived there.'

Edwina leaned forward. 'That's what age does for you. Mummy doesn't know her own mind from one minute to the next. I told her she should move in with me and I'd look after her, but no, she wanted to have one last fling, said she might even go on a cruise before she had to take to a wheelchair. As if! I said to her, "What a waste of money that would be," and she shrieked with laughter! That just shows what she's like.'

'Well, it was her money—'

'So she's changed her mind again, has she? Not at the home, you say?' Edwina ran her tongue over her lower lip. 'And you have no idea where's she gone?' There were more beads of sweat on her forehead.

Ellie shook her head.

Edwina's eyes skittered around the room. 'She'll have gone off with another man and come to no good, flashing her diamonds around, made up to the eyeballs with false eyelashes and all. At her age!'

Ellie maintained the smile on her face with an effort, thinking that Edwina's looks might be improved by the application of false eyelashes. Or would they? No, perhaps not. The venom issuing from her mouth would shrivel any lashes before they touched her skin.

Edwina nodded, not once but several times. 'That's what it is, all right. She's gone off with another man. Then she'll pop off, leaving him all the money that isn't hers by right, that ought to have come to me and my daughter. My own dear mother that was – she passed away years ago – must be turning in her grave.' A false note in her voice; she wasn't as sure of her facts as she pretended?

'Mrs Pryce's car's gone.'

'Well, she took it with her, didn't she?' But something was worrying the woman. She gnawed at her lower lip, her eyes darting hither and yon but never meeting Ellie's. She burst out with what seemed like the truth. 'It's giving me ulcers, wondering where she is and what she's doing. She said she didn't want me visiting her till she'd settled in, that she'd send me a card when she was ready to see me, but not a word have I had from that day to this.'

'You had the address of the home?'

An unbecoming flush. 'Yes, of course. Have you tried the hospitals? Maybe she's met with an accident.'

'Not yet. Have you?'

'No.' The woman drew back, clutching her bag tightly. 'She wouldn't like me interfering, she's made that plain.'

'Do you have the licence number of her car?'

'I don't drive.' A stare. 'Why would I have that?'

'If she'd met with an accident in the car and we had the licence number, we could ask the police to trace it.'

Another stare. 'Is that how it's done? I wouldn't know.'

'Do you know who her solicitor is?' Neither Vera nor Pet had known that.

'The family have always used Greenbody on Ealing Common. I told her to use him, but she had a perverse sense of humour. Regularly did the opposite of what I suggested. You know, Mrs Quicke, I really did my best to get on with Mummy, but she made it very difficult.'

'Did she make a will, do you know?'

An intake of breath. 'I have absolutely no idea, and I'm amazed that you should mention it. Now, if all you want is to find the things my nephew stole, I've given you his details, you can pass them on to the police and there's an end of it. I've had a difficult enough life without . . .' She pinched in her lips and stopped. 'I must be going. You'll keep me informed, won't you?'

'Certainly.' Ellie showed Edwina out, set her back to the front door, and wondered why the woman had come. The obvious answer was that she'd come in response to Thomas's message on her answerphone, but her visit had raised more questions than it had answered.

Edwina had implied that her stepmother was a flighty creature who had probably gone off with a new man. Really? Ellie didn't think that sounded like the hard-headed and responsible person Vera and Pet had described.

Then again, Edwina had seemed anxious to hear of Mrs Pryce's present whereabouts, but admitted she hadn't phoned the retirement home herself, or even enquired whether the lady had ended up in hospital for some reason.

She'd suggested that Ellie should make those enquiries. Why? Wasn't Edwina the most appropriate person to do so?

She'd had nothing good to say about her nephew Terry and had been quick to hand over his address. She didn't like Terry much, did she? Well . . . who did?

What on earth, Ellie wondered, was going on?

A movement caught Ellie's eye. A small brown figure was pottering around in the conservatory. For one heart-stopping moment Ellie thought it was her beloved aunt. Then she remembered that Miss Quicke had never in her life lifted a watering can to care for plants and couldn't tell one from another. It was Rose who cared for the plants, it was Rose for whom the conservatory had been built, and it was Rose who, with a watering can, was checking on the plants now . . . favouring her wrist.

'Rose dear, let me do that.'

'No, no. It's lovely being able to get up and about again, though I must admit I'm only using the little watering can because the big one would be too much for my wrist, which is healing nicely, I must say, and only gives me a twinge when I pick up something heavy. Isn't the plumbago a picture, all lacy and blue? And what about the hoya carnosa? I've counted over thirty flowers on it today.'

'I don't want you tiring yourself out.'

'Doing a little of what you want to do never tires you out. There, now. I'll sit down here for a while. As I said to Miss

Quicke a while ago, it was clever of her to put a chair here where I can relax and put my feet up for a bit, and she said she felt the same way but preferred her own chair in the sitting room, the one you like to sit in, too, and sometimes I come upon you and think it's her . . . if you see what I mean.'

Ellie relaxed. 'You're feeling much better.'

'Miss Quicke gave me such a scolding about going up on that ladder. She's worried about her old friend Mrs Pryce, though. I met her a couple of times, you know. Mrs Pryce.'

'What did you think of her?'

Rose grinned. 'A big lady with a big laugh, all in lavender with diamond earrings and a socking great diamond brooch so big you wouldn't believe. She came round one day soon after Miss Quicke had begun to put the place right and I'd moved in to look after her, and we had builders and decorators everywhere, and so many cleaners that we'd had were no good, all scamping their work and leaving the doors and windows open and needing cups of tea and biscuits every half hour. She – Mrs Pryce – had seen the scaffolding go up and heard the gossip from the cleaners, that's the lot we had before Vera and Pet, of course, and she'd wondered what was going on.'

She took a deep breath. 'They'd known one another for ever, Mrs Pryce and Miss Quicke, going up to town together for business meetings, but up till then Miss Quicke had always pretended she was short of money and Mrs Pryce had found out the truth and come round to have it out with her. She looked quite fierce when she arrived but Miss Quicke invited her in, and I served them tea in the drawing room and Miss Quicke introduced me as her dear friend and companion . . .'

Rose sniffed and delved for a hankie.

Ellie said, 'Which you were, indeed you were.'

'After that they used to meet up in town for lunch now and again until your aunt began to fail.'

'I wish I'd met her.'

'But you did. Don't you remember that cyclist knocking her over on the pavement in the Avenue and you rushing over to help her and pick up all her shopping that had got scattered all over the place?'

'Was that her? I thought her name was Fay something. I remember I wanted to get her to a doctor to check her over, but she just wanted to sit down and rest for a while.'

'Not Fay; Flavia. And you treated her to lunch—'

'And she asked me about my charity work and got me talking . . . She was a good listener. I remember I ordered a cab for her, to take her home, and she said she'd be in touch, but I don't think I ever saw her again.'

'She came to the funeral, but I don't suppose you noticed.'

'Really? That was nice of her. But no; I don't remember much about that day, I'm afraid.'

Rose was fidgeting. 'There really was someone in the window at the top of Mrs Pryce's house? I didn't imagine it?'

'No, you didn't imagine it. There really was someone.'

'But I did pull up the gladioli, forgetting you'd planted them beside the montbretias, and I do get things mixed up on the orders, and as for climbing the stairs . . .'

'We'll put in a chairlift, if it pleases you.'

Rose was horrified. 'Not on that beautiful staircase. Miss Quicke wouldn't like it, and neither would I.'

'Up the back stairs, then.'

'We'll see. I'll ask her what she thinks about it. Isn't it coming up to supper time? And here's me sitting here, not having done a hand's turn for it.'

'Sit still. I'll go and see what there is.'

So information had passed between the two houses, both ways? Miss Quicke's cleaners had gossiped to their mates about the turnaround in Miss Quicke's fortunes, and they had passed the gossip on to Mrs Pryce, who had probably checked with her financial contacts only to discover that Miss Quicke was not poor but a miser. Now the information was coming back the other way; from Mrs Pryce through Vera and Pet to Ellie.

The phone rang as Ellie was on her way through the hall, and she picked it up.

'Mrs Quicke? It's Vera here.'

'Yes, my dear?'

'I was talking to Pet about Mrs Pryce and the car being gone. Pet and her husband used to have a car once, and she used to collect him from work late at night until it died, the car died, I mean. I thought she might have remembered the number but she didn't. Then I thought Fritz might know, and of course I should have thought of him straight off, I can't think why I didn't.

'So I popped in on him on the way home . . . In a minute, Mikey; I'm just on the phone . . . Sorry, Mrs Quicke, but it's getting to the end of the day and he needs his tea. Anyway, I asked Fritz, and he says it was a silver Toyota with NYD on the licence plate. He remembers because Mrs Pryce was annoyed with herself about not getting her old plate transferred to her new car because she couldn't recall the new one for the life of her. So he made up words for her out of the new initials. It was "New York Detective" for NYD. So I said to Fritz that he should ring you about it, and he said no, it wasn't anything helpful. But I thought you might like to tell the police.'

'Yes, I will. Thanks, Vera. Though whether they'll listen to me or not—'

'Tell the truth, I get a funny feeling every time I think about her not getting to the retirement home and, well, I wouldn't like to spend a night in that house alone now.'

'Neither would I. Thank you, Vera. That's most helpful, but don't go . . . ! Did you ever hear Mrs Pryce talk about my aunt, Miss Quicke?'

'Oh yes, she told us she used to give Miss Quicke lifts to town in the old days, until she found out she was only pretending to be poor. Mrs Pryce said she'd been a bit cross when she found out, as who wouldn't be, and that she was going to pay Miss Quicke out some day for pulling the wool over her eyes. They went on seeing one another for a bit, but then your aunt frailed up and they stopped meeting. Mrs Pryce was ever so sorry when she heard Miss Quicke had died. Said it was seeing your friends go that made you realize the world was changing. We told her how good you'd been to Miss Quicke at the end, and how well you looked after Rose, and . . . well, something about your daughter, who's a bit like Edwina, isn't she?'

'I suppose she is. Thank you, Vera. It's good to know.'

Wednesday lunchtime

Hoopers, the estate agency
'The Shark's been looking for you. Where've you been?'
   'Trying to shift the Pryce mansion.'
   'He wanted to handle that himself.'
   'Well, I didn't know that, did I? The call came in, I took it.
Routine.'
   'Nothing's routine when dealing with the Quicke Foundation.
Apart from Middle Eastern sheikhs, who else would want to
buy that house as it stands?'
   'Mrs Quicke wants to have a second viewing, so I can't
have done too badly, can I? It's lucky I did go, for all the
mains had been left on. I dunno what the old lady was thinking
of, not seeing they were turned off; also there's a mountain
of post there that should have been redirected.'
   'You'd better go in and report. And don't blame me if he
chews your ears off.'

TEN

Wednesday evening

Another beautiful evening. House martins twittered across the clear blue sky, Ellie spent a soothing half hour watering the garden and all was right with the world. Well, sort of. Actually, her world didn't feel all right at all, and she knew why, though she tried not to think about it.

What was Diana up to? If Ellie refused to help her daughter, would she be made bankrupt? And, trying to think clearly, was Diana really trying to get custody of little Frank again?

By your actions you shall know them. Diana's actions showed that Frank fitted into her busy life way behind her work and any liaison she might happen to have going at the time.

Ellie wished she didn't have such a suspicious nature, but it crossed her mind to wonder if Diana might be using her stated desire to reclaim Frank as a ploy, to remind everyone how uncomfortable she could make life for them if they didn't give her the money she needed.

Ellie was also concerned about Thomas, who had gone back into his study after supper, wrestling with some problem that he hadn't seen fit to share with her. This was worrying because Thomas was usually calm and supportive when Ellie got into a state. She missed him.

Mia had gone out without bothering to tell Ellie or Thomas where. That was all right. They weren't her parents. She didn't have to account to them for her movements.

Rose was dozing in front of her telly. She seemed better, thank the Lord.

Normally, Ellie would have used this quiet time in the garden to catch up on her relationship with God. But not today. She had a feeling she knew what He was going to say: let Diana go chase herself. Well, not in so many words, perhaps, but that was the gist of it.

Ellie went over and over the arguments in her mind till she felt sick. Result: the same. She could not, would not approach the Trust to find more money for Diana, and she couldn't let Diana go bankrupt.

The doorbell rang. She turned off the water in the hosepipe and went to let her caller in. Surprise. It was Detective Constable Milburn with a large envelope under her arm and a smile on her face.

'Am I interrupting, Mrs Quicke?'

'Of course not. Come in.' Ellie led the way to the sitting room, cool and comfortable in the evening air. 'Would you like a soft drink?'

'Nothing for me, thank you. It's like this. I know that in the past when you've brought information to the police, there was always something in it. So I thought you might like to chat to me, unofficially, about . . . well, anything. Though if any official action were required, I would have to pass the information along and then . . .'

The spectre of Ears rose between them. Ears might well be deaf and blind to any suggestion raised by Ellie.

Shoulders were braced. 'Mrs Quicke, I'm off duty and on my own time.' Good girl.

'I tried this afternoon to pass on some information and—'

'Yes, I heard.' The DC produced some photographs from her envelope. 'But first, let's go back to the burglary. I found some pictures of cars that might help to jog your memory.'

'Can you trace a car if I give you half a licence number?'

'You've remembered the licence number of the car that the con man was driving?'

'No, not that car, but another one. And oh dear, your boss told me in so many words not to worry the police with my fantasies.'

'One thing at a time, eh?' DC Milburn sat down and spread out a number of pictures of cars: yellow cars, gold cars, lemon-yellow cars. 'Do any of these ring a bell?'

Ellie studied each one in turn. 'Too pale, too green, not that sort of gold. Ah, that's the right colour. Egg-yolk yellow.'

'That's a Peugeot. Does it look something like the car you saw?'

Ellie nodded. 'Definitely, yes. There aren't that many around, are there?'

'Too many to trace, unless you can remember the licence number.'

'A pity. But as you're here, let me tell you about another car that's missing.' She fetched the notes she'd made on Mrs Pryce's disappearance and went through them with the police-woman. After a while DC Milburn got out her own notebook, and she asked Ellie to repeat her story with as much detail as she could remember.

'So that's it,' Ellie concluded. 'Terry Pryce visited me in an effort to trace his great-aunt and ended up stealing from me. Although he told me a number of lies – especially when he was asking for money – there was a nugget of truth in there as well. His aunt Edwina gave me an address for him; can you follow up on that?'

'I certainly can. We can get him on a charge of theft.'

'His aunt, now.' Ellie frowned. 'I didn't like her, but I suppose I mustn't be judgmental. She tried to make me believe Mrs Pryce was a flibbertigibbet who might easily go off with a man without telling her family. I don't believe it. I've talked to other people who knew her, and it seems to me that Mrs Pryce was a lady with a strong personality, who put up with a lot of flack from her dead husband's family but knew when to draw the line.'

'What's the daughter's name again?'

'Edwina Pryce. I think she came to see me because she doesn't know where her stepmother has gone and is worried sick about her. I find it odd that she's not worried enough to check the hospitals or go to the police herself. She wants me to report her disappearance instead.'

'Are you absolutely sure Mrs Pryce hasn't gone off on some ploy of her own?'

'How can I be sure? I rang the retirement home; Mrs Pryce sent her furniture there and left Disneyland – sorry, but I call it that because the house does look like something from a cartoon – but never arrived at her destination. What I did find out when I visited the house was that somebody's been living in one of the attics and only just cleared out.'

'Squatters?'

'It looks more to me like a young couple in hiding. Question: how did they get a key, because there's no sign of anyone breaking and entering? There can only be a limited number of keys around; the cleaning company might still have a set, I suppose. The estate agency has one, and of course . . . Mrs Pryce.'

'You think the squatters killed her and took her key so that they could live in her house?' DC Milburn's eyebrows rose almost to her hairline.

Ellie reddened. 'I don't know what I do think, except that something is definitely wrong.'

DC Milburn gave Ellie a sceptical look but made a note of it. 'Well, I suppose I could check with the cleaning company and the estate agency to see if their keys are still around and haven't been "lost".'

'The water and electricity had both been left on – or turned back on, I don't know which. The vegetable garden's still being worked, probably by the gardener Fritz, who may or may not have had permission to do so. He lives in one of the flats above the Co-op in the Avenue, and no, I don't know the number. Mrs Pryce's car has gone. Maybe she's had an accident and is in hospital somewhere, but if so, no one has informed her relatives, which seems strange. Can you check the hospitals, see if she's been admitted anywhere?'

'Where? Throughout Greater London? The whole of the south-east of England?'

'No, I see that you need to narrow the search down. Well, can you trace her car – it's a large Toyota, silver, only a few months old, and part of the registration reads NYD? Or would that be wasting police time?'

DC Milburn tapped her teeth with her pen. 'Officially she hasn't been posted as missing, nor has her car been reported as stolen. Her great-nephew Terry obviously isn't going to go to the police on her behalf because he'd get done for stealing from you. You say that her stepdaughter doesn't want to get involved. Yes, that is odd, but I can't say I'm surprised at anything that happens in families. Well, a neighbour could report her absence. Would you be prepared to do that?'

'Here and now, to you, I am formally reporting my neighbour's absence.'

'Let me write down as many details as you can remember . . .'

Ellie remembered quite a lot, which was pretty good considering she'd only once met Mrs Pryce.

'Good,' said the DC, closing her notebook. 'Now you'll need to come down to the station and sign a statement. Are you prepared to do that? Because unless you do, I can't get anything moving. Meanwhile, I can get on to the computer to see if her car's turned up anywhere. Perhaps it's been sitting unclaimed in a car park attracting fines, or been hoicked off to a pound.'

'If I wanted to get rid of it,' said Ellie, 'I'd take it to a quiet residential street and walk away. The neighbours would think it had been parked there while someone living locally went off on their holidays, and they wouldn't dream of reporting it. The person who drove it there could walk to the nearest tube or bus stop and get back home that way.'

'That's brilliant. I do hope you won't ever think of turning to crime, Mrs Quicke.'

Ellie preened. 'I don't think I'd be any good at it, you know. I'd be sure to forget in which street I left the car.'

A laugh. 'Well, I don't think that particular scenario would work, because if they left a body in the car in this heat, we'd soon have had neighbours complaining about the stink.'

A body. Oh. Ellie hadn't allowed her imagination to stretch that far. 'So you think she's dead? I suppose I do, too. She loved life, you know. She put her make-up on every day, and her false eyelashes. She liked a good laugh. She was nobody's fool, and she was kind to my aunt when she was alive. By the way, I believe she had some rather good jewellery. I wonder if that's been the motive for her, er, disappearance.'

More note-taking. 'I'll see if I can get a list from the stepdaughter, and I'll check if anything's turned up through the local jewellers. While I'm about it, I'll enquire if any of your

stolen pieces have turned up as well. Now, what about the
gardener? Have you spoken to him yet?'

'No. You think he bashed her over the head and buried her
in the cabbage patch?'

'And then drove her car away somewhere? You did say he
could drive, didn't you?'

'So I was told. Ms Edwina says she can't drive, and I believe
her. There are recent car tracks in the front drive, but I think
they were made by the getaway car – I mean, the car which
the young squatters used to remove themselves and their
belongings. You'll want to take away the two bags of rubbish
we collected from the site, I assume? We can't prove that they
came from that house, but everything seems to point to it.'

'I'll collect them another day. If there was no breaking and
entering involved and they didn't do any damage, I don't think
we'll be taking that little matter seriously.' The DC put her
notes away and got to her feet. 'Set your mind at rest, Mrs
Quicke; you've given me plenty to get on with, and I'll be
doing just that. Meanwhile, may I ask you not to go round
muddying the waters, so to speak?'

'Leave it to the professionals? I know. Are you sure you'll
be allowed a free hand to investigate?' Which was one way
of asking if Ears would let Milburn proceed?

'Leave it to me.' DC Milburn offered her hand for Ellie to
shake, and Ellie did so. It was an enormous relief to think she
needn't worry about Disneyland any more.

Only after the policewoman had gone did Ellie remember
that Vera had said the back door key to Disneyland had disappeared. Oh well. Perhaps it wasn't important. Only, it was
important, wasn't it? Ellie shook her head at herself. She really
must stop poking her nose into other people's business.

What should she do next? Was it too early to soothe Rose
into bed?

The phone rang.

'Mrs Quicke?' A man's voice, accustomed to command.
'My name is Hooper, Evan Hooper. We have a mutual friend
who suggests we should meet. Are you free to lunch tomorrow?'

Hooper? Now how did she know that name? And what was
she doing tomorrow? 'I don't think I—'

'I apologize for my staff. You ought never to have been exposed to a dunderhead like Mr Abel this morning.'

Ah. Ellie was beginning to see where this was going. 'I thought Mr Abel dealt admirably with a difficult situation.'

'You are very forgiving, Mrs Quicke, but I feel I should make amends. Shall we say noon tomorrow at the Golf Club? They serve a decent enough meal. I will collect you, of course. Perhaps you will be ready by eleven forty-five, on the dot? Good. I'm happy to make your acquaintance at last.'

He put the phone down, and so did Ellie. She gazed into space, thinking hard. Who was their 'mutual' friend? It must be Diana. Who else would suggest that the senior partner in a successful estate agency should meet with Mrs Quicke, who had inherited money and headed up a charity based on an empire of property to let?

Definitely Diana.

Ellie picked up the phone again and got through to Stewart, who should be able to give her the low-down on the gentleman concerned.

'Stewart? Ellie here.' Noises off. Children playing; Mother saying: 'Bedtime, girls.'

'Ah. Ellie. Did you like the Pryce house?'

'No, not at all, and no, I'm not suggesting that we buy it.'

'Good. I had put it on the agenda for our meeting tomorrow.' The Trust had a regular weekly meeting at Ellie's to discuss the properties to let. 'I'll take it off, shall I?'

'Leave it on. I'll explain why when I see you. Meanwhile, a Mr Evan Hooper has rung me, wants to take me out to lunch tomorrow. He's—'

'I know who he is. They call him the Great White Shark.'

'You're warning me to be careful when I see him? You think he'll persuade me to buy the Pryce mansion against my will? Now, come on, Stewart. You know me better than that.'

A reluctant laugh. 'Yes, I do. Sorry, Ellie. A bit out of sorts today. Frank came back from school OK, but says he doesn't want to go to his mother's this weekend. Wants to come to you instead.'

Ellie quickly rethought their plans for the weekend. 'That's all right, though it is the time of the month when Thomas disappears from view to put the magazine to bed. Actually he's a trifle distracted at the moment, but don't worry; we'll manage. One more thing. Diana said she was merging with another agency. Does that mean Hoopers might be taking her over?'

'It is the likeliest one.'

'She also said she had a new man in her life. It wouldn't by any chance be this Mr Hooper, would it?'

'He's on his third wife, who's a model in her twenties. Four children so far, ranging in age from twenty down to one and a half. It's not likely he'd want another divorce in the near future. Too expensive.'

'Right. Thanks for the information. See you tomorrow morning as usual.' Ellie put the phone down.

So if Evan Hooper's 'mutual' friend was Diana, then what was in it for him? Or for her? The sale of the Pryce mansion, presumably.

Ellie checked to see whether or not the kitchen had been cleared after supper, and it had. She found Rose struggling out of her clothes, ready for an early night. Rose's wrist was still paining her, though the swelling had almost disappeared. Ellie helped Rose undress and have a shower before getting into bed.

Mia hadn't yet returned. Ellie hoped the girl wouldn't be out late, but there . . . It was a good sign that she was going out and about, wasn't it?

Midge the cat arrived, demanding to be fed, and got his own way, of course.

Thomas wasn't in his study, though he'd left the lights on there and his computer was running on a screen saver. She wished he'd tell her about the problem he was having at work. He hadn't joined her to watch telly or sit in the garden that evening. So, where would he be?

Ah, upstairs in his special place, the room in which he went to talk to God in peace and quiet.

Yes, there he was, sitting in his big chair in the dusk and holding his bible – which he put down when she came in. She clicked on the light.

He blinked, and she clicked it off again. 'Sorry, too bright?'

He held out his hand to guide her into the chair next to his.

'I was just about to come down. My dear, I've been neglecting you.'

'Your work is important.'

'It's not that important, but I've been acting as if it was. The bishop has been calling in favours, and one or two important people – or people who think they're important – are putting pressure on me to "oblige" him, which I am refusing to do. Threats have been uttered. I was so angry I came up to tell God about it. Halfway through with my rant, I realized He'd a smile on his face, which threw me completely. Then I realized, what does it matter if one or two people bad-mouth me? I can stand it, can't I?'

He picked her hand up and kissed it. 'After I'd come to my senses, He slid into my mind a picture of a young man so desperate that he stole some of our pretty toys, and of a kindly lady who used to give lifts to your aunt being tossed around between greedy relatives. He reminded me that Diana's in trouble again, and so is little Frank. He asked what I was doing to comfort Rose – who is deadly afraid of dementia – and Mia, who is torn between staying to look after Rose and moving out to get on with her own life. He made the point that I'd left you to deal with sorrow and sin all by yourself. I am ashamed of myself.'

'Oh, Thomas.' She patted his arm, pleased and touched. 'Don't be silly.'

'No, my love. I'm going down now to turn off my computer. We'll go and sit on the settee side by side, you'll tell me what's bothering you most, and we'll have a stab at dealing with it together.'

What was bothering her most? Diana. Tears came. She sniffed and felt for a hankie in her pocket. No pocket, no hankie. 'Sorry.'

He handed her one, only slightly used. She laughed, blew her nose, said she knew she was being silly, but it had all got rather too much for her, and it would be bliss to talk about it. Except that she wasn't going to tell him she couldn't pray about Diana, because he'd be horrified and sad and want to do something about it, and she couldn't see any way out of the situation.

On their way downstairs, she turned on the lights as the front doorbell rang. At the same moment Thomas's phone rang in his office.

He hesitated. 'Oh, let it ring for once.'

'You get it. I'll answer the door.'

He peeled off to his office while Ellie paused halfway down the stairs, wondering why the mere fact of turning on the lights should be so significant. And shook her head at herself.

A stranger in a sleeveless T-shirt and cut-off jeans was on the doorstep. Fiftyish, strong-looking, recently shaved head showing the advance of male-pattern baldness. A tan that hadn't come out of a bottle, crow's feet round his eyes from working outdoors. Big hands. A tatty-looking green van stood in the driveway. There was no sign on it, but the man himself advertised his trade: gardener.

Ellie opened the door wide. 'Come in. You're Fritz, I take it?'

'Fitz, as in "son of". A joke that started at school. My dad was George, his dad was George, and I'm George. So my first teacher called me "Fitz George" to distinguish me from the other two Georges in the class. Mrs Pryce said it should be Fritz for some reason, something to do with French fries, I think. Whatever. It stuck.'

He wiped his feet with care on the doormat. Big feet in trainers. 'Vera dropped in on me and the wife, said you were taking an interest. Must admit I been worried, too. But the wife, she says, not our business, nothing to do with us, don't start something you can't finish. She's right, of course. But I can't stop thinking, can I?'

Ellie nodded. 'Will you come through into the garden? It's cooler there at this time of the evening.'

He checked that his trainers weren't leaving tracks across the polished floor and followed her through the conservatory and into the quiet, shadowy garden. He looked round with a professional, critical eye; he'd probably noticed where the rambling rose had come off the trellis work and the gardener had missed a stranglehold of ivy, but he wasn't going to say so.

She patted the bench for him to sit beside her. 'You're worried about Mrs Pryce.'

'I wasn't, not at first. She did say I could take what I wanted from the vegetable garden, you know. No sense it going to waste.'

'Sensible.' And we won't talk about water not being turned off at the mains so that he could continue to work the plot. 'Your runner beans look a treat.'

'If we get some more rain, they'll be all right, maybe.' Did he know the water had been turned off that morning by Mr Abel? Would Vera have told him? Probably.

She said, 'Did you put the padlocks on the outside doors?'

He shifted his feet. 'Jack the Lad did that. Window cleaner.'

'Later you took two of them off so that you could get into the back garden?'

He shifted big feet again, didn't reply. The answer was obviously 'yes'. But there was no need to admit it, was there?

'Tell me about Jack.'

'Big man. Hard. Tattoos all up his arms and legs. Divorced. Got a timeshare in Spain. Mrs Pryce said we mustn't be prejudiced, and if he *had* done a stint in prison, he'd been straight for a long time and we should make allowances. Cleaning the windows used to take him all morning. He did a fair job, I'll grant you that. It was him that offered to put the padlocks on, knowing the house would be empty for a while. I said I'd have done it, but he give me a look which I didn't like, me thinking he might have a knife in his back pocket, if you follow me.'

'I think Mrs Pryce was a brave woman, giving people the benefit of the doubt.'

He relaxed, met her eyes. 'When he said he'd put the padlocks on, I thought he might be wanting to keep a key for himself so's he could poke around, perhaps lift something he'd no right to. I wouldn't have trusted him, not an inch, but she was like that. Gave everyone the benefit of the doubt.'

'What might he have wanted to steal from an empty house?'

'Fireplaces, bathroom and kitchen stuff. Lead guttering. There's a market for them, if you know where to look. And he'd know.'

'When did Jack put the padlocks on the doors?'

'It had to be after Mrs Pryce left or she couldn't have got

her car out of the garage. I suppose he gave the keys to the estate agents.'

'Was it you or Jack who took the spare key to the back door?'

A startled look. 'Not me.' He shifted his feet, cleared his throat. 'I took the padlocks off the doors into and out of the yard and that's all. We'd had such a dry spell, I had to get back in to check on my potatoes and runner beans, didn't I?'

She probed a little more. 'But now you're worried about her.'

He nodded his head violently. 'I wasn't at first, but I am now. See, she promised to send me a card for my birthday which was two weeks back, and we – that's Vera and Pet and me – we was all going down to see her next month for *her* birthday. When my card didn't come, the wife says to me, why did I think she'd remember, and I couldn't say anything except that Mrs Pryce wasn't like that. Then, this and that's been happening . . .'

'You mean, the young couple in the attic.'

A closed look. 'I don't know nothing about that.'

Wednesday evening

On the phone.
   'Vera, is that you?'
   'Pet? Is there a problem?'
   'No, of course not. I asked my husband if he could remember the licence number of Mrs P's car, but no go.'
   'Well, I don't suppose he ever saw it, did he? I got part of it from Fritz, though. NYD. Don't you remember him trying to think up words, so that she could remember it?'
   'You told the police?'
   'No, I told Mrs Quicke. She's in touch with the police.'
   'Is she? I didn't know that. Do you think they'll take any notice?'
   'Dunno.' A sigh. 'It's a mess, isn't it?'

ELEVEN

Ellie said, 'Fritz, I believe you when you say Mrs Pryce gave you permission to go on gardening at her place –' fingers tightly crossed – 'but you must have wondered if she'd given someone else the right to use the premises when you saw or heard something of her other "visitors".'

'I never.'

She gave him a Look. 'If I've understood the matter correctly, they weren't breaking any law by using a key to get in and staying in the attic for a while. But while you were working in the garden I expect you heard water run off . . . when they used the toilet, for instance. Or perhaps you spotted footprints in the garden. Did they pick any of your produce?'

A shake of the head, a half smile. He wasn't going to admit that he knew anything. 'I never saw nor heard nothing.'

'Did you think they'd taken the back door key?'

No reply except for a frown and a shrug.

Ellie thought about it. 'There were no tracks in the dust on the floor in the kitchen which means no one has been there recently, so they didn't come and go that way. I think they must have had a front door key. How do you think they got it?'

'Dunno.' He was puzzled. 'I haven't got one. Vera and Pet, they handed theirs in. If Mrs Pryce had said for anyone to stay, they wouldn't have needed to keep themselves to themselves.' He cleared his throat, backtracking like mad. 'That is, if there were any visitors, which I doubt.'

'How soon after Mrs Pryce left did you begin to think someone might have moved into the house?'

'Not long. She left on the Friday, just before the last of the vans took her stuff away—'

'Hold on a minute. How many vans, and how many times did they come?'

He was happier talking about this. 'She told me how she'd planned it; like a battle, she said, bringing up the troops. First there was the top auctioneers, international they were. They came early in the week to wrap up the silver and the china that she didn't want to take with her, and to take all the valuable stuff away including the big pictures and the best pieces of furniture that she didn't want to keep.

'The next day it was the local auction people – another great big lorry for that; all the furniture including her own king-size bed. When that had gone, I moved a smaller, single bed into her room from across the landing, for her to sleep in. That was the one she was taking with her, see. Almost everything else went: the three-piece suite and the good carpets. From the downstairs rooms she only kept her walnut bureau, her own special chair, her fold-down table, and the flat screen telly from the playroom.

'Then came the house clearance people and the man she sold the kitchen bits to, and the people who took the billiard table, and someone from the garden centre who came for the big electric mower and the urns – great big urns full of geraniums – I was sorry to see them go. Men were coming and going all the time.

'I come in most evenings to help move this and that, and to see she was comfortable with what she'd got left for the last few days. She cried a bit one evening, saying she'd loved her time in that house, but on the whole she was looking forward to being waited on, and having people around to talk to all the time. She planned to take up playing bridge, she said, so's she'd always have company in future.

'That stepdaughter of hers was under our feet, coming in and out every day, driving everyone crazy, criticizing every decision Mrs Pryce had made. "Why do you want to take this with you?" and: "You could have let me have that." A right pain.

'I went round special at lunchtime to say goodbye on her last day, and I saw the van being loaded up to take her own special bits and pieces to go to the home, but her car had gone and so had she. Couldn't stand to see the last of it, I suppose.'

'What day was that, and who was in charge of seeing the last things loaded on to the van?'

'That would be the Friday. A lad from the estate agency was there with the keys. He said Mrs Pryce had arranged to leave early and have them clear up afterwards, as she wanted to be settled in her new home by teatime.'

'What did this man from the estate agency look like?'

A shrug. 'Youngish, dark. Asian, probably born here. Posh.'

Not Mr Abel, then. 'Removal people always leave bits of paper and cardboard here and there. Was the house swept clean by someone after she left, and do you know who did that?'

'The estate agency organized that. I passed by at lunchtime on the Monday—'

Doubtless wanting to see if he could get into the garden and check if his beloved vegetables needed watering.

'—and there was this cleaning company's van outside, and they had the windows and doors open and they was working through the house with industrial hoovers, you could hear them even from the road. Three men I counted, and it was more, maybe. I didn't go in to ask. That Asian guy was there again.'

'Which cleaning company was it?'

'Didn't take no notice. The estate agents would know. I'd expected she would have Vera and Pet to clean the house through after she left, but when I thought about it I realized they'd got their own everyday jobs to do. I suppose it was easier to get the estate agents to do it.' He delved into an inner pocket and produced a tooled gold cigarette lighter.

'She give me this, as was her husband's. She'd forgot I'd given up smoking some years back. I didn't say nothing. The wife says we should sell it, but I think maybe I won't.'

Ellie said softly, 'She was kind to my aunt, too.'

There was a film of tears in his eyes. 'Something's happened to her, hasn't it? There can't be no other reason for her not being in touch.'

'It seems like it. Tell me, was it you or was it Jack who turned off the water and electricity at the mains?'

He took a deep breath. Preparing to lie again? 'That last Friday the estate agent said they'd to read the meters and told me to turn everything off at the mains. The gas was easy to turn off, and so was the electrics. I tried to turn off the water, but it was stiff and I couldn't manage it. I thought I'd go back with a wrench and do it later, but I left it over the weekend, and after that I couldn't get in, could I?'

Of course he could have. He could have got back in on the Monday when the cleaning firm were in. But he hadn't done so because it was more convenient for him to go on using the water supply for his garden.

'The cleaning company came in on the Monday, and you say they were using industrial hoovers, which run on electricity. Do you think they turned the power back on? And forgot to turn it off again?'

Another shrug.

It seemed important for some reason to find out when the electricity had been turned off, and then turned on again. Ellie tried to work it out after she'd sent Mr Fritz on his way.

The hall was dark now that the sun had gone down. She switched the lights on. And then off again. And on.

She knew – as did Vera and Pet and Fritz – that something bad had happened to Mrs Pryce. The lady was no longer around. She was, she must be, dead.

If her body had been left in her car, then it must have been parked well away from human habitation, or somebody would have smelt decomposition by now. Perhaps it was in a secluded country lane somewhere?

She was not in the house. Even if she'd been shoved in a cupboard somewhere, by now the smell would be noticeable.

The cellar? No, the door to it was rusted shut. Mr Abel had not been able to get the door open, and Ellie had respect for Mr Abel's capabilities. Strike the cellar.

As Ellie went through into the kitchen to make sure everything was tidied away for the night, the fridge sprang into life.

She'd heard a motor like that start up when she'd been in the covered yard and again when she'd been in the back garden of the Pryce house.

Oh dear. Oh dear, oh dear. Ellie knew exactly where Mrs

Pryce's body might be, and why nobody had smelled anything all this time.

She must tell Thomas straight away what she suspected, and if he agreed with her they could inform the police together.

He'd be in his office, wouldn't he? He'd gone along there to take a phone call when Fritz had come to the front door.

She found Thomas sitting at his desk. His head was bowed, and he had to drag himself upright to give her a caricature of a smile.

'Whatever is the matter? My dear Thomas . . . !'

He had a singularly sweet smile. 'It's all right, Ellie. Worse things happen at sea.'

She pulled up a chair and sat beside him, taking one of his hands in hers. 'Tell me about it.'

'Pressure. This time from the man who appointed me to this job. I might have to resign.'

'Well, I'd certainly like to see a little more of you, but . . . Can you tell me why, or is it confidential?'

'It's no secret, I suppose. The book they want me to serialize is a clever attack on women, and by extension on their being ordained and everything that follows from that. A number of important men have backed it, and a major publisher has offered a contract. There will undoubtedly be a lot of media interest. I don't approve of the line the book is taking but I foresee it will become a best-seller in its own way and do a great deal of damage to the unity of the church.'

'I don't understand. If the book has got so much going for it already, why are they bringing so much pressure to bear on you to serialize it?'

'They believe that, although my magazine is of little interest to the general public, it is read by people of influence. Therefore they wish me to, er, toe the line. I can't do it, Ellie. I shall have to resign.'

She stroked his hand. 'Only a little while ago you were saying that God thought you were worrying unnecessarily about this.'

He laughed in genuine enjoyment. 'So He did. You're quite right, Ellie. This is a storm in a teacup and I suspect . . .' He looked at her sharply, 'Something's happened, hasn't it? Have

I been neatly diverted from helping you, just when you need me?'

'Perhaps. But it's getting late. Too late to do anything about it now. It's just that I suddenly realized . . . No, that's too strong a term. I can't be sure, but I *suspect* I know where Mrs Pryce might be. I'll ring the police tomorrow and tell them.'

He rubbed his eyes, and yawned again. 'She's dead, isn't she?'

'Oh yes,' said Ellie. And then: 'Of course, I might be quite wrong because I do tend to jump to conclusions; but I rather think she is.'

'You wonderful woman.' He switched off his computer and got to his feet. 'Do you know how she died?'

'Don't be silly. How could I know that!' Laughing, she drew his arm within hers, and they went up to bed together, leaving the hall lights on for Mia's return.

Thursday morning

Thursdays were always busy. Pat, Ellie's middle-aged and, to tell the truth, somewhat frumpy part-time assistant, arrived to bully her into dealing with the paperwork that had been piling up during the week.

After that they adjourned to what had once been the formal dining-room of the house, for the weekly property meeting. Their finance director was on holiday, but Stewart had brought along his assistant. Ellie wondered why he'd done that. To back him when he brought up the subject of Disneyland?

Stewart was, as usual, able to provide meticulous and succinct reports concerning what properties were vacant and needed work done, which ones were ready to be let out again, and so on. So far, so good. They whisked through the usual load until they came to Any Other Business.

'Disneyland,' said Stewart, looking pugnacious. 'Even in this depressed market the price tag on such a large house in extensive grounds is going to be three or four million, maybe more.'

His assistant played devil's advocate. 'It's a prestigious site. Why not? We've taken on larger projects before: buying a big house in poor condition, knocking it down and putting up a block of flats instead. That's what's needed around here: more housing stock. Miss Quicke had an instinct for it.'

'I realize,' said Stewart, 'that since Miss Quicke died we haven't gone down that road, but there is no reason why we shouldn't. Besides which, if we don't step in now, someone else will. An unscrupulous developer could put up a couple of tower blocks which would overlook all the houses and gardens around here and destroy your privacy.'

Ellie said, 'They'd never get permission, not in this area.'

'Want to bet?' Stewart was grim. 'We've all seen blocks of flats go up on tiny plots of land around here. This one is going to attract some serious money.'

Ellie struck out for sanity. 'Our core business is in buying, converting and maintaining properties to rent out. I know my aunt did occasionally buy a house in order to develop the site, but I'm not sure it's in our best interests to do so in a recession. I'd like to keep this item on the table to be looked at again later. Coffee anyone?'

Coffee was provided. Chat ensued. Everyone left, except Stewart.

Stewart was like a Rottweiler once he'd got his teeth into something, and Ellie knew he was not going to let this one go easily.

'Stewart, I have my own reasons for being interested in the Pryce house, but I definitely don't want to buy it. It's a monstrosity and ought to be shrunk to a miniature and kept in a glass bowl. Converting it into flats would be hideously expensive, and clients who might want to live in a Disney fantasy are few and far between . . . which means we'd be lumbered with a huge outlay and unable to clear our costs. And no; I do not want to develop the site myself – not in a recession. Too dicey.'

As he opened his mouth to object she added, 'I can quite understand that Hoopers would be delighted to move such an important property in this area, but to the best of my knowledge they have no right to offer it. You told me yourself that Mrs Pryce withdrew the house from the market, and now I can tell you something that you didn't know; the lady has gone missing. That's the real reason why I've been sniffing around the place.'

Stewart leaned back in his chair. 'Now how did you find that out, Ellie? And what else do you know that I don't?'

'I don't *know*, but I do suspect that something bad has happened to her. I have no proof, if that's what you mean, and I'm not entirely sure that I've got the right end of the stick, although I rather think I have. I'm going to set the police on to it, so we'll know soon enough.'

She saw Stewart out and went to her office to ring the police.

'May I speak to DC Milburn, please? Mrs Quicke calling.'

Muffled voices, a hand over the receiver? Ellie was put on hold. Now what?

Finally, someone deigned to return to her. 'DC Milburn is tied up on a case right now and will be for some time. If you have a complaint, perhaps you'd like to put it in writing.'

Complaint? Ellie looked at the receiver and heard the line buzz. She'd been cut off, without even so much as a suggestion that she should speak to someone else.

Something had gone wrong with her plans. Yesterday DC Milburn had been eager to follow up the leads which Ellie had given her, but now she wasn't even available to speak to Mrs Quicke. Hm. Did one detect the fine hand of Ears? Had he learned that the DC wanted to follow up Ellie's suggestions and pulled rank to stop her doing so?

That was, of course, implying that Ears disliked Ellie so much that he was prepared to sidetrack any investigation that she might instigate. A nasty thought, and one which Ellie knew she ought to throw out of her mind without delay.

Unfortunately, she thought it might be all too true.

Which meant . . . which meant that Ellie was going to have to become more involved in finding Mrs Pryce than she had hoped to be. After all, it would only take a few minutes with a screwdriver to check out her suspicions. She regarded her plump wrists with dissatisfaction. She wasn't good at opening the lids on jars and usually handed them over to Thomas to deal with. She suspected that getting screws out of wood might be rather too much for her.

What about Thomas? She went down the corridor to his

study, only to be met by him coming out. 'Sorry, sorry. Got to rush.' A quick hug and a kiss. 'I've just had an idea, got to check it out. Be back before lunch, with luck.'

Another kiss on the tip of her nose, and off he flew. Thomas was trying not to be stressed half out of his mind, but she realized that he couldn't help worrying about his future. Perhaps, thought Ellie with a smile, Thomas wasn't trusting in God to sort out his problems as much as he ought to?

Now, if she were going out for lunch, she must make sure that either Mia or Pat would be around to keep an eye on Rose. Mia had gone out, not saying where or for how long.

Right. Well, Pat would usually agree to stay on for a while if Ellie made it worth her while. And yes, today she would do so with pleasure. Rose was up, dressed and pottering around in the kitchen, almost like old times. Good.

So who did she know who had strong wrists and a screwdriver? Hm. Oh well, if all else failed, and it meant she'd have to eat humble pie . . . Well, why not? One more phone call, and then it would be time to decide what to wear for her lunch date with Mr Hooper, a lunch date which might turn out to be very interesting indeed.

Ellie didn't 'do' business clothes. She'd decided long ago that she was no great shakes as a business woman, but since she'd inherited money and couldn't deal with it herself, she'd find people she could trust to do whatever business people did with legal this and financial that. Her function was to give praise for work well done, and to trust her instincts. Rather like Mrs Pryce, in fact. Except that in the latter's case, she might have been a little too trusting.

Ellie put on one of Thomas's favourite dresses, a pretty blue and white floaty affair with a frill around a low neckline. She popped on a pair of dark blue sandals to match and eventually managed to find her lipstick; pale pink, nothing too strong. She brushed her silvery curls out till they shone.

There. She was the very picture of a sweet little housewife, wasn't she? Er, no. Perhaps too much cleavage for that. She grinned, remembering that Thomas called it her 'flirtatious frock'. Which reminded her to send up an arrow prayer. *Please, Lord. Look after Thomas?*

She remembered, too, that little Frank would probably be around most of the weekend. What were they going to do with him this time? Perhaps Thomas might have an idea – if he could disentangle himself from this nasty little problem with the bishop.

Evan Hooper – tall, beaky, and wearing an expensive mohair and silk mixture suit – called at the house to collect Ellie, driving a Lexus. She knew it was a Lexus because he told her so as soon as she got into the car. 'The very latest, of course. I change my car every year, don't you?'

'I'm afraid I never learned to drive.'

He relaxed into a Great White Shark smile. Stewart had been spot on about this man. Did Mr Hooper think he was dealing with an unworldly little old lady, whom it would be easy to bully? Mm. Well, she didn't mind him thinking that. She had a question or two which might be easier for him to answer if he were not on his guard.

He'd chosen to take her to the Golf Club, whose restaurant was only sparsely occupied. Ellie had eaten there in the past. She remembered that the menu then had been old-fashioned and the food rather filling for one who had to watch her weight. It hadn't changed, but the wine list was definitely more extensive – and expensive – than it had been in the past.

Mr Hooper was the sort of host who liked his guests to eat what he recommended, and to drink glass to glass with him. He swept the menu away, told the waiter he'd have his usual, and informed Ellie that she'd like the steak and kidney pudding, with a starter of prawn cocktail.

Ellie said, 'Actually, I'd prefer a salad and no starter. And I don't usually drink at lunchtime.'

'Nonsense, nonsense. My treat. Waiter, two prawn cocktails, with some of the Riesling I had the other day. With the steak and kidney puddings, we'll have a bottle of claret; you know the one I like.'

Ellie wondered if Mr Hooper planned to get her drunk and incapable of making suitable decisions. She asked the waiter to bring her some iced water and took only a sip of the wine Mr Hooper pressed upon her.

'Your husband is not a member here?'

The idea of Thomas playing golf made her smile. Mind you, he ought to take more exercise than he did. 'No, I'm afraid he—'

'Well, we'll soon put that right. What do you do to fill your time? It must hang heavy on your hands nowadays, with indoor staff to look after you.'

Ellie thought of her busy life and was amused. 'Well, not really, because—'

'You play bridge, of course?'

Ellie opened her eyes wide. 'No, I'm afraid I—'

'Never mind. There's a beginner's class, I believe. Must keep the old brain ticking over as you get into the sere and yellow. Drink up, there's plenty more where that came from.'

Ellie was annoyed. He looked much older than her – probably well into his seventies – and she was pleased to note there were threads of red in his cheeks. Did he drink too much? Probably. She remembered he'd screwed up his eyes when offered the menu, and she thought she'd spotted the bulge of a glasses case in the top pocket of his jacket. Ah-ha. Was he short-sighted but too vain to bring out his specs in front of her? She smiled to herself and tried to stop him topping up her glass.

'Come on,' he said, 'we have to drink to our special relationship. Cheers!'

She let him touch her glass with his and took a small sip of wine. It was too dry for her taste, but she told herself she was no connoisseur. 'What relationship is that, Mr Hooper?'

'Call me Evan.' He laid one large hand over hers and patted it. The back of his hand was dotted with liver spots. 'My dear Ellie; surely it's no secret?'

She removed her hand, letting the waiter take away her half-eaten starter. 'You have the advantage of me, I'm afraid.'

He was annoyed with her. He opened his mouth to issue a rebuke, remembered he needed her cooperation – or whatever it was he might be after – and treated her to a blinding Shark smile. Very good false teeth. Or, more likely, implants.

'Do I need to spell it out?' He'd gone all roguish. 'It can hardly be kept a secret much longer, can it?'

Diana! thought Ellie. To Mr Hooper, she said, 'Perhaps you'll let me in on this secret of yours then?'

His smile faded. 'I believe your daughter . . . ?' He waggled his eyebrows.

'Yes?' said Ellie, with a bland smile.

The waiter laid a huge plateful of steak and kidney pudding in front of her, with a side dish of new potatoes, carrots and broccoli. All swimming in butter. It looked delicious.

The wine waiter brought up a bottle of red wine, opened it, and poured a little out for Mr Hooper to taste. He did so, nodded, took a swig. Looked pleased with himself. Indicated that the waiter should give some to Ellie, and should fill up his own glass, too.

'Surely,' said Mr Hooper, 'your daughter has let you into our little secret?' Perhaps the wine was going to his head, if not to Ellie's?

'Ah,' said Ellie, putting carrots and broccoli on her plate. 'She did say something about business looking up. You are buying her out, is that it?'

'No, of course not.' Shocked. 'I'm not in the business of rescuing lame ducks.'

He took another swig of his wine, ladled potatoes on to his plate. Clicked his fingers for the waiter. 'Mustard.'

'My poor daughter.' Ellie shook her head, enjoying the rare treat of a steak and kidney pudding done exactly as she liked it. 'Does she know you think of her as a lame duck?'

'No, of course not. Has she really not discussed this with you, Ellie?'

'Discussed what?'

His fingers went white, clenched round the stem of his wine glass. 'Your putting some money into her . . . into our combined agency.'

So that was it? A straightforward demand for money. Oh well. What else had she expected? She allowed her brow to crease. 'But I thought – forgive me – she indicated that you and she were on excellent terms.'

'So we are.' He refilled his glass. Ellie hadn't touched hers.

'But that's a different matter. I don't mix business and pleasure.'

So now Ellie knew where she was. 'Let me get this clear. You plan to use my daughter for sex—'

'Hush! For heaven's sake! I'm a happily married man.'

'Who likes a bit on the side? You are not proposing to set up house with her and little Frank, then?'

'Certainly not!'

So Diana had lied about that. 'Well, you're both well over twenty-one and – may I have some of that delicious mustard, please? It's so long since I tasted such a good pudding – and though I can't say I approve, the law says that whatever consenting adults do in private is no business of mine. Or have I got my metaphors mixed?'

'My dear Ellie, you are missing the point.'

'Enlighten me. You say you're not in the business of rescuing lame ducks, but that you've come to an agreement with Diana – sex aside – to take over her agency. Now you are saying that this is contingent upon my investing in it? Dear me. I think you may have been misinformed; I don't have money to spare for rescuing lame ducks either.'

'But I understood . . .' He gobbled the words. Attacked his food, which was getting cold. Drank some more of his wine. Smiled falsely. 'You're having me on, as they say.'

Ellie watched him nod to himself, over the rim of her glass of water. Was he really so sure of himself that he thought she'd shell out a small fortune, just like that?

'To you,' he said, lifting his glass in a toast.

She touched her own lips to her glass in return. She liked his claret better than the white they'd served first, but she wasn't going to have more than one more sip of it. She tried the water instead. Iced, and with a slice of lemon in it. Excellent for quenching the thirst. She wondered what the sweet trolley might have to offer.

She said, 'Tell me, do you have a young Asian man working in your Ealing office? Well spoken.'

'What? Who?' He dabbed at his mouth with his napkin. 'Oh. Yes. Young Nirav. What's he done now?'

'Nothing that I know of.' Well, not much, anyway. Only purloined the keys to the Pryce house in order to move his girlfriend in. And turned on the electricity, which set a whole lot of other problems in motion. 'He seemed efficient. Not married, is he?'

'How should I know? Hardly out of school. Always well turned out, I'll give him that.' He scowled. 'Not like Abel. Turned up in my office in a filthy shirt yesterday. Not what I expect from my staff.'

'Mr Abel was trying to save Mrs Pryce money. It was turning off the water – a difficult job – that got him dirty. I give him full marks for efficiency.'

He took another swig of wine, pushed his half-eaten food away, and turned on the charm. 'Now that you've brought the subject up . . . You realize, of course, that the Pryce house is not officially up for sale at the moment?'

TWELVE

Ellie was delighted with the dessert trolley. 'I wonder, do they have a chocolate mousse? I shall have to go on a diet after this.'

'There's a lot of interest already from developers. If you are interested, we'll have to move quickly.'

'Oh, just look at that pavlova! I must admit to a weakness for meringues. Yes, please; waiter, the pavlova. And double cream? Lovely.'

Mr Hooper was not accustomed to being deflected but, to his credit, rose above it. 'No sweet for me, waiter. Just coffee. Black.'

One-upmanship? Ellie could play that game, too. 'Yes, waiter. Coffee for me as well. Sugar and cream. I must say; it's a long time since I had such an enjoyable lunch.'

Mr Hooper glared at her and morphed the glare into a number-three Shark smile. 'You told Mr Abel you wanted to have a second viewing. There is, of course, a great deal to think about when considering the purchase of such an important property, but I'm afraid this one won't be on the market for long, so if you're interested, we should—'

'What address do you have for Mrs Pryce?'

'What? I'd have to look in the files, but—'

'She's disappeared, you know. Never arrived at the retirement home. I'm hoping the police will turn up her body soon.' She looked wistfully at the sweet trolley. Could she manage some chocolate mousse after the pavlova? No, better not.

'What-what?'

'I wonder if she made a will. If she didn't and she's had an accident or something, it's going to be a bit of a mess, working out who inherits. I mean, it might be a distant cousin, living in Canada. Or some charity or other. She had two cats, I believe. Perhaps she left it all to the pussies.'

Mr Hooper croaked, 'Waiter; brandy!'

Ellie looked at her watch. 'Dear me, is that the time? Thanks for the lunch, most enjoyable, lovely to have met you, but must go. My son-in-law Stewart is collecting me. That's Diana's ex-husband, you know. Such a nice man, honest and reliable. But of course you must know him because he deals with all the house purchases made by the Trust. He was terribly shocked to hear of Diana's financial woes, as I was, but as you say; who throws good money after bad?'

She left him gaping after her and made her way, floating rather than walking, to the Ladies. Seeing how flushed her cheeks were and easing the waistband of her dress, she considered that she might perhaps have indulged a little too much in her 'free' meal. But there; there was no such thing as a free meal, was there? She hoped, insincerely, that Mr Hooper felt it had been worth his while to wine and dine her.

She grinned at her image in the mirror, deciding that she didn't care what he felt about it.

Plus, she'd put a nice spoke in Diana's wheel. Hah!

Thursday afternoon

A Second Time Around clothes shop.
'Will you just look at this! Perfect for my daughter's wedding. My size and all.' To the shopkeeper: *'How much for the lilac dress and jacket?'*

'Thirty. It's a designer label, hardly worn at all.'

'And a matching handbag? Looks like real leather. You haven't got a hat to go with it, have you? Ah, yes. Right up to the minute. I must say you've got some good stuff in at the moment, haven't you? Better than usual.'

'Depends who brings stuff in. There's some shoes to match over here.'

'Not my size. How much for the dress, the handbag and the hat?'

'Sixty the lot.'

'Done.'

Thursday afternoon

'What are you smiling at?' asked Stewart, handing Ellie into his car. 'And what is this urgent matter you want me to deal with?'

'Take me to Disneyland!' said Ellie, with an uncharacteristically florid gesture.

'What? Why?' He set the car in motion.

'We're going to do a spot of breaking and entering.'

'What? Ellie, you can't be serious.'

Bother. She'd forgotten how strait-laced he was. Thomas would have trusted her and not asked questions. Oh dear, she did hope he could sort his bishop out . . .

'It's quite all right. I've just had lunch with Mr Hooper.' She wasn't lying, exactly.

'I suppose that's all right, then.' He turned into the Disneyland drive and parked. 'So why did you ask me not to forget my tool kit?'

'Can you bring it along with you?' The door to the yard wasn't locked, was it? No. Perhaps Fritz had been frightened away, and perhaps not. The house itself ought to be empty. She pushed through the door into the yard.

Pooh. A trace of rot on the air. Damp? Well, no. Not the drains.

Stewart had followed her in. 'Ellie, what are we doing here?'

The padlock on the door from the covered area into the garage looked strong and new but, as Fritz had demonstrated, a padlock was only as effective as the screws that held it into the wood. 'Stewart, can you take the screws out of that padlock, please? I need to get into the garage.'

'*What?*' She might have been asking him to sacrifice one of his children! 'I can't do that. Ellie, what's going on?'

'Trust me, Stewart. It's important. Mrs Pryce has gone missing, and I have a horrid feeling she's been stashed in the garage. I'd get the padlock off myself, but I haven't got a tool kit and I know my wrists aren't strong enough to get those screws out.'

'No.' Stewart downed his tool kit and folded his arms at her.

She danced with impatience. 'Look, there's a big freezer in there. I know because I've heard it start up and—'

'You're imagining it.'

'No, I'm not. The electricity's been turned off since yesterday morning, and if she's in there, she's going to start decomposing again any minute now.'

'What? I can't smell anything.'

Ellie rather thought she could. Or was she imagining it? Was it perhaps too early for the body to become smelly?

Stewart picked up his tool kit. 'I'm not being a party to this, Ellie, and neither are you. If you think Mrs Pryce is in there – which I doubt – then you should inform the police.'

'I've tried that and they won't listen.' She calculated distances and swung her handbag against the garage window, stepping back as it broke.

'Ellie! Whatever . . . ?' asked Stewart. 'Are you all right? Have you hurt yourself? Of all the . . .' He sniffed the air.

As did Ellie.

A buzzing sound came from the garage, and a number of blowflies found their way out into the open air through the broken window.

Ellie sucked a cut finger.

Stewart found a large screwdriver in his tool kit and set to work. One screw out. Another. He took the padlock off and opened the door.

'Phew.' He blenched. Drew back.

'We have to make sure,' said Ellie. She took a deep breath and stepped into the garage, batting flies away.

The freezer stood on a concrete floor, tucked into the shadows at the back of the garage. It wasn't locked. In fact, a piece of heavy material seemed to have prevented the lid from closing completely. In order to aid decomposition?

Ellie held her breath and pushed up the lid.

More flies. How quickly did flies settle on a body? Of course, just after Mrs Pryce had been killed, there'd been a period of two or maybe three days when the electricity had been turned off. Decomposition must have started at that time and been arrested when the electricity had been turned on again by the squatters . . . and not turned off again when they left.

The motor had been labouring to cope, since the lid hadn't been closed properly. All this time the freezer had been on until Mr Abel had turned the electricity off again yesterday. And that had started decomposition once more.

Stewart pushed Ellie gently aside to see for himself what had been lying there for so long. Mrs Pryce looked up at them, hair carefully blonded, false eyelashes still clinging to her cheeks. Head at an odd angle. A gash on one temple with dried blood around it. She was wearing a long purple housecoat in a velvety material. One fold of the garment had not been tucked into the freezer with her and had kept the lid from closing properly.

Stewart helped Ellie out into the yard, only to come face to face with someone Ellie knew.

'So you found her, then?' said Fritz.

Ellie made it to the nearest drain before throwing up her lunch. Oh dear.

Stewart gagged, controlled himself, took out his mobile phone and punched numbers.

An arm around Ellie's shoulders guided her through the far door into the garden. Fritz helped her to sit on the side of a raised bed. He left her for a moment to run the garden tap, wetting his handkerchief and bringing it back to help her wipe her face. There was still some water in the system, then.

She managed to say, 'Thank you, Fritz.'

'My pleasure. You keep sitting right there. I don't think it'll hurt that pretty frock of yours. Will you be all right by yourself for a bit? I need to see her for myself.'

She nodded. Found a hankie, blew her nose.

She was trembling. It would pass.

Fritz left the door to the yard open when he went back in. Ellie could hear Stewart on his mobile, telling the police what they'd found. Practical Stewart. A screwdriver and strong wrists.

Oh dear, oh dear. *Dear Lord, forgive them, for they know not what they do.*

Now why on earth had she thought that?

Stewart loomed into view. 'I phoned the police. Are you all right, Ellie? How did you know?'

'Long story short. She's been missing for a while, but nobody wanted to do anything about it for different reasons. Then her great-nephew came looking for her and stole from us – which set me off on her trail.'

Fritz shuffled back into the garden. His face gleamed with
sweat, but he didn't actually vomit. He went to the garden tap,
turned it on, and drank some water out of his cupped hands.

Stewart turned on Fritz. 'Who are you, and how did you
come to be here at the very moment that we found her?'

'She knows.' Indicating Ellie. He squatted on the ground,
put his head back, took deep breaths.

Ellie tried to think straight. 'Fritz, no need for you to stay,
especially if you've work to do.'

He cracked open his eyes, tried to smile. 'Thank you, but
no. I'll stay, face the music. They'll take one look at the garden
and know I was here. To think . . . all this time . . . and me
believing . . . The car being gone, see. The youngsters didn't
have nothing to do with it, did they?'

'No. Except that they turned the electricity back on.'

'I only ever caught sight of the girl once. Dressed in black,
head to foot, with a scarf around her head. Scarpered the
moment she saw me. I knew she was around, seen her footprints. Could see where she'd cut herself some roses. Poor
thing; I didn't grudge her a few flowers, locked up in that top
room all the time.'

'What?' said Stewart. 'Who?'

Fritz said, 'Dunno their names. Do you, missus?'

Ellie shook her head. She thought she might know one of
their names, but was it right to give it to the police if they'd had
nothing to do with Mrs Pryce's death, and they'd gone to such
lengths to hide themselves away? If Mrs Pryce hadn't minded
Fritz coming in to tend his vegetables, wouldn't she also have
given permission to the young couple to stay in her empty house
– that is, if she'd known about it? Which, of course, she hadn't.

Ellie rubbed her forehead. She was getting a headache, not
thinking straight.

Stewart was hard to deflect. He addressed Fritz. 'So, how
did you happen to come along at the right time, eh?'

'It was her –' he poked an elbow in Ellie's direction –
'talking about the electrics. All this time I thought Mrs P had
gone off in her car and got herself lost somewhere. Tell the
truth, I'm not much in the thinking line. But when Mrs Quicke
asked me when the electrics had been turned off and put on

again, I kept remembering that I'd heard the freezer running all this time and thought her stepdaughter was supposed to have emptied it out and I'd seen her doing it. Except that she should have switched it off at the power point on the wall when she'd done that, shouldn't she?

'So I come along in the van and see a car turning into the drive. I wasn't sure who you might be, so I parked a little way back on the road and walked in just as the lady was breaking the window . . . which I'd better tell the police as I did it, no need to get you into trouble, missus.'

'Don't do that,' said Ellie. 'I did it, and I'll own up to it. You've got enough to worry about.'

'Don't I know it! They'll have me down the station, boxing me in, getting me to say black is white, and before you know it, they'll have me in handcuffs, thinking I killed her for her cigarette lighter. Which I didn't.'

'No, I'm sure you didn't,' said Ellie. 'Stewart, would you do something for me? Do you remember my solicitor, Gunnar Brooks? A heavyweight – in all directions. What I mean is . . . Oh, never mind about that, now . . .'

Remembering Gunnar was a happy thought. He was indeed a heavyweight; he weighed in at eighteen stone, but being over six foot two in height, his weight didn't look anything out of the ordinary. He was also the senior partner in a prestigious firm of solicitors in town, he'd known and respected and admired Ellie's aunt for ever, and he was always happy to oblige her niece in such trivial matters as finding corpses. In fact, her adventures amused him.

She said, 'Mr Fritz and I will be happy to make statements to the police but we'll need Gunnar's help so that we can get home in time for tea. Can you find his telephone number and get hold of him for me?'

Stewart succeeded in getting through to the solicitor's office on his mobile as the first of the police cars turned into the driveway. He hesitated. 'Ellie, can you take the call? I'd better show the police where to go.'

Ellie asked for Gunnar, and as soon as she was through, cut off enquiries about her health to say, 'Dear Gunnar, I've found another body. Yes, a neighbour of mine. We've informed

the police, who are about to descend upon us. The only thing
is; I tried to report her missing earlier and they fobbed me
off. They're going to be furious at being proved inefficient, if
not worse. Can you get here to protect me – and the gardener,
who is innocent of causing her death – as soon as possible?
Or are you tied up with something more interesting?'

'I'll be with you instantly. Routine bores me to death, and
it seems a long time since I visited you for—'

'A glass of Madeira and a slice of Rose's Victoria sandwich.
Well, I'm not sure I can promise you the cake, but I think we
can find a bottle of Madeira for you.'

'Give me your address, and I'll be on my way.'

Ending the call, she spotted action through the open door
into the yard. Predictably, it was Ears who hove into sight
first, followed by a cowed-looking DC Milburn. 'Phoo!' Ears
blenched at the smell.

'This way,' said Stewart, indicating the open door to the
garage.

But Ears had seen Ellie in the garden and pounced on her
first. 'Mrs Quicke! *Now* what have you been up to?' His ears
had turned bright red. Never a good sign.

'Let me give you a hand up, missus,' said Fritz, helping
Ellie to her feet. 'And don't forget your handbag.' He passed
that over to her as she brushed herself down.

Ellie told herself to be brave. Ears couldn't eat her. 'I found
the missing lady for you, that's all. She's in the garage behind
you, and she's very dead. This heat, you know.'

DC Milburn caught Ellie's eye and mouthed, 'I did try!'

Ellie relaxed into a grin. Poor girl. Of course she'd done
her best, but what could she do against Ears?

'And what's so funny?' blared Ears.

'Nothing,' said Ellie. 'Now, before my solicitor gets here,
do you want to have a look at what I've found? And then I'll
sketch in the background for you, although really, you should
have got all that from DC Milburn, right?'

Ears disappeared into the garage for five seconds and came
out looking pale, except for his ears, which remained bright
red. DC Milburn followed him, stayed ten seconds and emerged
again, also looking pale.

'So,' said Ears, breathing heavily. 'Who did it, then?'

Ellie summoned up her sweetest smile. 'Oh, I leave all that clever stuff to the professionals. I'm sure you'll find out in next to no time.'

Thomas had not returned by the time that Ellie got back home, but Pat was still there. Pat lived in a flat and had never done any gardening, but Rose had enticed her outside and was instructing her in the difference between a weed and a flower. Somewhat to her own surprise, Pat had discovered how pleasant it was, on a gentle summer's evening, to do a little light gardening under supervision.

Mia was in the kitchen, putting something in the oven to eat. What a blessing that girl was, and how were they going to cope without her?

So where was Thomas? Ellie checked, but he hadn't even left a message on the answerphone for her.

Her handbag seemed surprisingly heavy, so she opened it.

A glint of gold, and a wooden handle. Fritz strikes again! Ellie worked it out; he'd gone to the Pryce house armed with a screwdriver so that he could look into the garage for himself, only Ellie had beaten him to it. Then, when the police were on their way, Fritz had realized they might misinterpret his possession of a screwdriver and charge him with going equipped to burgle. So, he'd dropped it into her handbag as he handed it to her. He'd added his gold cigarette lighter, for much the same reason.

Ellie started to laugh and found it difficult to stop.

It occurred to her that Mrs Pryce would have been much amused by all these goings-on. Perhaps she was hovering overhead somewhere with a smile on her face, patting her blonde coiffure, and batting her false eyelashes. Enjoying the fuss.

Ellie plodded up the stairs. 'A long relaxing bath is what I need. And a change of clothes.'

She went to her bedroom window and looked out. Far off to the left she could see the turrets of the Pryce house and that one particular window in which Rose had seen the girl in the black scarf.

Where was that girl now? And why had she been in hiding?

Not that it mattered, since the police had taken over with dire warnings from Ears if she interfered in his investigations once more. Which she hadn't the slightest intention of doing, as she had quite enough on her plate without that.

She turned the bath taps on. Everything she'd been wearing went into the laundry basket. Although Thomas didn't like her to take their radio into the bathroom in case it got wet and short-circuited, she rather fancied some soothing background music and did so now, plugging it in by the washbasin. She found a channel of orchestral music – Elgar, anybody? – and turned the volume up to drown out her thoughts.

Thomas had given her a huge bottle of Badedas, a luxury she wouldn't normally have allowed herself. She poured a plentiful amount into the bathtub, swirled it around till the whole surface was deep in bubbles, stepped in, and slid down into the water. She was really going to enjoy this . . .

For ten seconds. And then, even above the orchestra, she heard a screech of rage.

Diana erupted into the room, screaming. 'How could you! You ruin everything I try to do!'

'What?' She sat upright. 'Diana, I'm having a bath.'

Diana was beside herself. 'How dare you tell him I'm a dead duck!'

Ellie raised her voice. 'It was he who . . . Turn the volume down, will you? Over there. The radio.'

'What?' Diana clutched the air, her mouth squared into a scream. 'You ruin every chance I have to . . . !' Violins surged to a crescendo.

'TURN THE VOLUME DOWN! THE RADIO!'

Diana looked wildly around, seized the radio and tugged on the cord, which resisted her. She stared at it, lifted it . . .

Dear God!

Was she going to toss it into the bath?

If she did . . .

Dear God!

Ellie looked into her daughter's face and saw . . . death.

Diana was going to throw the radio down into the water and kill her.

THIRTEEN

Ellie prayed. *Dear Lord above, if this is the end . . . Into your hands . . .*

She clutched at the sides of the bath, but her hands were slippery and she lost her grip . . . Her head hit the side of the bath and she slid down into the water.

Dear Lord, in your mercy, forgive my sins . . . Look after Thomas.

She flailed around, gulped water. Choked. Floated away . . .

A confused babel of sounds. A strong pair of hands lifted her head and shoulders out of the water. She coughed and spluttered. A man was shouting. 'Ellie! Wake up!'

Who was Ellie?

She tried to speak, to open her eyes. Failed. Coughed some more.

She was pulled up out of the water by strong hands.

Someone screamed.

The man's voice said, 'Ellie! Oh, dear Lord . . .'

She managed to open her eyes. She saw a tiled wall, a bright overhead light. Inside her head she was in a dark place, full of howling winds. The Slough of Despond.

A bearded man held her up in a deep-sided bath from which the water was receding. He pulled a towel around her. What was happening?

The man looked anxious. He held her close. She could feel his heartbeat. Too fast. Thumping away. She knew him, didn't she?

Someone . . . a woman . . . screamed, hands to head, mouth ugly, eyes closed.

The woman had tried to . . . What was it the woman had tried to do?

The man plucked her out of the bath and seated her on a stool. She had no strength, was a rag doll. She looked beyond her feet. There was a radio on the floor, smashed out of shape. Why was it there?

She was in shock. Split in two.

One part was in a bright bathroom. The other part was in the wilderness. She tried to join the two parts together and failed. All she knew was that the woman standing by the door had tried to do something bad to her.

She could hear herself breathing. Her throat was raw. The man was towelling her dry. He was being rough, trying to pull her back to life. But her life had been twisted out of the true, and she didn't think she'd ever get it straight again.

Someone was having hysterics, laughing, crying . . .

It wasn't her, was it? The man held her head and looked into her eyes. 'Is it safe to leave you for a moment, Ellie?'

Her name was Ellie? She had no words, couldn't even nod.

The man left her to tower over the dark woman. A slap. Silence. He thrust the woman out of the bathroom.

Angry voices came from a distance.

Ellie. Her name was Ellie? She was confused, couldn't make sense of what had happened. She was in an icy cold place. Brown and icy. She began to shiver. The towel was wet, uncomfortable. She let it drop from her shoulders. There was a white fluffy robe hanging on the back of the bathroom door. That would be warm, wouldn't it? She lifted her arm in an effort to reach it. It was too far away.

She was cold, so cold. If only she could put that robe on . . .

With an enormous effort she managed to stand and reach it. And put it on. There, that was better. Perhaps the trembling would stop now.

More shouting from the other room. What was going on? Did she, in fact, care? She shuffled to the door and pushed it open. The man was furious about something. She thought his blood pressure must be going through the roof, and that was a comforting thought, reminding her of the world in which she used to live.

A dark-haired woman was with him, in tears, pale as ash except for a red mark on one cheek. 'Mother, he hit me!' The voice came from far, far away, tuning in and out. Was there water in her ears? 'He says I was going to . . . but I . . . I couldn't find . . . control to turn the sound . . .'

The words meant nothing to her. Mere sound and fury, signifying nothing.

Ellie? Her name was Ellie? She was too tired to stay on her feet. The man leaped to her side, helping her to reach the bed. She sat down with a bump.

The man was speaking. The words meant nothing. They echoed round her head. 'She had . . . ready to throw . . . Another minute . . .'

'. . . lying! Why would . . . Believe . . . ?'

It was all a dream. A dream . . .

She fell back on the pillows, beyond speech. My name is Ellie . . . ?

'I meant no harm,' the dark woman whined, twisting her hands together.

Curling herself into a foetal position, Ellie slipped down into the brown hollow where the ice-cold winds whistled around her.

The man shouted something. He grasped the dark-haired woman's arm and thrust her away from the bed.

Ellie was trembling. It started small, with a quiver, and grew worse. The dark woman's voice was raised in protest, going fainter . . . going away.

The man picked her up, held her tight. 'There, there. There, there.' He rubbed her arms and back, and then her legs, bringing her back to the present, trying to hold her from slipping back into the wasteland. At last the tremors subsided, and she relaxed against him.

'I'll get the doctor.'

Why would she want a doctor?

He held her away from him to check that she had stopped shaking, got her out of his damp bathrobe, and tucked her up in the duvet. Nice. Warm.

It was a bright day. Too bright. She closed her eyes against the brightness.

There was something she needed to ask the man, but she couldn't remember what it was. She half-opened her eyes. He smiled down at her. She liked this man a lot.

He was saying something . . . praying over her? That was good, too.

She drifted away into sleep.

Thursday night to Friday morning

She woke. It was dark. Someone was murmuring words in her ear. Soothing. She'd been wound up tight as a drum. She couldn't make out the words, but the tone was . . . gentle, hopeful. Tears slipped down her cheeks and were wiped away. Her breathing slowed. She relaxed and slept again.

How many times did that happen before she half woke to the realization that the dark-haired woman had meant to kill her, perhaps only for a couple of seconds . . . but in that couple of seconds she had intended to throw the radio into the bath and electrocute her.

The radio was plunging down towards her . . .

She started upright. She was in bed. She prised her eyes open. Someone had drawn the curtains, muting the power of the sun outside. Or was it dusk already?

A little brown woman sat in the chair by the window, smiling a nutcracker grin. Was that . . . could it be . . . Miss Drusilla Quicke, Ellie's much-loved aunt? 'Good girl. Coming out of it? I'm so glad you found Mrs Pryce. You'll sort out what . . .'

Who was Mrs Pryce?

She slid down in bed and closed her eyes again. She dreamed she was walking in a garden full of roses in the dusk. The fragrance of the roses was all around her. The dripping tap was the only sound she could hear, except for the birds . . . mostly sparrows, twittering to their nests as the dusk deepened to night. She stood by the pond, watching the reflection of a cloud as it passed overhead, and then she was in the water, looking up at a dark-haired woman's furious face and seeing the radio hurtle down towards her.

She sat upright, breathing hard. Tears formed and slid down her cheeks. She lifted her hands . . . oh, the effort that took . . . and wiped them away.

She knew who she was. Ellie, that was her name. She knew where she was. At home in bed.

A little brown woman was sitting in the chair by the window. No, it wasn't Miss Quicke. Ellie recognized her dear friend Rose, snoring gently. The curtains had been drawn against the light outside. Ah, so Rose had managed to climb the stairs again? That was good.

Ellie eased herself out from under the duvet. Naked. Ah, well. She did sometimes sleep naked, because . . . She smiled, remembering Thomas chasing her round the bed pretending to be a bear . . . Yes, well. Her smile morphed into a grin. Thomas was just great in that department, as in all others. Thomas had saved her life and prayed over her. But Diana . . . ! No, she would not think about Diana now.

She turned her head with difficulty. Yes, Thomas had slept in bed with her last night. In fact, she seemed to recall waking at some point from a nightmare and him comforting her. Praying for her? She supposed she ought to be thanking God for giving her back her life, but she wasn't sure she could. Not yet, anyway.

She turned her thoughts away from prayer. She'd been anxious about Thomas for some reason. Why? The reason eluded her.

With an effort she swung her legs out of bed and reached for her dressing gown, which someone had thoughtfully put on the chair nearby . . . just too far to reach. The room went round and round. And steadied.

There was a carafe of water and a glass on the bedside table. Good. She was thirsty. She drank some water. She had a slight headache. She touched the back of her head gently. Yes, it was sore. Oh, Diana!

She shuddered. She pushed the horrible memory to the back of her mind. Don't think about that now. What time was it? Eight? In the evening? Or was it the next morning? What day would that be? Thursday or Friday?

In her chair by the window Rose woke up with a start. 'Gracious me, don't tell me I dozed off. He made me promise to call him the moment you woke up, and here's me wasting time—'

Ellie managed to speak though her voice was hoarse. 'I'm

quite all right, Rose. Honest.' Well, not really all right. But improving. 'You made it up the stairs, then.'

Now, Ellie, don't start crying again. It doesn't help.

'Of course I did, and without anyone helping me, either.' Rose eased Ellie into her dressing gown. 'I'll call him in a minute, as I expect you'll be wanting the bathroom before you do anything else.'

Which was true. Her big bath sheet lay in a heap on the bathroom floor, sodden. Some people never understood that towels do not dry themselves if left in a heap on the floor. Thomas, though a wonderful man in many ways, had never grasped this principle.

A wrecked radio had been shoved under the stool. So it had all been true? She'd hoped that it had been a bad dream.

Rose had drawn the curtains back by the time Ellie returned. 'Another lovely day. A really blue sky. I've told Thomas you're awake and looking tickety-boo, and he'll be up shortly. You'll be wanting some breakfast I've no doubt, and if you'll tell me what you fancy, I'll get straight on to it for you. You look a bit shaky. Let's get you back to bed.'

'Do I have to?' She sounded like a whiny child.

'It's my turn to scold you for not looking after yourself properly. For days now Miss Quicke has been saying to me that I've been falling down on the job. "You've let yourself fall into the doldrums, Rose," she says. "You're no good to man or beast at the moment, and this has Got to Stop!"'

'Oh. Has it?' Ellie was still finding the slightest movement a drag. 'Do you know, I think I might be better going back to bed for a bit.' She couldn't think when she'd last pampered herself like this.

Rose helped Ellie replace her dressing gown with a pretty cotton nightdress and plumped up her pillows before helping Ellie back to bed. 'There, now. Don't you worry about a thing because I'm back in charge again. You've all been very good to me these last few months when I was feeling so down, and that dear child Mia, although meaning to be helpful, has turned me almost into an invalid, which as you know is not really my cup of tea at all. Not to say she didn't mean well, because she did, but what I say is that she ought to be going out and about now and picking up her life where she left it off, and if she won't take it from me that that's what she ought to do, then you'll have to put your foot down with a firm hand, Ellie, and see that she does it.

'Now, I should think you could manage a boiled egg with soldiers, and perhaps a pot of Earl Grey tea rather than coffee, which I shall have coming up in next to no time, right?'

Rose whisked herself out of the room, and Ellie closed her eyes, thinking that she really needed to take some aspirin, but couldn't summon up enough energy to get out of bed to fetch it . . .

Friday noon

Someone was stroking her hand, kissing her cheek.

She opened her eyes, and there was her dear husband Thomas with her breakfast. Her headache was almost gone.

He was smiling. 'You're better.'

She smiled back. 'I found Mrs Pryce, I sicked up my lovely lunch, and then I hit my head on the edge of the bath. Concussion.'

In the same moment he said, 'Shock.'

Yes, it had been a terrible shock, and she hadn't got over it yet. Diana . . .

'I rang the doctor, explained. He said to watch you like a hawk, wake you every few hours, let him know if you had any visual disturbance. But you haven't. You look so much better, but you're staying in bed today.' It wasn't quite a question.

'Yes. I love you, Thomas.'

He blinked hard and turned his head away. 'I was worried. Ellie, you really are the light of my life and . . .' His voice faded out, and he swallowed, hard.

With an effort she reached for the box of tissues and handed it to him.

He tried to laugh. Almost made it. 'Now I know you're better, thinking of others before yourself.'

She pushed herself further up on the pillows and reached for the tray. 'And you? I seem to remember wanting to ask you something but . . . oh, I've remembered what it was now. Did you sort the bishop out?' The 'soldiers' of toast and butter were crisp, the egg perfect.

Thomas poured tea for her. 'I shouldn't have left you. A couple of minutes more and—'

'Don't let's think about that. What about the bishop, Thomas?'

'The bishop is in full flight. Or, at least, he's no longer on my tail.'

'How did you manage that?' Around another mouthful.

'He called in some favours; so did I. My favours were bigger than his favours.'

'Tut,' said Ellie, mock serious. 'Two boys battling with conkers.'

'Me, conker champion!' Thomas flexed his biceps.

She did her best to laugh, pushed the empty plates away from her and accepted the mug of tea. And sobered up. 'Diana?'

He was wary. 'I caught her just as she lifted the radio above her head.'

Ellie winced. Surely it would be best to pretend it never happened?

Thomas said, 'She was beside herself.'

'My fault. I shouldn't have taken the radio into the bathroom.'

'I, er, threatened her with the police.'

Ellie stifled a qualm. Nodded. 'You did right.' It had never occurred to Ellie before that she should be frightened of her daughter, but now she was. Oh Diana, where did I go wrong that you could even think of doing such a thing?

'I didn't call them, because she wept and begged and . . . I suggested she go on an anger management course.'

'Thomas, you are brilliant!' She had tears in her eyes, didn't know what to do with her mug of tea, needed paper tissues. He took the mug off her and handed her the tissues. Suddenly, she was tired. And wanted to cry again. She slid down in bed. 'You'll keep everyone away?'

'Of course. It's about time you had a rest, give everyone a chance to realize how much you do for them. The cleaners are here, or rather Vera's here but she's got another girl with her and neither Vera nor Rose is happy about that – but that's not something you need to worry about, and they'll not come in this room, I promise.'

'I'd like to see Vera. She must have heard about our finding the body by now, and she was fond of Mrs Pryce. Besides, she could clean and dust in here and in the bathroom . . .' Don't think about the bathroom. 'No hoovering. Just a quick dust. And maybe change the sheets on the bed?'

'Are you sure?'

'I'm sure.'

'All right. Then I'm going downstairs to Google up a holiday for us. Where would you like to go? I thought we might take off somewhere for a fortnight or so. Do you fancy the Great Wall of China, or the spectacular scenery of New Zealand? Or perhaps Disneyland?'

'Anything but Disneyland.' She closed her eyes. He drew the curtains and took the empty tray away.

Early Friday afternoon

Vera tiptoed into the room. Ellie had been dozing, but she made herself sit upright and held out her hand in welcome to the girl.

Vera dropped her cleaning things and began to cry. 'I'm so silly, don't take any notice of me, but Fritz came round to tell me last night and I haven't been able to stop crying since. You know how fond I was of her . . . and now you're poorly and Thomas said I wasn't to tire you out and look at me!'

'I know.' Ellie motioned the girl into the chair beside her bed. 'It's all right.' Ellie pushed the paper tissues towards Vera. 'I see you're still wearing the earrings she gave you.'

Vera blew her nose and sniffed. 'At first I thought I wouldn't, and then I thought I would; so I did.'

'She'd have been pleased to see you wearing them.'

Vera tried to laugh. 'She would, wouldn't she? Every day she put on her make-up and picked out some jewellery to wear. She wore her diamond drops most times, but she had all sorts, all colours of the rainbow. And then her rings! Oh, my! Mostly diamonds again, though her eternity ring was

alternately emeralds and diamonds, and she had others that
she wore from time to time to match different outfits, you
know. She would say, "Do you think this goes with my dress?"
And we'd say, "Yes," of course.

'She was lonely, you know, because many of her friends
had moved away or died, and she looked forward to our
company. She'd sit down with us while we had a cuppa, and
ask us what we were doing at the weekend, and tell us what
she'd been doing. And she'd sort of flirt with Fritz, although
it wasn't really flirting, but asking if he liked her new
eyeshadow, and was her skirt length all right, that sort of
thing.'

Vera blew her nose again. 'I'm glad you found her. I've
been wondering, was she in the garage all the time we were
going round the house? So near?'

'I'm afraid so. But she'd been gone a long time before.
Think of her as you last saw her, making plans for her future.'

'Mikey's been asking after her, wanting to see the lady with
the pretty things again. I had to tell him this morning that . . .
Well, I didn't tell him she was dead. I said she'd gone a long
way away and wouldn't be coming back. He was so sweet,
he said, "Never mind, Mummy, I'll draw you a picture of her
to remember her by." Wasn't that lovely of him?'

'It was.'

'Do you think she suffered much? Fritz said she was wearing
that long housecoat of hers and must have fallen downstairs
and broken her neck. Do you think that's what happened?'

'I don't know. The police, thankfully, have taken over and
no doubt will let us know sometime.'

'The only thing is –' Vera's brow wrinkled – 'if that was
how she died – and that seems very likely to me – then how
did she come to be in the freezer?'

That was the question, indeed. Ellie shook her head. 'I don't
know.'

Vera sniffed and stood up. 'Oh well, this won't get the baby
his supper, will it? What you must think of me, carrying on
like this! You'd like your bed changed, right? And the bathroom
cleaned.' Still talking, Vera went into the bathroom and came
back with the radio. 'You had an accident? Thomas said you'd

had a fall . . . over the radio? What a shame.' She clicked the switch several times. 'It's quite dead. What shall I do with it?'

Ellie suppressed a shudder. She wanted to say, 'Throw it away,' but decided against it for some reason. 'Put it in the bottom of the wardrobe for now.' She struggled into her dressing gown and made it to the chair by the window. What was the time? Perhaps she could manage some more food soon? She told herself not to think about who would have to make it; Mia or Rose. They'd have to sort that out between themselves. Perhaps Thomas would do it?

'Vera, Thomas tells me you've got a new partner today. What's happened to Pet?'

'Holiday time, innit?' Vera set about changing the bed. 'Didn't give us much notice this time. Some cousin of her husband's wants them to house-sit, down on the Isle of Wight. Jammy whatsits. Wish I had a cousin in the country who wanted me to house-sit. Lovely weather, too. When we go out for the day, it's raining, likely as not.'

The doorbell rang downstairs. Ellie had heard it ringing every now and then that morning but had managed to ignore it.

Vera floated a clean sheet on to the bed. 'That'll be another bouquet for you no doubt, and Fritz said he'd be popping round sometime. Said you have something of his you were keeping for him.'

Ellie suppressed a grin. Yes, Fritz should be grateful to her for concealing evidence on his behalf. She wondered what form his gratitude might take. A basket of vegetables taken from the Pryce garden, perhaps?

Vera shook up pillows and placed them on the bed. 'There was one huge bouquet came, but Thomas told the florist to take it to the church or something. From your daughter?' Curiosity leaked out of her eyes.

'Possibly,' said Ellie, trying to be non-committal. 'Who else called, do you know?'

'Dunno. Thomas said as how he was guarding the fort, and no one else was to answer the door or the phone. He got Rose to lock the back door, too. He don't do things by halves, do he?'

No, he didn't. Ellie relaxed, closing her eyes. Vera whipped around the room, almost without sound. Vera was very good. Better than Pet . . .

Ellie dozed off again . . . and woke out of another nightmare, dragged herself up out of the howling wind and the water closing around her as Diana lifted the radio above her head . . .

She was sweating, crying, fearful, her heartbeat far too fast. She wiped her eyes, made herself breathe deeply. Look, you're at home in bed, no one else in the room.

The house was quiet around her. She relaxed, yawned, and stretched. She felt her strength returning. She was also hungry.

She found her watch and discovered it was past three o'clock. Hadn't anyone thought to bring her some lunch? There was no sight of a tempting snack in her room. Had they all forgotten her?

FOURTEEN

Every movement was a drag, but she pulled on the minimum of clothing – it was a warm day so she could manage with fresh undies and a light grey cotton frock. She brushed her hair, didn't bother with make-up. Had she lost weight? Possibly. Good.

She found it necessary to hold on to the banister as she went down the stairs into the hall. She could smell freshly-made coffee and wondered peevishly why they hadn't thought to bring her some.

Everyone was in the kitchen. Rose and Mia, Thomas. Vera and her new sidekick were picking up their bags, ready to depart. They chorused, 'Bye, Rose. Bye, Mia. Bye, Thomas. See you next week.'

And Fritz. Of course. This was the time of day when Fritz would normally have popped into the Pryce garden to attend to his vegetables, but he couldn't go round there with the police on the spot, could he?

Thomas hastened to pull out a stool for her. 'My dear, are you sure you ought to be up?'

'I'm fine.' Though she wasn't, really. But getting there. 'I could do with a bite to eat and some tea perhaps.'

'Coming up,' said Rose, smiling away. 'Tuna sandwich on brown bread, salad on the side?'

Mia scowled at Rose. 'I wanted to take something up for her half an hour ago.'

'And I said, "Wait till she wakes."' That was Thomas. 'Ellie, why don't you go to sit in the other room and we'll bring it in to you?'

Ellie nodded and made her way to her sunny sitting room. Fritz followed her, as she'd known he would. She sank into the big high-backed chair by the fireplace, and he stood before her, brown hands clenching and unclenching, looking around him. Not caring to sit unless she told him to do so.

'Sit down, Fritz. I've got your things in my handbag. I'll get them for you in a minute.'

He nodded, didn't take a seat. 'I wanted to say "thank you" for helping me out. I owe you, big time. They'd have had me for breaking and entering, if they'd found that screwdriver, and if they'd known about the lighter . . .' He shrugged, spaniel eyes on hers.

Oh dear. She'd made a friend for life. 'Think nothing of it. I didn't discover them till I got back home. Besides, I know you didn't kill her.'

'She fell down the stairs, you think? That housecoat of hers was on the long side.'

'It could be. But if it was an accident, then why did someone put her in the freezer?'

'I been thinking about that. Only reason would be to delay discovery; so it wouldn't be that nasty stepdaughter of hers, who'd want the body found straight away so that she could inherit, right?'

'I don't think Edwina Pryce had a clue where her stepmother had gone and was worried sick about her.'

He shifted his feet. 'She might still have pushed the old dear down the stairs, which is what it looks like. But she's a poor, weak sort of creature and could never have picked the missus up, her being well built and all, to put her in the freezer. My money's on that pesky window cleaner, Jack. I reckon he popped back that last day on some excuse, putting on more padlocks maybe, and asked her for a "present" or maybe found her with her jewel box in her hand and snatched it, making her tumble. He panicked, put the body in the freezer, padlocked the doors and bingo, off he went.'

Ellie was tiring fast, but could still see the flaw in that argument. 'Taking her car off for sale somewhere, you think? What about his own transport? He must have a van or a car to carry his ladders and other equipment around with him. I suppose he might have left it round the corner somewhere while he took her car away, and then come back for his own. But if so, why didn't he put her in her car or his van and take her off somewhere to bury her? None of this makes sense to me. Fritz; you should tell the police what you've told me, and if they think the window cleaner's involved, they'll search for him.'

A sideways look. He had no intention of approaching the police about anything. 'That your handbag over there?' He nodded towards where it was sitting on the settee. 'Shall I . . . ?'

'Help yourself.' Which he did, taking only what was his.

Preparing to go, he twisted his hands. 'I brought you an orchid, left it in the kitchen. One of my customers has a big greenhouse, big as this room maybe. I grow orchids for him, and he won't be missing it. Thought you might like it. Semi-shade, water not too often, right? It'll do nicely on that table near the window.'

He left Ellie trying not to giggle and wondering how many other customers let him use part of their gardens or greenhouses to grow his own plants. Well, that wasn't her concern, was it?

Thomas brought her a tray of luscious looking food. She ate most of it and felt better. He sat nearby, watching her every mouthful.

'Diana called. She brought a bouquet of flowers. I told her to take it to the hospital and sent her away.'

Ellie nodded, sipped tea.

'The police came round. I said you weren't up to seeing them.'

She nodded. She wasn't.

'Diana said . . .' His eyes dropped from hers. 'She's got a black eye.' Was there something else on his mind? Well, if there was, it could wait.

Ellie pushed her tray away. 'I think I'll have another little nap. All this detecting is tiring.' And having a near death experience was even more so.

She transferred to Thomas's big La-Z-boy and relaxed.

She woke again in the twilight, feeling much, much better. She flexed her arms and stretched. Yawned. Felt almost well enough to tackle a domestic problem . . . Well, only if it were a very small domestic problem, like deciding what she wanted to eat for supper.

She'd been conscious, vaguely, of the door and telephone

ringing from time to time. Thomas must have muted the bell on the phone, but nothing could be done about the doorbell. She stretched once more, heard the doorbell ring out again. And again.

Thomas put his head round the door. 'You have a visitor from Hoopers Estate Agency. Most insistent. I said I'd ask if you were up to seeing him for five minutes.'

Mr Abel? This ought to be interesting.

It wasn't Mr Abel. It was a slightly built, dark-skinned youth with beautiful eyes and springy black hair.

'Nirav?' she said as he came into the room, nervous, looking around him.

He nodded. She indicated that he should sit down. He did so, on the edge of the chair. 'I need . . .' He stopped. Blushed. He was very young still.

She decided to help him out. 'Why have you come to see me?'

'He gave me the sack today. Said I hadn't done my job properly, had failed to look after his interests. But I had. I tried to tell him that, but he wouldn't listen.'

'Mr Hooper, you mean? A man of hasty temper.'

He nodded. 'I need to work, because . . .' He stopped, but she could complete that sentence for herself. He needed to work not only for himself but also to look after his girlfriend. He settled himself more firmly in the chair. 'I thought you might have a job for me.'

Did he want her to find him a job in Stewart's office? Really? He was an optimist, wasn't he, when he'd betrayed his previous employer's trust by moving into Disneyland?

Well, there were extenuating circumstances, and she supposed a job might be possible, but first she must clear up a little mystery. 'When you were with Hoopers, you were responsible for seeing that the Pryce house was cleared, the meters read and the services turned off?'

He nodded. 'I did all that, to the very letter of the law.'

'Don't let's talk about the law here, or we'll be discussing how trespass comes into it.'

He winced.

'You expected to see Mrs Pryce on that last day, but she didn't turn up. She left you a message of some sort?'

He was eager to explain. 'On the answerphone. It is my job to listen to the messages first thing in the morning and make a note of what needs to be done. She said she'd decided to leave very early on her last day so that she'd be settled in her new home by teatime. She wanted us to see to sending off her last bits of furniture, and then we were to close up the house for her and get it cleaned. Which is what I did.'

'Hold on a minute. Did you recognize her voice? Had you ever met her?'

A wide-eyed stare. 'No, of course not. Mr Hooper made all the arrangements.'

'It was an old woman's voice?'

'Yes, of course.' A shrug. He didn't understand what she was getting at.

'Do you keep the answerphone messages?'

'No. Why should we?'

So anyone could have left that message on the answerphone on behalf of Mrs Pryce. Or perhaps it had indeed been the lady? 'Go on. You were sent to her house to see to the last load of furniture being cleared out and to read the meters, but you didn't check that the gardener had turned off the water properly. The tap was stiff, and he had to leave it. You didn't report that, did you?'

He shifted his feet. 'I didn't know he'd not done it properly until, well, later. I asked him to do it, and he said he had.'

But, thought Ellie, you didn't check, did you? She said, 'So after the weekend you went back with a cleaning team. Now, for them to be able to work, you turned the electricity back on?'

'Just for the day. The client would pay.'

'And the water?'

'The team had orders only to sweep and vacuum throughout, which they did. You must understand that there was a lot to be done. I trusted the gardener had done what I'd asked him to do. Mr Hooper says I should have checked and got a plumber in if the mains water couldn't be turned off, that I deserve to lose my job. But I've worked well for him all this time, and I don't think—'

'Does he know you were dossing down there?'

Silence.

Ellie sighed. She thought Nirav had given ample grounds for his dismissal. 'Well, let's leave that for the moment. When did the window cleaner put padlocks on the outside doors?'

'The day she left. Friday.'

'Was that before or after the car disappeared?'

'The car? Mrs Pryce took the car before we arrived on Friday.'

'I see. And did Jack, the window cleaner, give you the keys to the padlocks when he'd fitted them, or did he hang them up in the kitchen somewhere?'

'He gave me two, and I handed them in to the agency with the other keys for the house.'

Ellie counted on her fingers. How many padlocks had there been originally? Garage outer door, one each to get in and out of the covered yard, one for the door from the yard into the garage, and one for the tool shed at the end. Had there been another door from the yard? She couldn't remember. Well, make it five, minimum.

'How many keys did you say that Jack gave you?'

A puzzled stared. 'I said. Two. I handed them in to the office.'

So Jack had kept three keys for himself?

All those keys . . . it made her head ache to think of them, coming and going, spinning around. Think, Ellie; think. 'Let's talk about the front door key. Did you keep one for yourself, or did you have it copied for your own use?'

No reply.

She sighed. 'All right. Moving on. When did the "For Sale" board go up?'

'About a week before she left, I suppose; I don't know exactly when because Mr Abel handled that side of things. There was another message on the answerphone afterwards—'

'How much later?'

He thought about that. 'On the Tuesday after she left, I think. I logged it into the telephone message book as usual. She rang to say she was taking the house off the market. Mr Hooper was very angry. He said I must have done something to annoy her, but I hadn't, really I hadn't. I never even saw her.'

'Only, you forgot to tell the signs people that the house had been taken off the market?'

'I told you, that wasn't my job. I did pass the message on to Mr Abel, but then I heard Mr Hooper tell him to leave the sign up, in case someone happened to show interest and they might get the sale after all. I thought that was wrong,' said Nirav, virtuously, 'so when I saw the sign was still there, I knocked it down and threw it aside.'

'When did you move into the house?'

'Thursday evening.' He lifted his hands in despair. 'You must understand, Kyra and I were at school together and hoped that one day . . . But that evening she rang me, they'd had a family council and said she'd disgraced them by going out to a friend's party with me and that she was to be sent to Pakistan to marry a cousin she's never seen. She made an excuse to fetch something from the kitchen, slipped out of the back door and ran away.

'She phoned me in a terrible state, didn't know what to do, they were all out looking for her. I thought of the Pryce house lying empty, where she could hide for a few days. I took the front door key and got her there in safety. They forced their way into my father's house to search for her and threatened me when I got back. I've had to take all sorts of precautions in case they followed me when I went to see her. I don't suppose you understand, but that's the way it is.'

'I've heard about such things, yes. So you hid her in an empty house, where you knew you could turn on the electricity and had water on tap?'

A despairing nod. 'We thought, just for a few days, till I could think of something better. We want to get married, and we will as soon as she's eighteen, though even then . . . you know? They may come after her.'

'You tacked thick black cotton over one window and card over others, screwed in a new long-life bulb, swept the floor, and every day took her food and, perhaps, slept with her?'

'I bought her a futon, and food and clothes and . . . everything, but we did not sleep together. We are waiting to be

married, which is the right thing to do. She walked outside in
the garden in the evenings when it was safe. She saw the
gardener come almost every day, and then she hid herself away
but it was so hot that sometimes she lifted the cloth over the
window to let the air come in.'

'My housekeeper saw her at the window and thought she
was going mad.'

'Sorry about that.' An ingratiating smile. 'When you came
into the garden Kyra heard you talking about searching the
house, so we cleaned up and moved out.'

'Where to?'

His smile disappeared. 'That is a secret.'

Of course. And perhaps the pair would some day marry and
not be pursued by her angry family. And perhaps not.

'So,' he said, tossing his hair back, pretending nonchalance,
'any chance of a job?'

There was a lot against it: the possibility of action being
taken by Kyra's family, which might well involve him in fisti-
cuffs if nothing more lethal, and the fact that he'd undeniably
slipped up over shutting off the water at the Pryce house. On
the other hand, it would annoy Evan Hooper immensely if she
gave Nirav a job, which was, of course, not at all Christian,
but might be amusing. Yes.

'Give me your mobile phone number and I'll see if Stewart,
my property manager, can find something for you. But don't
count on it.'

'Thank you, oh thank you. You are as delightful as everyone
says, and I swear I will be totally efficient and never miss a
trick.' He gave her a slip of paper with his number on it and
bowed himself out.

Overdoing it, what? But he was an attractive young man
who'd gone out on a limb to help his girlfriend, and that must
count for something. He'd need watching, of course. But
Stewart could do that.

She reached for her handbag, found her mobile phone and
left a message on Stewart's office phone, explaining the circumstances, and asking him to interview Nirav – giving Stewart
the phone number – for a temporary post. That done, she
fished out her diary, found a clean page at the back, and started

to make some notes on all that she'd seen and heard recently. The pages were too small. She moved across to her aunt's roll-top desk and settled herself down with some larger sheets of notepaper.

First of all she made a timetable for Mrs Pryce and her removal from her house. Most of this she had got from Fritz. All of it needed to be checked.

One week, possibly two before she disappeared . . . Mrs Pryce asks Mr Hooper to arrange the sale of her house, and a contract for the lawns to be cut. The 'For Sale' board goes up.

Monday: the big auction firm take the best of the antiques.

Tuesday: the local auction house takes the everyday furniture.

Wednesday: the house clearance people take the rest.

In between whiles, different people come for: two cats, the kitchen equipment, urns, lawnmower, etc., from the garden, and the billiard table.

Thursday evening or early Friday morning: Mrs Pryce – or someone impersonating her – rings Hoopers, to say she's leaving early. She asks them to supervise the last day's clearance, read the meters and organize a clean-up.

Friday morning: Nirav takes the message, arrives at Disneyland, supervises reading meters. There's no sign of Mrs Pryce. The last load of her furniture leaves for her new home. Fritz arrives; notes the car has gone. Nirav asks Fritz to turn off the utilities. He tries and fails to turn the water off, but does turn off the electricity and gas. Jack puts at least five padlocks on, gives two keys to Nirav. Keeps three?

Saturday: Mrs Pryce, or someone impersonating her, phones the retirement home to say she's changed her mind and won't be arriving. Nothing else happens over the weekend.

Monday: Nirav supervises cleaning crew of three men. Turns electricity on. Turns it off when leaving. His men don't need to use the water.

Later that week: (Tuesday?) Mrs Pryce or someone pretending to be her leaves a message on the answerphone at Hoopers asking them to take the house off the market. Hoopers decide to keep the sign up, still hoping to get the sale, but cancel the contract to keep the lawns mown.

Thursday of that week: Nirav gets a despairing call from Kyra and moves into the house with her. The water is still on. He turns on the electricity, which he forgets to turn off when they eventually leave. He takes the 'For Sale' sign down and throws it in the shrubs in the front garden.

Ellie hummed to herself. So the electricity was on from that point until Mr Abel turned it off weeks later, when showing Ellie and Vera round.

Ellie got out another sheet of notepaper. This business of the electricity . . .

Why was the big freezer left behind in the garage when everything else was moved out? By mistake? Perhaps someone had been booked to take it, but at the last minute failed to do so? Had it been emptied of food by that time? The power had probably been switched off at the plug on the wall at that point.

Ellie thought that needed checking, too, and made a note to herself to do so.

On the other hand, perhaps it been left there by design? In which case, the murder – if that is what it was – had been premeditated.

Ah, but shoving the body in the freezer looked like a panic-stricken move to hide the body somewhere as a temporary measure. Whoever had done it had been in such a hurry that they'd failed to tuck all of Mrs Pryce's robe inside, so the lid hadn't shut properly, which had aided decomposition.

One person might have done it, but it was more likely to have been a two-person job. They hadn't wanted her found straight away, so they'd turned the electricity back on at the plug on the wall. This had frozen her body and prevented the start of decomposition.

Ellie looked back at her notes. The last time anyone had seen Mrs Pryce in the flesh had been on the Thursday. Ellie didn't count the phone messages, which could have been left by anyone, really.

So, let's suppose Mrs Pryce had died – never mind how for the moment – and been put in the freezer on the Thursday night. The car had gone by Friday morning when Nirav arrived. Then Jack had arrived to put padlocks on all the doors,

including that of the garage. He might or might not have
entered the garage, but he wouldn't have noticed any smell
because at that stage there wasn't any.

How quickly does a body decompose and start to smell?

Ellie checked her notes. Back to the beginning . . . The
mains electricity had been on till Friday when Nirav cleared
the house and checked the meters. Nirav got Fritz to turn the
electricity off, and it remained so till Monday morning, when
he returned with the cleaning crew.

It takes a good twenty-four hours to defrost a large chest
freezer. Decomposition might have started on the Sunday, but
not enough to be noticeable even in the garage, because on
the Monday it had been turned on again for the day. The
freezer had got down to temperature and frozen the body again.

When the cleaning crew left on Monday the electricity had
been turned off and the freezer started to defrost. Decomposition
started once again, until Thursday when Nirav moved in with
Kyra and turned the electricity on again, which held up further
decomposition. Stop and start. The garage had been securely
locked up and no one had had cause to visit it . . . except
blowflies.

This ruled out Jack the window cleaner as the murderer
since – as he'd retained keys to the padlocks – he could have
got into the garage at any time and taken the body away for
burial. Nobody would have been any the wiser.

Nirav and Kyra had left the electricity on when they fled.
The motor in the freezer had been under stress during the
period of their occupation, because the lid hadn't been properly
closed, but it had kept decomposition at bay until Mr Abel
turned the electricity off for good.

Which takes us to this last Wednesday. Give it a day to
defrost again. The current heatwave had speeded up decomposition, and death had at last begun to spread its message
through the garage and out into the courtyard beyond. By
Thursday afternoon when Ellie had gone to investigate, the
telltale smell was unmistakeable. Not to mention the blowflies . . .

Ellie put down her pen, sighing, easing her back.

She thought she'd probably got the timeline right, but there was a sheaf of unanswered questions in her head. What had become of the car? What had happened to Mrs Pryce's personal effects and, in particular, her jewellery box? Who had phoned Hoopers and the retirement home, saying they were Mrs Pryce? And who had killed her in the first place?

FIFTEEN

Friday evening

'The police are here again,' said Thomas, putting his head round the door. 'Do you feel up to seeing them?'

'Probably not, but I'll try. Thomas, would you photocopy these two pieces of paper for me? It's a bit macabre, but may explain what's happened.'

In came Ears. It would be him, wouldn't it? His ears were red even before he started, which indicated he was already in a state about something, and that something was bound to be Ellie's 'interference'. After him came DC Milburn, looking subdued.

Ellie wished she hadn't said she was up to seeing them. She didn't feel up to it, not at all. Ears said, 'No solicitor present?' with snarling irony. 'Well, what a surprise. How long have you been obstructing the police in their enquiries, may I ask?'

'Have I?' said Ellie. 'About what? I'm not aware that—'

'No, you never are aware, are you? Always so innocent, making out you're helping the police but actually hiding information from them.'

DC Milburn said, 'We found Mrs Pryce's car in a long-stay car park at Heathrow Airport.'

Ears shot her a look of annoyance and returned to focus on Ellie. 'You should have told us it was missing.'

Ellie blinked. She got up with an effort and made her way back to her own chair by the fireplace. 'Forgive me. I've had an accident and am not quite the thing. I suggested you look for it in conjunction with Mrs Pryce's disappearance.'

'No, you didn't.'

The DC shot a resentful glance at her superior officer, lowered her eyes and clenched her mouth shut.

'The airport?' said Ellie, feeling tired but making an effort.

'An excellent place to leave it. No one would look twice until the car overstayed the amount of time they'd paid for. Did you find her belongings, including her handbag and a leather jewellery case?'

'The cupboard was bare,' said the DC.

'Jewellery case?' Ears swung round on the DC. 'What do we know about a jewellery case? Has one been reported missing?'

Ellie waved her hands in the air. 'She was packing to leave home for good, so wouldn't she have intended to take her most precious possessions in the car with her? There'd be at least two big suitcases containing her clothes; a make-up box; the tin that she kept her costume jewellery in; probably also a briefcase and laptop, but certainly a handbag and her jewellery box. And, I suppose, whatever she kept in the safe . . . if there really is a safe.'

Ears breathed in and out, audibly. 'Just how does it happen you know what she took with her?'

'I guessed,' said Ellie. 'By the way, I didn't look all that closely when I lifted the lid on the freezer . . . Was she wearing earrings when she was found?'

'No,' said the DC.

'What business is it of yours?' asked Ears at the same moment.

'Oh, do go away!' said Ellie, sinking back into the chair and closing her eyes.

'What! You look here, Madam!'

Still with her eyes closed: 'If you shout at me, I shall burst into tears, and then you'll be sorry.'

He made a tearing sound in his throat, and she heard him charge out of the door. A gentle touch on her hand. Ellie opened her eyes to see the DC leaning over her. 'I'm so sorry. Look, I can see you're not quite . . . May I come back to see you tomorrow?'

'Of course, my dear.'

Thomas came in, looking over his shoulder to where Ears was stamping out of the hall. 'What's up with him?'

'Chronic frustration,' said Ellie, 'due to his own incompetence. Thomas, have you photocopied those lists? Would you give a copy to the Detective Constable here? I was trying to work out when Mrs Pryce was killed, and my notes might be of interest.'

The DC took them. 'Thank you. Most helpful. I don't want to tire you, but is there anything else?'

'Lots; but for a start, can you find out why the freezer was left behind in the garage when everything else was removed?'

'I can tell you that. The discovery of the body was on the local news this morning, and the man who'd bought all her kitchen equipment rang us to say that he'd arranged to buy the freezer, too. Only, it was too big to get on his van at the last minute, so he left it behind and adjusted the amount of cash he paid Mrs Pryce for the rest of the stuff.'

'Which day was that?'

'About six o'clock on Thursday evening.'

'It must have been after the house clearance people had been through the house and gone. I suppose the freezer was forgotten about after that; nobody checked because they assumed it would have been taken away with the rest of the kitchen equipment, and Mrs Pryce wasn't around to tell them otherwise. We know the car had gone by Friday morning, when Jack arrived to put padlocks on the doors. So putting her in the freezer – which must have been done on Thursday night – wasn't premeditated. An opportunistic hiding place. Mm. Well, let me know how you get on, won't you?'

'Take care of yourself,' said the DC, and left Ellie in peace.

Except that she could feel Thomas hovering; wanting to say something? She said, 'What is it you're afraid to tell me?'

'You know me too well. I think we should get the facts about what happened with Diana down on paper. Not for the police, I hasten to add, but as insurance.'

'You want me to sign a paper saying that Diana tried to k–k . . .' she gagged. 'Isn't it better forgotten?'

'The very existence of such signed statements should avoid a recurrence. Yes, I can see why you wouldn't want to do it, and I'm not sure you're up to it, but I mentioned it to Gunnar—'

'Surely the fewer people who know about it, the better?'

'If she's tried to kill you once—'

Ellie winced.

'—and there's no repercussion, then the next time she loses her temper with you, she might try again.'

'No, no. It was a moment of madness.'

'I'd agree with you if it were possible to reason with her, but it isn't. She was beside herself with fury. If I hadn't caught her, she would have thrown that radio into the water.'

'She might have drawn back at the last minute.'

'I can't risk it. Suppose you were having an argument in the kitchen and there happened to be a knife handy. You'd be gone in an instant, and I'd be left thinking I could have done something to stop her.'

'But she doesn't inherit anything much under the terms of my will. Killing me wouldn't get her what she wants.' Ellie didn't want even to think about this. Tears threatened.

'True, but she was in such a temper she didn't consider the consequences. If I hadn't been there, you'd have died. Where reason fails, fear might keep you safe. Gunnar agrees and is coming round to talk to you about it.'

Tears came, slipping down her cheeks.

He took both her hands in his. 'Oh, my dear love.'

'I know I mustn't give in. It won't solve anything if I do. I can't in all conscience ask the Trust to bail her out, and even if I did she'd spend it and come back for more at a later date. Of course you're right, and she has to be stopped now. Vera put the radio in the bottom of the wardrobe. There'll be her fingerprints on it, of course, but also Diana's. Perhaps you could let Gunnar hold it for us?'

There was a stir in the hall, people shouting. A scream?

The door burst open. Rose staggered backwards into the room and fell. Diana strode in, one side of her face puffy and discoloured. She was wearing a closely fitting neck brace and was followed by an unhappy looking little man carrying a briefcase before him as if it were a breastplate.

After them came their young guest, Mia, red rags of temper in her cheeks.

'Ah, there you are!' Diana gestured to the little man who'd been following at her heels. 'Serve the writ on that man with the beard!'

'What,' demanded a bass voice, 'is going on?'

Everyone fell back to let Ellie's solicitor, Gunnar Brooks, enter. He was a massive man, with a big presence. He took up his stance before the fireplace and immediately became the focal point of the room. Both judge and jury, as it were.

Mia helped Rose into a chair. 'Are you all right, my dear?'

Rose was on the verge of tears. 'No real damage. Don't fuss. I must get Mr Brooks his tea.' She tried and failed to get up.

Mia pressed her back into her chair. 'You sit still. I'll get it in a minute.'

Gunnar raised one bushy eyebrow. 'So, Diana. To what do we owe the pleasure?'

Diana's black eye was a stunner. She herself was a stunner, face white, clothes black. A vengeful fury. 'I'm glad you're here, Mr Brooks. You can be a witness to my complaint. I have here a writ to serve on my stepfather for assault!'

Ellie managed to get to her feet, holding on to Thomas's arm. 'Oh no, you don't, Diana.'

'He assaulted me. He can't deny it, and neither can you. I am going to sue the pants off him and nobody can stop me.'

'I doubt it,' said Ellie. 'If you'd really intended to serve a writ, you'd just have done it. Instead, you're playing the tragedy queen, and this audience is not impressed. Yes, Thomas hit you. But there was a reason, wasn't there? Do you want me to spell it out in front of witnesses?'

'I was trying to talk some sense into you, and he thought . . . I have no idea what was going on through what passes for his mind, but clearly he must be deranged and in need of psychiatric attention, for he turned on me without warning and gave me such a punch that I felt my neck snap. My doctor says I have a whiplash injury, and I am going to need full compensation.'

Thomas said, 'If you serve that writ and the case comes to court, then what will be my defence?'

'She doesn't intend it to come to court,' said Ellie. 'Gunnar, this is just the latest in Diana's ploys to get me to give her some more money, and I'm not playing. I'm glad you've come because Thomas and I need to make statements about what really happened when Diana caught me in the bath the other day.'

Gunnar smiled with his usual benevolence. 'Dear Rose, are you much hurt? Would you like me to sue Diana for her assault on you, pushing you into the room and knocking you to the floor like that? I would be happy to serve as a witness.'

'So would I,' said Mia.

'And I,' said Thomas.

'And I,' said Ellie. 'Diana; go!'

Diana was furious. 'If I do, you know who will suffer, and that's your precious Stewart, because I'll take my son away from him for good!'

'I don't think so,' said Ellie. 'No court would take you seriously when they hear what tactics you've been employing to get your own way. And please note; I've had enough. You've finally managed to kill the goose that lays the golden eggs.'

'You can't cut me off. I'm your only daughter.'

Gunnar beamed at Diana. 'I'm sure the courts will appreciate everything Ellie's done for you – and everything you've done for her.'

Diana was trembling with rage, but managed to control herself . . . with an effort. She turned on her heel, gestured the man with the briefcase to follow her and made a fine exit. Needless to say, she slammed the front door after herself.

'Are you all right, Rose?' Ellie was anxious.

'Tickety-boo, and all the better for hearing you give Her Highness a piece of your mind, which I never did think to hear and am all the better for it, thank you very much. Now, Mia; Mr Brooks always has a piece of Victoria sponge and a glass of Madeira. What do you think we can find for him today?'

When Gunnar had taken their statements, ingested a piece of Mia's chocolate cake and drunk his ritual glass of Madeira, he departed with the broken radio and two handwritten and witnessed statements as to Diana's recent actions.

Ellie sank back into her chair. She had to admit she was tired, and yet she'd hardly done anything that day, had she?

Thomas took her hand. 'My dear, that was brave of you. I know it would have been a lot easier to pretend it never happened.'

She nodded. Every time she closed her eyes, she was back in the bath, with Diana raising the radio over her head and . . . She tried to turn her thoughts away from that moment, knowing that next time she closed her eyes, the same scene would be replayed in her head. Perhaps if she could pray about it . . . but she was too tired. Tears threatened again.

'Now,' said Thomas, 'supper will be ready soon, and then you're going back to bed. In the morning we are going shopping in Paris, to replace my Kindle and your engagement ring.'

She tried to smile and failed. 'Oh, no; I couldn't.'

He took no notice. 'Mia will pack all your prettiest clothes, and tomorrow morning early you and I will get into a minicab – which I've already booked – and we'll leave everything behind us. We'll have our breakfast on Eurostar, first class, and be in Paris for lunch. I've booked us into a five-star hotel, and for five days and nights you and I will pretend to be Lord and Lady Muck, swanning around to different restaurants, buying you several new outfits, replacing your ring, visiting the Louvre, going to the opera or ballet, perhaps? After that, we may go on down to the south of France for a breath of sea air, or perhaps we'll decide to go on a tour of famous French gardens.'

'I can't just—'

'While we're away, Stewart is going to have our bathroom remodelled, with new tiling, a new bath, and a walk-in shower cabinet. We thought about a wet room, but on the whole I think I'd prefer a shower. Oh, and there's to be gold-plated taps on everything. Rose insists.'

'Thomas, no!'

'The alternative is that I take you to a private clinic where they will prod and poke you, and prick you with needles and practice all sorts of mumbo-jumbo to find out what's wrong with you . . . Whereas you and I know it's grief and sorrow and shock that's laid you low, and I dare to think my remedies will do you more good than anything a doctor would prescribe.'

'Yes, but—'

'You never let me spend my money on you, so this is my

chance to give you a treat. I need a holiday, too. When did we last go away together?'

'I can't possibly. There's so much to do, so many problems—'

'We've had a conference, Rose, Mia, Stewart and I, and we have decided you should go, and go you shall. I phoned Pat, and she agrees. Stewart and Pat will cover everything which Rose and Mia can't deal with. Let the police deal with crime – that's their business; ours is to help you recover.'

'But Diana might—'

'Gunnar has our statements and the radio. I suggested that he get someone to look into her finances. He will see that Stewart is well represented if it comes to a court case. I've spoken to Stewart and told him why we can't have little Frank this weekend, and he quite understands. It suits him better, anyway, as he was supposed to be taking his family on a river boat excursion, which Frank doesn't want to miss.'

She couldn't find the words to object, though she knew she ought to. Running away from your problems was all wrong. 'But your work—'

'I've seen off the bishop, haven't I? And this last couple of days I've been working all hours to get the next issue out. I'll take my laptop with me, of course, but honestly I can afford to take a few days off without the world coming to an end.'

'Diana wanted to k–k . . . I can't say it.'

He sighed. 'Yes.' He smiled, began to laugh. 'You have to admire her nerve. Fancy claiming whiplash! Whatever will she think of next!'

Saturday morning

'Kyra? Nirav here. Relax. It's good news. I've landed a job with Mrs Quicke's outfit. Almost the same money, too. I'm to work on the team that updates accommodation in their rented sector. I had to promise I'd never take advantage of my position to move into one of their vacant properties, but I don't think they trust me completely because they've only

given me a three-month contract. I suppose I can see their point of view.'

'But we don't need to now, do we? We can stay where we are for a while?'

'No problem. But to be on the safe side, I'll put out one or two feelers, have another bolt-hole ready, just in case.'

On the third morning of her stay in Paris, Ellie struggled out of the cold brown wilderness that trapped her whenever she fell asleep and made an effort to pray. It was a worry to find how difficult it was. The usual words such as 'please' and 'thank you' were no longer appropriate. She tried them out and felt she was getting an engaged signal, rather than an open line to her best friend.

What could be wrong? She'd cried out to Him when she was in danger of death, and Thomas had saved her. So why couldn't she thank Him?

Thomas had got up a while ago and was in their sitting room – they actually had a suite! What luxury! – saying his morning prayers.

She delved into her mind and found a dense fog blocking further thought. So, was this something to do with Diana?

She was seized with a bout of the shakes. Fear. All right, face it, Ellie. Your daughter tried to kill you.

Ellie had been in danger before and felt fear, but had been confident that life would return to normal in due course. In this case, it was impossible. Life could never be the same again, for Diana had broken the last taboo: that of trying to kill the person who had given her life.

In her mind's eye Ellie saw herself shrinking into a small dark place, unable to move. Broken. Imprisoned. When she returned home, she'd never be able to venture out of the house in case Diana were lurking nearby. If Diana were to contact her by phone, Ellie would be tongue-tied, unable to speak. Were Diana to demand more money, Ellie would have to give it to her. Though where she'd get it from . . . ?

She pulled her thoughts away. Living like that would mean there could be no growth, no bright mornings, no hope. Even now she could feel the tendrils closing around her, tightening around her forehead, warning her not to consider crossing a road lest she be run over, or walk down a steep staircase in case she fell.

This would never do; she was being reduced to a shivering shadow of herself. She would not go down that path!

Dear Lord, out of the depths I cry to you.

At long last, she heard his voice in her head. *Forgive and grow.*

Forgive Diana? Impossible! She heard the word echo down a long corridor in her mind. *Impossible, impossible, impossible.*

Yet our dear Lord had done just that; He'd forgiven those who were in the very act of putting Him to death.

Not possible, possible, possible. She couldn't imagine herself doing it. It was too much to ask.

Dear Lord above, help me to grow big enough to forgive.

She felt the tendrils which had wound tightly around her head release their grip on her a little. Was it possible that one day this fear would leave her, and that her spirit would be quiet again?

Thomas came bustling in. 'Aren't you up yet? Breakfast's here. Shall we go for a walk afterwards?'

He'd decided that a walk a day kept diets at bay, and who was she to argue? His very presence banished her fear.

'Any news?' Every day he had the *Times* newspaper to read at breakfast, but what she really wanted was news from home. Or did she? Wouldn't it be easier never to go home, but to wander around the Continent in idle fashion for the rest of her life? No, perhaps not. Too boring.

Thomas beamed. 'I rang them all while you were still asleep. Rose and Stewart and little Frank all send their love. Stewart says the bathroom's not finished yet, so we have to stay away another week at least. Rose is fine, ordering spring bulbs for the garden. Mia was out already; she's started going in, mornings only, to the printing works that she's inherited. Oh, and Rose says that the police have got someone for Mrs Pryce's murder.'

'That's good. Who was it?'

'Dunno. A relative, I think.'

'Terry Pryce, I suppose.' She frowned, thinking this didn't sound right, and then shook her head at herself. It was no longer her problem. 'Does it look like rain? Because if not, I'm going to wear one of my new dresses.'

One day soon perhaps she would only feel pity for the damaged creature who'd tried to kill her.

Saturday afternoon

Two weeks to the day after they'd left London, Thomas and Ellie journeyed back to Ealing. Ellie would have liked to prolong their holiday, but Thomas had begun to worry about work. He'd tried to hide it, of course, but he'd been spending more and more time on the phone and on his laptop.

Home at last. As they stepped out of the minicab, Rose flung open the front door to greet them. 'Welcome back, lovely to see you, did you have good weather, but oh, mind that cat, she's not ours of course, but she's been coming round begging for titbits and it's true I have been letting her have a saucer of milk now and again, but if Midge sees her there'll be another fight . . .'

A tiny brindled cat with white paws pressed herself against the front door and had to be picked up by Rose so that Ellie and Thomas could get in with their luggage.

Once they were in, Rose put the cat down and shooed her out of doors before saying, 'Don't you look pretty, Ellie, and isn't that a new outfit? I do like that colour on you, and will you look at that socking great ring! Now that's what I call a sapphire, fit to knock your eyes out. Yes, I can hear the little cat yowling, but we can't let her in, and don't let Midge out of the front door or he'll have her for starters. Tea will be up in just a minute. Mia wanted to make some of her chocolate cake, but I said no, it had to be a Victoria sponge to greet you on your return.'

Rose was back on form. There was colour in her cheeks for the first time for months. Perhaps the break had been good for her, too.

There was a fresh bowl of sweet peas in the hall and, through the conservatory, Ellie could see that the garden was full of colour. It was good to be home.

She was pleased to see there was no pile of post waiting for her to deal with on the hall table. Thomas had said Pat and Stewart were dealing with all her correspondence, and there was no need to think about it till next week.

Thomas gave Rose a smacking great kiss. 'Ah, it's good to be back. I've missed your home cooking.' He patted his front, which made both Ellie and Rose laugh, since he certainly hadn't lost any weight while they'd been away.

Ellie went upstairs, unpacked and admired her revamped bathroom – yes, there was real gold-plating on the taps – and the changed layout was impressive. Even the tiles were different. Why hadn't she thought of putting in a walk-in shower before? There was a new towel rail, too, with hot water running through it, wow!

She must remember to congratulate Thomas on his plan to change everything.

She stood in the middle of the room and slowed her breathing. Was the shadow of the past going to reach out and paralyse her again? No, it wasn't. With a rush of thankful praise she said aloud: 'Thank you, Lord.'

The phone rang downstairs. She tensed. What if it were Diana, checking to see if her mother had returned? What was Ellie going to say when she next met Diana?

Dear Lord, give me courage. Help me to grow . . .

SIXTEEN

The doorbell rang. Ellie walked down the stairs, fearing that it might be Diana . . . but it was only that nice DC Milburn, who said, 'Sorry, Mrs Quicke, I know I shouldn't interrupt when you're only just back. I've been round several times to see you, and Rose told me you'd be returning today.'

'Come in, and tell me all about it.' Ellie led the way into the sitting room and sank into her favourite chair by the fireplace. The French windows were open to the garden, and there was another bowl of sweet peas on the occasional table at her elbow. A pretty white orchid flaunted its petals on the mantelpiece. Where had that come from? Ah, she remembered, and smiled to herself. Fritz, of course. 'Do sit down. I hear you got someone for the murder.'

The girl grimaced. 'Not exactly. We're holding Terry Pryce on a charge of theft, and that's what I wanted to see you about. We need you to come to the station to see if you can identify your ring and the china box.'

'Good. You didn't find Thomas's Kindle? I suppose it's long since been sold on. Oh well. You're not holding Terry for murder, then? I must say he convinced me he didn't know where Mrs Pryce was. What did the autopsy tell you?'

'Some time before she died – maybe as much as an hour or even two – she'd fallen and hit her temple. We found an area of wallpaper in her bedroom where blood had been spilled and someone had tried to wash it away. We assume this was where the first injury took place.'

Ellie remembered Vera's saying how distressed Mrs Pryce had been when she'd spilt coffee on the wallpaper – on the other side of the bed. Poor woman . . .

The DC continued: 'The pathologist says that head wounds usually bleed profusely, but this first injury wouldn't necessarily have been fatal. He thinks she may have been stunned for a while, but managed to get back on her feet. We think she was well enough then to wash the blood off her face and change into her housecoat. Perhaps it was she who tried to clean the blood off the wallpaper, too.'

Ellie remembered the odd angle of Mrs Pryce's neck as she lay in the freezer. 'So she had another fall later, one that did kill her?'

'Yes, we think she probably fell down the stairs some time later and broke her neck.'

'So her death might have been an accident.' Ellie shook her head. 'One accidental injury is acceptable, two . . . ? Would a jury go along with that? Do the police want to downgrade her death to manslaughter?'

A gesture of frustration. 'Terry swore he was nowhere near the house on the night she died and produced an alibi; a stag night in Amsterdam, would you believe?'

'Dear me. I thought he might be gay.'

'He does give that impression, and the civil ceremony was between two of his male friends. The only problem is that the celebrations lasted over several days, involved a huge intake of alcohol and no one can be sure he was there all the time. He might have come back, trying to get money out of his great-aunt, and done the deed before returning to the party in Amsterdam. We're working on his alibi. The inspector is certain we've got the right man.'

'That's good news, if it was him,' said Ellie. 'I'm really glad you've found my ring and my aunt's little box. Did he confess to stealing them, and how did you trace him? Ah, I remember; Mrs Pryce's stepdaughter Edwina gave me his home address, and I passed it on to you.'

'I went round to his house only to spot a yellow car answering to your description outside his flat. So I phoned Ears – I mean, the inspector – and he came storming down and took Terry to the station for questioning. The inspector was so sure that we'd got our murderer that he, well, he let the news out that we'd cleared the case up before we realized Terry had a reasonably good alibi. So . . .'

'Egg all over faces?'

A guarded smile. 'Then the chief super came back from

her course, and she . . . Well, fireworks, you know? Faced with a charge of murder, Terry denied everything but the theft, so we've got him for that. He told us who he'd sold the goods to, and how much for. The jeweller still had your ring and the little box though I'm afraid the Kindle was sold on to an unsuspecting customer the following day.'

'Thomas has bought a replacement Kindle already because he needs it for work. It was an opportunistic thing, wasn't it? Terry didn't come here planning to steal anything, but to see if he could borrow some money. Did he tell you why he needed it so badly? He spun me a wild story about his sister which I didn't believe even at the time.'

'He shares a flat with a man who'd developed a drug habit and got Terry into it, too. They were both heavily in debt to their dealer, who'd threatened them: pay up or else. Terry really was desperate.'

Ellie leaned back in her chair. 'Are the police going to write Mrs Pryce's death off as accidental? But no; how can they? There's far too many unanswered questions. If her death was an accident, then why bother to cover it up? Who put her body in the freezer? Who drove her car away, emptied it and left it at the airport? And who phoned around to make her excuses, in order to give the impression that she'd disappeared of her own accord?'

'I know, I know.'

'Who else are you looking at now? The stepdaughter, Edwina, seemed a bit odd to me, but she's far too puny to have picked up Mrs Pryce, carried her to the garage and dumped her in the freezer. And anyway, why should she? If she'd seen or caused the accident, she would have left Mrs Pryce where she was and called for an ambulance. It wasn't in her best interests for Mrs Pryce to disappear. I assume she inherits under the will?'

'Something, yes.' Caution, here. 'You've heard all about that, haven't you?'

Ellie shook her head.

The DC looked as if she had something else to say, but changed her mind at the last minute. 'Do you fancy anyone else for it, Mrs Quicke?'

'Why ask me? There's a son, I believe, and a granddaughter. But the same problem arises; why try to hide the body? What about Jack, the window cleaner?'

The DC took out her notebook. 'We heard there was one, but the inspector doesn't think he's of interest. What's his full name, and where does he live?'

'No idea. He probably does a round of houses in that area once a month. Some householder will be able to give you details.'

'You don't fancy Fritz the gardener for it?'

Ellie smiled, shaking her head. 'He's a bit of a rogue, but not in that league. He was fond of her, you know.'

'The inspector favours him for it.' Non-committal. 'We've had him in a couple of times for questioning. He's admitted to trespass and to theft of tools and such like from Mrs Pryce, and to using her water supply without permission, which can be construed as theft.'

'Oh, poor Fritz. No, you can't be serious.'

'The inspector is. He's talking to all of Fritz's other employers, uncovering a long list of minor offences. The man admits he was always hanging around, that last week of her life. What's more likely than that she confronted him with his petty thefts and he pushed her down the stairs, perhaps not meaning any harm . . . and then put her body in the freezer until he could dig a grave for her later?'

'Nonsense. It was a woman who phoned the retirement home to cancel her stay there, and it was a woman who phoned Hoopers to rearrange the removals, bring in a cleaning team and take the house off the market.'

'We don't say he did it by himself. We assume his wife helped him.'

'No, no. He hasn't got that sort of mind. Besides which, he has a little van that he runs around in. If he'd caused her death, he could have put her in that and taken her off somewhere to bury her—'

'Or have driven her car away himself?'

'Why would he do that?'

'We assume that she was in the middle of packing up her car with her personal possessions on the night she died, when she was interrupted by someone probably asking her for money—'

'Assumptions, again.' Though it did sound likely, didn't it?

'You've said yourself there was probably quite a bit of saleable stuff in her car; a laptop, a briefcase, jewellery? I wondered if she might have possessed a fur coat or two. She was the kind of lady who wouldn't have bothered with political correctness and would have worn fur coats whatever people said, wasn't she?'

'None of that was in the car when you found it?'

'It had been emptied of all personal items and valeted professionally before being left in a long-stay car park at the airport. Edwina Pryce has given us a list of the things she thought Mrs Pryce would have packed to take with her. Apart from the stuff you've mentioned, there should have been some valuable Victorian jewellery, a carriage clock in a leather case and a couple of small but valuable seascapes, not to mention silver candelabras and photograph frames containing pictures of her husband and parents. All those were saleable. Fritz would have seen that the car was full of valuables, and he could have driven it away to dispose of them at his leisure—'

'Leaving her body behind in the freezer? Oh, come on.'

'Yes, because he planned to bury her later in her own garden.'

'Then why didn't he do so?'

'Because the window cleaner fitted padlocks on the doors next morning and he couldn't get in.'

'Nonsense. Fritz knew how to remove padlocks with a screwdriver. It was he who removed those on the doors in and out of the courtyard, so that he could tend his vegetables in the back garden. If he'd known Mrs Pryce's body was in the garage, he could easily have got in there and done something about it. But he didn't.'

'I'm only telling you the way the inspector is thinking. The other suspect is, of course, the cleaner Vera.'

Ellie shot to her feet. 'What? That's even more nonsensical.'

'Ah, but you've forgotten her little boy, who by all accounts has behavioural problems. Suppose Vera took him there after school that last day, perhaps innocently enough, to see if Mrs Pryce were coping all right? The little boy might have demanded something from the old lady, and when he didn't get it, gave her a push . . . down the stairs.'

Ellie told herself it was no good to lose her temper. 'Then why not call a doctor?'

'She was protecting the boy from the consequences of his actions, of course. That's why she hid the body in the freezer and drove off in Mrs Pryce's car.'

'Vera did not know where Mrs Pryce's body was. Believe me, she didn't. And in any case, Vera doesn't drive. I'm not listening to this. Would you please go?'

'I think this was a two-person job. She had help.'

Ellie deflated, staring into space. A two-person job sounded right. She'd been thinking it had needed a strong man to put the body in the freezer, but two women . . . ? That was just about possible. Also, it had been sloppily done, leaving a fold of Mrs Pryce's housecoat outside. Panic. Yes.

But it couldn't have been Vera. Ellie would stake her life on that.

The DC got to her feet. 'You'll think about what I've said, won't you? And perhaps you'll remember some little thing which might help to prove or disprove our theories?'

Saturday afternoon

An exclusive jewellers
'These two rings and the diamond earrings was give me by an old lady as I used to ferry around and run errands for. A neighbour, like. They're worth a pretty penny, aren't they? A couple of thousand each, say?'

'Mm. The settings are dated, but the stones look good. How did you come by them, did you say?'

'There's a problem, is there?'

'Have you any provenance, Mr . . . er? That is, a piece of paper in her writing to show that she's given them to you?'

'I don't do business with those as doubt my word. You give them back to me.'

Saturday evening

Ellie wandered into the kitchen, only to be told by Rose to make herself scarce, as she was busy. Midge the cat turned his back on her; as far as he was concerned, she'd deserted him for half his lifetime and he wasn't prepared to kiss and make up.

There was no sign of Mia, who was, Rose said, out visiting old friends. Ellie drifted down the corridor to her office, where a pile of letters had been dealt with and left for her to read. For information only. Pat had left her a note saying there was nothing there which required urgent attention.

Two envelopes marked 'Private & Confidential' had been propped, unopened, against Ellie's computer. She eyed them with dislike and left them where they were. After all, Thomas had said she needn't do any work yet, hadn't he?

She could hear his voice, faintly, as he talked on the phone in his study. No doubt he was making up for lost time and ought not to be interrupted.

Out into the sunny garden she went. The gardener had mowed the lawn recently, and someone had dead-headed the roses. There was nothing for her to do.

Instead of being grateful, she felt, well, excluded. As if she were no longer essential to the life of the house and those who lived in it.

She glanced up as two parakeets squawked their way across the sky on their way to the nearby park, and then dropped her eyes to the gables of Mrs Pryce's house. She wondered who had inherited it and what they'd want to do with it. She supposed it would be torn down soon and the neighbourhood made hideous with the screeches and bangings of a new build. Stewart was probably right, and an ugly block of flats would shortly rise in what had once been Mrs Pryce's rose garden. Ellie shrugged. Not her problem.

Thomas came out of the house and put his arm around her. 'Everything all right?' He meant, was she coping now she was back home?

'I'm fine. Rose won't let me into the kitchen, Mia's out visiting friends, Pat says there's nothing for me to worry about and Midge won't talk to me.'

He laughed. 'Is your internal clock out of kilter? Mine is. But it's still broad daylight and not time for supper yet. Let's have a gentle stroll, work up an appetite.' They'd done a lot of walking while they'd been away, and had agreed it was good for them.

For a moment Ellie hung back; suppose Diana was waiting for them outside? She set her teeth. Well, if so, she wouldn't dissolve into a puddle on the pavement, because Thomas would be beside her. 'Yes, a walk would be a good idea.'

There was no Diana outside. Good. As they passed the first few houses, Ellie thought to herself that one or two of them needed their windows cleaning – which reminded her to ask Rose who cleaned their own windows. Not Jack the Lad, presumably. Someone like him, though? Rose always dealt with that sort of thing. They could have walked towards the shops or in the direction of the church, but instead they went round the block and so, of course, by the Pryce house.

'That's odd,' said Thomas as they passed it.

'What?' Incident tape was no longer blocking the drive.

'Nothing.' Yet he was frowning. 'I thought I saw a light . . . It must be a reflection, or the sun shining through the hall from the back of the house.'

She turned back. The house was now showing definite signs of neglect. The front garden was a tatty version of a hayfield, and the windows looked grubby. Of course, windows quickly became grubby in a dry spell of weather. On the other hand, it did look as if there were a light on in the hall, and another in the television room immediately to the right of the front door.

She started up the drive, expecting to confirm that they were merely seeing a reflection of sunlight from the windows of the house opposite.

The porch was deep and dark. The front door was solid, but on either side were panels of stained glass, purple and green in a diamond pattern. The glass was old, thick and bubbly, difficult to see through, but when Ellie pressed her nose to a paler green diamond, it was obvious that the light they had seen came from the ceiling in the hall.

She stepped out of the porch to check on the television room. 'There's a light on in this room, too. Do you think that the young lovers have returned now the police have finished here? I wouldn't put it past them.'

'They wouldn't leave lights on downstairs, would they? And do they still have a key?'

She stepped back. 'I didn't bring my handbag, and I haven't got my mobile with me.'

He patted his pockets. 'I've got mine.' He pressed the door-bell. A resounding silence. A rustle inside the hall, and something scratched on the inside of the door. Thomas pulled up the flap of the letterbox.

'It's a cat. It looks like the one which was trying to get into our house.'

The cat mewed, and a tiny white paw appeared, reaching up towards them. Thomas released the flap and stood upright. 'Didn't you say Mrs Pryce had two cats, which were rehoused when she left? I've heard that cats dislike change and will make their way back over vast distances to their old homes.'

'How on earth did it get into the house? Someone must have let it in, but . . . I don't like this, Thomas.'

'I expect there's a cat flap somewhere, and it can get in and out as it pleases. Now that the house is empty, it's probably going round the houses to beg for food. Rose has been feeding it on the sly, remember.'

Ellie tried to remember if there was a cat flap in the Pryce house, but couldn't. 'We should ring the police, anyway, tell them that lights have been left on.'

He nodded, took out his mobile. Ellie wandered round to the garage. A fresh padlock had been put on the door which led into the courtyard. No one had recently got into the house that way, which meant that whoever had turned the lights on must have had a key to the front door. Surely the police wouldn't have left lights on when they departed?

Thomas was still on the phone when she got back. He grimaced at her, shut it off. 'They said they'd get a patrol car to drop by some time. I'm not sure they believe me.' He put his eye to a piece of pale green glass and froze.

Ellie waited, feeling prickles up and down her spine.

He stood back. 'Tell me I'm imagining things. It looks as if someone's lying on the floor at the foot of the stairs. Perhaps one of the young visitors?'

'Another dead body?' Ellie applied her eye to the same place, her heartbeat going into overdrive. What she saw – or thought she saw, because it was hard to see clearly through stained glass – was shocking. 'I think you're right, though it's hard to tell. Oh!' She started back. 'Did she move? Perhaps she's still alive.'

He knelt down to look through the cat flap. 'Out of the way, puss. That's it. Just let me have a good look at . . . Yes, there is someone there.' He raised his voice. 'Hello, are you all right?'

Ellie was still glued to her piece of clearish glass. 'I think – I'm not sure – did she move her hand? Thomas, if a starving cat is locked up with a dead body, there's no knowing what will happen . . . or rather, I've heard that a hungry cat can attack a—'

'I'd better phone for an ambulance.' He got his mobile out again and this time asked for an ambulance. Ending the call, he wondered: 'How can we get in?'

Ellie spotted the discarded 'For Sale' sign in the long grass and retrieved it, careful of splinters. 'It's your turn to break a window, Thomas. I did it last time.'

He grunted. 'Haven't broken a window since I was eight. A new experience every day, what?'

He selected a suitable section of coloured glass and bashed at it until it broke into shards and fell, tinkling, inside the door. Pulling his jacket over his hand, he thrust through the hole he'd made until he could find and release the catch on the door. The cat shot out and wound round their legs, but they ignored her to rush to the side of the girl on the floor.

Ellie was horribly afraid it was Vera lying there, for this girl was also big-boned and had fair hair. She'd been punched and kicked around, to judge by the damage and the boot prints on her jeans. Blood spatter showed where she'd been tossed against the walls and stairs. Her nose had been broken, and blood had pooled under her head. Bruises marked both arms and her throat. Her left arm lay at an odd angle from her body.

She'd been wearing a sleeveless white cropped top, no bra, over low-cut jeans; very low-cut jeans. Was she wearing a thong beneath the jeans? Hm. Possibly not. Both top and jeans were bloodstained and torn. She'd been wearing flip-flops, which had come to rest some distance away from her body. Her finger and toenails were painted black.

Ellie didn't think the girl had been raped, for the jeans were still fully zipped up. It wasn't Vera, because this girl's ears had been pierced not once but several times, and she wore a number of rings and studs in her earlobes: five each side.

Ignoring the blood on the floor, Ellie knelt beside the girl. 'Hold on. Help is coming.' Ellie took the girl's right hand and stroked it. One of the girl's eyes was fast shut, but the other gazed upwards.

'What is it?' Ellie asked. 'Who did this to you?'

The hand she was holding felt cold and clammy. The girl's eye didn't move.

Thomas knelt on the girl's other side and felt for her pulse, muttering, 'Hold on, hold on. Don't give up.' He looked across to Ellie and shook his head. 'It's no good. She's gone.'

A backstreet jewellers

'What'll you give us for these bits and pieces. Worth a bit, aren't they?'

'They're only glass, gold settings, rather dated. Women want something classier nowadays. Fifty quid do you?'

'They are diamonds, I tell you.'

'Take it or leave it.'

'Give us fifty, then.'

SEVENTEEN

Saturday evening

Ellie released the girl's hand, which fell back on to the floor. She'd been dead for some time. Ellie had been deceived into thinking the girl had moved, by the distortion of looking through stained glass. There was a piece of string tied round the girl's wrist with a couple of keys on it, one with a sparkly tag attached. The front door key to this house, and one to her own place?

Thomas began to say the prayers for the dead.

Faintly at first, becoming louder, Ellie heard the whine and bleep of a paramedic's car.

She got to her feet. The little cat pressed against Ellie's legs, mewing. Ellie picked her up and stroked her. The cat nibbled Ellie's ear by way of thanks. An affectionate animal, unlike their own Midge.

The paramedic's car turned into the drive. Thomas would not interrupt his prayers, so it would be up to Ellie to explain the situation. What exactly had happened here? Still holding the cat, Ellie took a good look around.

Dried blood streaked down the inside of the front door. The girl had tried to get out and been hauled back, her hands clutching in despair at the wood. Kicked into the corner behind the door was an empty gym bag . . . intended for carting away whatever was in the safe?

There was dried blood on the newel post of the stairs and on the bottom three steps . . . and a smear descending. The girl had been thrown against the newel post, had rebounded on to the stairs and slipped down again.

More blood, dried, was on the doorknob and the panelled door that led to the television room. She'd been thrown against the doorknob, and had slid down the door.

There was no blood on the doors leading to the sitting

room and study, so she hadn't tried to get out that way, but there were dark streaks on the floor leading to the garden room . . . the room where the cats had been kept, the room which led out on to the garden. The girl had tried to flee that way and been brought down, dragged back again, not allowed to escape.

In the corner by the door to the television room lay a torch, one of the wind-up kind. Pristine, no blood on it. The girl's, presumably? She'd come prepared with a torch, which meant she'd expected the electricity to have been turned off . . . which meant someone else had turned it on?

She'd had a key with her. Had someone followed her in, someone who'd been watching her or the house? Or had someone got there earlier, turned the lights on and been looking for something when the girl arrived? And if so, how had he got in?

'Hello there? Someone called for an ambulance?' A woman's voice at the front door. The paramedic.

'In here,' said Ellie, not moving. 'She's already dead, though.'

The paramedic looked at the body and then at Thomas, whose lips were moving in prayer. The woman knelt beside the body, felt for a pulse, found none and sighed. 'Any idea who she might be?'

'I'm not certain because I've never met her, but I think she's Evangeline Pryce, granddaughter of the Mrs Pryce who used to live here.'

The paramedic said she didn't remove dead bodies and left, saying she'd report what she'd found to a doctor and the police.

A patrol car arrived containing two large policemen, who knew only that they'd been asked to drop around by the Pryce house to investigate a possible break-in. The police phoned for reinforcements. One of the patrolmen took an initial statement from Ellie and warned her not to leave.

The policemen strung incident tape around and spoke, low-voiced, into their radios, not touching anything or making eye contact with Thomas or Ellie.

Thomas sighed and stood up. He fished out his mobile again;

this time to phone Rose and tell her they'd been delayed but
to keep supper for them.

Ellie was nursing the little cat. 'Thomas, do you think you
could check to see if there's a cat flap in the garden room
under the stairs? I suspect that's how the cat got in.'

He investigated and came back to report: 'Yes, and it was
open both ways. I've locked it now.' It wouldn't be a good
idea for the little cat to get in and out as she pleased in future.
She had no collar on, but the Cats Protection League would
know where she belonged.

Ears arrived, in a towering rage. Of course. There was a
detective constable with him, but it was another man and not
the pleasant DC Milburn.

Ears barked at Thomas and Ellie to stay where they were,
not to move, not one inch. And then proceeded to ignore them.

Thomas raised his eyebrows, but obeyed by folding his arms
and finding an unstained piece of wall to lean against. The
men from the patrol car left, and Ears' constable took up his
position by the door . . . to prevent Ellie and Thomas from
leaving, or to prevent other people from coming in?

Ellie needed to sit down, and the cat needed to be nursed.
It was very young; still a kitten, really. Ellie climbed up the
stairs till she was well above the bloodstains and sat down.
The little cat turned round and round on Ellie's lap until she
had her head tucked under one paw. And was quiet.

Two men in disposable white clothes arrived and donned
white slippers. One set to work photographing the scene, while
the other dusted for fingerprints.

'Well, Mrs Quicke; so we meet again,' said Ears, condescending to acknowledge her presence at last. 'Over yet another
body. Things were nice and quiet while you were away, and
as soon as you get back . . . ! So what's your excuse this time,
and who is it you have so conveniently found?'

'At a guess it's Evangeline Pryce, granddaughter of the
elderly Mrs Pryce who used to live in this house.'

'The lady whose body you just happened to discover a
fortnight ago? You're making quite a habit of discovering your
neighbours dead, aren't you? So, do tell me how you managed
to come across this one?'

Ellie sighed. How long was this going to take? She was getting hungry, and Rose would be getting anxious, trying to keep supper warm for them.

A female doctor arrived, carrying a large bag. She greeted Ears without enthusiasm and went straight to examine the body.

Thomas explained, 'We went for a walk, saw there were lights on inside the house – just as you see them now. We thought it odd, so I phoned in a report. I was told a patrol car would be along to investigate. Then we heard a cat – the one Ellie's holding – scrabbling around inside the hall here. I looked through the letterbox and saw someone lying inside. I broke the window and released the catch to get in because—'

'You should have left it to the police to investigate. Don't you know it's against the law to go around breaking and entering houses?'

'We thought we saw the girl move. It's difficult to be sure through stained glass. And the cat—'

'So you broke into a house you knew was empty, in order to rescue a cat?'

Thomas kept his temper, just. 'We thought the girl might still be alive and in need of urgent medical attention. Also, we wanted to save her from being attacked by a hungry cat.'

The doctor stood up. 'She's been dead for some hours.'

'How many?' barked Ears.

The doctor refrained from rolling her eyes, just. She didn't seem to like Ears much either, did she? 'It's hard to be sure, in this heat. It was a brutal attack, and she lost a lot of blood. She was probably knocked unconscious by one of the many blows to her head, but didn't die straight away. She might have lived for some considerable time after she was injured.'

The doctor indicated a dark patch some way away from where the body had finally come to rest. 'You can see that she lay over here for a while.' Blood had been spilt there, and it had soaked into the floorboards. 'After some time, either she moved of her own accord, or more likely someone shifted her to lie nearer the stairs, where there is this second pool of blood. The body is cold, but rigor mortis hasn't yet set in. At a guess, she died some time in the early hours of this morning. I'll know more when I do the autopsy.'

Ears turned on Ellie. 'Admit it; you moved the body.'

Ellie shook her head. 'I lifted the girl's hand for a moment, then laid it down again.'

Thomas said, 'I touched her neck to see if there was a pulse. There wasn't. Neither of us moved her head.'

The photographer commented in a cheerful voice: 'She put up a good fight, didn't she? There's blood everywhere.'

Ellie sighed. 'I'm tired, and I want to go home.'

Ears put his hands on his hips, almost hissing: 'And what else have you to tell me before you go? Have you any more advice for me on how to conduct an investigation? More tips for beginners? Tell me. I'm all ears.'

An unfortunate thing to say, since his ears were bright scarlet at that very moment. Of course, he would be in a state, since his boss had hauled him over the coals over his earlier conduct of the Pryce case.

Thomas flexed his muscles and opened his mouth, but Ellie shook her head at him. She could handle this. She gave Ears a limpid stare. 'One and one makes two. Would three be a better number, or four? And which came first; the chicken or the egg?'

He reared up, flushing to his forehead. 'What?'

Ellie said, 'The lights were also left on in the television room, remember. Don't let anyone go in there till they've dusted for prints, will you?'

Ears swung round wildly. 'Which room?'

Ellie pointed to the door. 'I've been told Mrs Pryce had a safe in that room, but that it's well concealed. It's probably behind the panelling somewhere. Why don't you take a look?'

The man who'd been dusting for fingerprints approached the door to the television room and dusted it for prints.

Everyone waited.

The technician shook his head. 'Smudged. Useless.'

Ears sent Ellie a look of pure acid, threw open the door and recoiled. Ellie climbed down the stairs with the cat in her arms and followed Thomas as he went to peer over Ears' shoulders.

It looked as if someone had taken a crowbar to every piece of panelling in the room, starting from the door. Plastered wall showed through each shattered panel until, nearly in the opposite corner, the steel door of a safe stood revealed. Still locked, but dented.

Ears' voice shook. 'Mrs Quicke, you were watching through the window.'

'No. I used my eyes and my ears.' She concluded artlessly: 'People are always anxious to tell me things, you see. I'm sure you're going to be busy for a while, and we've had a long and tiring day, so I think we'd better go home now. Supper's waiting, and this little cat needs to be fed, poor thing.'

She walked past Ears' constable, who was supposed to be guarding the front door, but who, as she approached, stepped aside to look over their heads, grinning widely. Out she went into the fading light of the evening, the cat awake but not struggling in her arms. Thomas followed her, making clucking sounds.

'What's the matter with you?' she asked when they were safely away from the house.

He doubled over, gurgling with laughter. 'Ellie . . . Ears!'

She was conscious of irritation. 'He deserved it!'

'You made him look like an incompetent oaf. His team took it all in and will no doubt be repeating what you said in the canteen.'

'Oh. Was I very rude?'

'Magnificently. I wouldn't have missed it for anything. Ellie Quicke, you are not only the light of my life, but my delight. But what did you mean when you said "which came first, the chicken or the egg"?'

'I haven't the slightest idea,' said Ellie, quickening her pace. 'The words came into my head and I let them out. And, I need the loo.'

Thomas kept pace beside her, looking worried. 'Midge isn't going to be pleased if we introduce another cat into the household, is he?'

'We'll contact the Cats Protection people and find out who's responsible for her, but it's too late to do that today. We'll have to keep her in my office or the dining room out of Midge's way overnight and return her to her owner in the morning.'

No, Midge wasn't pleased. He was in the hall when they got back. He took one look at the tiny cat in Ellie's arms and hissed in outrage, curving himself into an upside-down 'U' shape, his tail fluffing out to the size of a lavatory brush.

The little cat burrowed her head under Ellie's arm and squeaked in terror.

'Oh, behave yourself, Midge,' said Ellie, cross with him for once. 'We all know you're king of the castle, and nobody – and especially not this tiny morsel – is going to challenge you for that position. Rose!'

Rose appeared, looking flustered. 'Oh, there you are, I've been so worried. What kept you? And we've got Herself in the sitting room. I told her you wouldn't want to be bothered tonight, but you know what she's like. Oh, it's never that stray cat again, is it?'

'I'm putting her in the dining room for now. Have we a litter tray she can use? She was in the Pryce house, got in through the cat flap which hadn't been fastened properly and . . . oh!'

Diana was standing in the doorway to the sitting room. Dressed in black, as always. White of face.

Rose tried to take the little cat from Ellie. She mewed piteously and clung to Ellie's dress. Ellie tried to unhook her. Thomas tried to unhook her. Rose helped.

Midge spat and hissed.

Diana said, 'Well, really!' She exhaled and tried to help. And got scratched for her pains. 'Ow! The little devil!' She sucked her fingers.

Rose managed to get the cat off Ellie at last and bore her away.

Ellie shook herself down, eyeing her daughter with a jaundiced eye. 'Diana, I don't know what you've come for. If it's to say you're sorry, I'm ready to listen – in the morning. I've no time for you tonight, so please go.'

'But I've got the most marvellous proposal to put to you. You can't just—'

'Oh, yes, I can.' Ellie started to climb the stairs. 'Goodnight, Diana. Thomas will see you out.'

Thomas opened the front door, waited till Diana had made her exit, then shut and bolted it behind her.

Rose hovered. 'That little thing's pretty wild. She'll be up and down the curtains, I've no doubt.'

'The cat, or Diana?' said Thomas.

'Both,' said Ellie, from the landing above. 'I've had today up to here. I'm hungry and tired and need a wash. I'm just going to change and I'll be right with you for supper, Rose.'

Sunday morning

Thomas went to an early morning service at the nearby church. Ellie overslept.

She got downstairs later than usual, in time to take a phone call from Thomas, phoning to say he'd been asked to visit an old friend who was ill, and could she manage if he didn't get back till lunchtime? Of course she could.

The kitten had ignored the improvised cat tray, peed on the carpet and torn a rent in one of the curtains. Midge was on sentry duty outside the dining room door, snarling whenever he heard the little cat mew.

Ellie phoned the Cats Protection League, only to get an answerphone. Of course, it was Sunday. She tried to make a fuss of Midge, to assure him he was the most important person in the household, but he was having none of it. He knew what he knew, and he wasn't going to compromise. He hunkered down outside the dining-room door.

Ellie had to get Rose to come and hold Midge while she darted in to feed the kitten minced up beef and milk, which the little cat attacked as if she hadn't been fed for a week – which was just possibly the truth. She was pathetically glad to see Ellie and didn't want to be left alone. Ellie felt like a traitor as she shut the door on the appealing little face within. As soon as Rose released Midge, he settled himself back into the angle of the door, waiting for it to be opened again.

What should they have for lunch? Mia and Rose laughed when Ellie asked them. What did Ellie think they'd been doing since breakfast time? A half leg of lamb was roasting in the oven and potatoes had been peeled, ready to be popped in later. As for fresh greens – how about some mangetout peas?

All Ellie had to do was praise and withdraw. And worry about what she should say to Diana.

The doorbell rang, and it was – wouldn't you know? – Ears, plus DC Milburn.

'You left without signing a statement last night.' Ears was trying to contain irritation without much success. He attempted a smile. 'You must be aware you are not supposed to leave the scene of a crime without giving us all the information you have at your disposal. I could charge you with wasting police time.'

'Surely you know as much as I do? If not more.'

He breathed hard through his nose. 'You have a reputation . . . possibly undeserved, but . . . I have to ask you what, if anything . . . In short, I would welcome any comments you might care to pass on.' Through his teeth.

DC Milburn stood behind him, her expression bland.

Ellie tried not to giggle. Poor Ears! Had he been hauled over the coals again?

'Well, you'd better come in and sit down. As you say, it is just possible that I may have heard one or two items of gossip which might be useful to you, although my poor brain does occasionally take off into flights of fancy. First of all; was the girl really Evangeline Pryce?'

'How did you know it was her?'

'I didn't really. Only, Vera told me that Evangeline Pryce didn't wear a bra or knickers, and neither did that girl.'

Ears sucked in his breath. 'That is not sufficient to—'

'She was the only other young girl I could think of who had access to a front door key and might be searching for something in the house. Edwina Pryce – that's the old lady's stepdaughter – had a key to the house because she used to take food in for her. The victim obviously wasn't a middle-aged woman, so it must be her daughter, Evangeline.

'I don't know anyone else who had a key to the front door –' here she thought of Nirav and crossed her fingers behind her back – 'except for the estate agents, and they wouldn't be likely to pop in after hours in the dark, would they? Have you checked for fingerprints on the torch? Did it belong to her?'

'Too rough a surface to hold prints, but her mother says she had one just like it.'

'Did you have to get her mother to identify her?'

He nodded, grimacing.

DC Milburn murmured, in such a low voice that Ears could ignore her intervention if he wished, 'Ms Pryce is distraught.'

'I can imagine,' said Ellie, wincing.

Ears said, 'Let's get to the point. How did you know there was a safe in that room?'

'Vera told me there was a safe in the house and she thought it was probably in that room. It made sense for it to be there because the room was panelled, which disguised the presence of a safe much better than merely hanging a picture in front of it. Vera didn't know exactly where it was, she didn't know the trick of opening the panelling, and she certainly didn't know the combination.

'I don't know how long the safe has been there. If it had been installed by the late Mr Pryce, then his daughter would have known where it was, and she might well have told Evangeline. What's not so clear is whether or not it still contains what it used to hold, which I believe is Mrs Pryce's most valuable jewellery and possibly some other treasures. Have you had it opened yet?'

'We've got a man coming in later on to get it open for us. You're not implying that Edwina Pryce attacked her own daughter, are you?'

'Certainly not.'

'So what was the girl doing there?'

'Yes, that's the big question, isn't it? Why now, after so long? What has changed recently that made her decide it was worth a look?' Ellie wanted to be quiet so that she could think this through.

Ears was impatient. 'It's obvious she was going to see if there was anything left in the safe, right? We've recovered Mrs Pryce's car, but there was no sign of her jewellery or other valuables. Presumably whoever took the car has disposed of everything they found in it. We've issued a description of what's missing, but nothing's turned up yet.'

'I suppose,' said Ellie, 'it depends on whether or not Mrs

Pryce had time to empty the safe before she died. Was Evangeline desperate for money, do you know? Surely she must inherit something from Mrs Pryce? Has the will been read yet? Ah . . . did they wait for the will to be read, were disappointed with its contents, and only after that became desperate enough to try opening the safe?'

Ears made a chopping gesture and turned away.

The DC replied, 'We understand from her mother that Evangeline had borrowed a large sum against her expectations and spent it on a deposit for a flat and a sports car.'

Ears took a chair and sat, his knees rather too close to Ellie. 'But you know all that, don't you?'

'Me? No. Why?'

The DC pressed on. 'You're sure you haven't heard?'

'Absolutely. Go on.'

'Evangeline found she'd only inherited five thousand pounds, which wouldn't cover what she'd laid out. So, yes, she might well have been desperate for money and decided to see if some of Mrs Pryce's valuables were still in the house.'

Ellie was puzzled. 'I don't understand. Whatever was in the safe would be the property of the estate, and she had no right to it. Ah, I'm being naive. She was doing a spot of burglary on her own account?'

'Possibly,' muttered Ears.

Ellie tried to work it out. 'Let's see now; she took her mother's key to the front door of the house – it was on a string round her wrist, wasn't it? And she also took a torch because she knew the house was empty. And, because her mother had been in and out of the house during the last week of Mrs Pryce's life, Evangeline knew the services were supposed to have been turned off. She didn't have any tools with her, which indicates that she knew where the safe was and how to open it.'

Ears bent closer. 'So who killed her? An accomplice?'

'The assailant must have been a big man, don't you think, to have done such damage to the girl?'

'Who are you pointing the finger at?' said Ears. 'How about the gardener, Fritz? A no-good boy, if ever I saw one.'

EIGHTEEN

Sunday morning

E llie flushed with irritation. 'Certainly not Fritz.'
    'He's put up his hands to theft from everyone he's
ever worked for—'

'And will any of his employers prosecute? Of course not.
It wasn't Fritz who killed Evangeline.'

'Come on then,' said Ears. 'Give us a full description of
the killer: height, weight, colour of hair and eyes, with name
and address, including both Christian names. You know you
can do it.'

She thought of saying that sarcasm didn't become him, but
resisted the temptation. 'Have you considered her uncle, who
works as a school caretaker somewhere?'

'Don't be ridiculous!' snapped Ears. Then he softened. 'No,
we did check, but he was at a poetry reading in a bookshop
until late and, let's face it, he's a bit of a weakling and hasn't
the guts or the strength to knock a healthy young girl about
like that.'

'Have you considered Mrs Pryce's window cleaner, whose
name is Jack? I have no idea where he lives or what he looks
like, though someone told me he was a big, hard man with
lots of muscle. There was something else I was told about
him, but no . . . it's gone. Ms Milburn can find him for you
by asking around the neighbourhood. There can't be that many
window cleaners around. He must have a van or car that he
takes his ladders around in. Perhaps someone saw it there a
couple of nights ago?'

'Come on! A window cleaner!'

The DC tried to say something, but he overrode her. 'Why
would a window cleaner want to kill Evangeline?'

Ms Milburn looked agitated.

Ears stopped prowling and barked out, 'What!'

'The window cleaner was close to Mrs Pryce because, if you remember, he inherited something under her will.'

'Oh. Ah.' He didn't like to say he'd forgotten, but turned on Ellie again. 'It doesn't sound at all likely to me that a window cleaner would want to kill Evangeline. How like you to smear the reputation of an honest man who keeps his nose clean and has never strayed from the straight and narrow.'

'Well, yes. Except that I think you'll find he has a record and has spent time inside.' Also, Fritz didn't like him; Ellie would trust Fritz's judgement on this.

Shock, horror. Hadn't they checked Jack out? Incredible!

Ears breathed hard. 'So tell me why a window cleaner would want to kill the girl?'

'I don't suppose he wanted to. I suppose they were both after the same thing – the contents of the safe.'

'You're saying he was an accomplice of hers?'

'Certainly not. All she had with her was the torch, no tools. She expected to be working in the dark, but knew where the safe was and how to open it. If they'd been in it together, he wouldn't have had to wreck the panelling to find the safe, because she would have told him where it was. He must have brought a crowbar or some such with him, intending to tear the panelling apart till he found the safe.

'What a shock it must have been to both of them to find the other there! I imagine there was an argument; perhaps she threatened to call the police, and he assaulted her in order to stop her leaving and raise the alarm. She was dragged around the place and punched until she lost consciousness.'

The DC said in a soft voice, 'Edwina Pryce admitted they did know where the safe was, but says she didn't know the combination. She says Mrs Pryce did give it to her once, a long time ago. She says she wrote it down on that year's calendar, which has since been thrown away.'

An unlikely tale, thought Ellie. Edwina throw away the combination to the family's safe? Pull the other one.

As for Evangeline, from what Ellie had heard about that young lady, she'd certainly not have passed up a chance to memorize it, or to write it down somewhere.

'Evangeline presumably took her mother's front door key

. . . We'll have to check on that,' said Ears. 'So how did this mythical window cleaner get in?'

'Well, I suppose there are two scenarios. The first is that he spotted Evangeline going into the house and pushed his way in after her. That's very possible. There was another way. He didn't have a front door key, but he's had access to the house for years and knew the layout. He was in and out of the house on that last day when the utilities were turned off. He was there to put padlocks on all the outside doors – and incidentally, he didn't hand over all the keys to the padlocks, but kept some for himself so he could get into the yard at any time he liked.

'Now the back door key, which usually hung on a hook in the kitchen, is missing. I think he took it. You'd better check whether or not it got handed in to the estate agents, but my guess is that it wasn't. Once inside the yard, using the keys he'd kept to the padlocks, he had access to the house through the back door.'

'Why would he want a back door key to an empty house? And don't tell me he was after the contents of the safe on the day she moved out, because at that point everyone thought Mrs Pryce had gone off with all her bits and pieces.'

'Well, not everyone, perhaps. Those who were involved in her demise would have known better. But, getting back to Jack; an empty house is an open invitation to people with contacts in the building trade. Good fireplaces and plumbing fixtures go missing from empty houses all the time. Jack hasn't a good reputation. The only puzzle to me is why he waited so long to go in.' There was something else in the back of her mind about that, too, if only she could remember it.

'Oh,' she said, with a little jump. 'Have you checked to see if the back door was jemmied open?'

'No sign of a break in.'

Ellie sighed. 'Oh dear, it does look as if it was Jack, and that he planned to rob the place right from the start.'

'So you say,' said Ears, heavily sarcastic.

Ellie pursued her own line of thought. 'When he got in through the back door, the first thing he did was to turn the electrics on. He must have done this after the girl arrived and before she got as far as the safe. If she'd noticed that lights had been turned on in the house she wouldn't have gone in, would she? It must have been a shock to her when the place lit up.'

'All right; she knew where the safe was. What makes you think she knew the combination to it?'

'I don't think Edwina has been straight with you. What, throw away the combination to the family's safe, when she knew that a number of valuables had been stored there over the years? Of course she didn't!'

'Then why is she pretending that she did?'

'She's dissociating herself from her daughter's attempt at burglary. I suppose you can't blame her for that. But the idea that Evangeline would have come to the house armed with nothing but a key and a torch is a giveaway. She must have known the combination.'

'You think Edwina gave her the key and the combination, that she was in it with her?'

'I really don't know. It could be that, or it could be that Evangeline had the combination all along and took her mother's key, acting on her own initiative. There wasn't any blood in the television room, was there? The man must have caught her in the hall, perhaps as she came through the front door. The blood spatters tell us it was a hard fight with lots of blood shed. Have you checked to see if all the blood was hers? Maybe she managed to scratch him as he threw her around. She tried to get out of the front door at one point, didn't she? Finally he knocked her out and left her lying on the floor at the bottom of the stairs. He went off to work on the panelling, but once he'd found the safe, he couldn't open it. She was still alive at that point—'

'Why do you say that?'

'Because she was moved after she'd been rendered unconscious. I suppose that when he found the safe he went back to try to shake the combination out of her. She couldn't or wouldn't help him. His earlier blows to the head might have knocked all the sense out of her, or perhaps she was so bloody-minded she wouldn't tell. Poor girl. He panicked and left, leaving the lights on, perhaps not realizing that she was dying. I hope he didn't realize it.'

He made a gesture of defeat. 'You've told us nothing we didn't know already. I expected better of you.'

She ignored the sneer in his voice. 'There's plenty I don't know. Which came first, the chicken or the egg? And why did the chicken cross the road?'

'Don't even think it!'

She allowed herself a small smile. 'All right. I can't even guess who might have caused Mrs Pryce's death until we find out whether the safe was empty or not. You say Evangeline was disappointed when the will was read. When did that happen, may I ask?'

The DC replied, 'The will wasn't read till early this week. On Tuesday, to be precise. After that, Evangeline must have been psyching herself up to check on the safe, and finally made it on Friday night.'

'And why did Jack the Lad hold back till now?'

The DC said, 'We believe his name is really John, and he is listed among the beneficiaries of the will, but he didn't attend the reading. In fact, only the immediate family attended. The others mentioned will be informed of their good fortune by letter. We have an address for him. We'll follow that up. You do know that you—?'

Ears cut her short. 'If she wants to play games with us, that's all right. It takes two to tango.'

Ellie blinked. What on earth did he mean?

'Enough,' said Ears, gathering himself together. 'I'm really disappointed in you, Mrs Quicke. I'd thought you'd want to help us, instead of withholding information, so—'

'What?'

'When you're prepared to be open with us, we'll be happy to continue this discussion. As it is, we'll be on our way.'

Ellie couldn't think what he meant. 'I've done my best, but . . .' She shrugged. 'Let me show you out. I'll be down in the morning to see if I can identify my bits and pieces, all right? I can sign a statement then.'

As she passed out of the door the DC muttered something about a letter, which Ellie didn't catch because she was so happy to see the back of them.

She shut the front door with a bang. Good riddance.

She tried to turn her mind to some other matter, but for some reason couldn't think straight. Was she missing a piece of the jigsaw puzzle? Several pieces, in fact. Facts and figures whirled around in her mind, refusing to settle into a pattern.

Perhaps there was no pattern. Perhaps it was all panic and stupidity.

Dear Lord, this is nothing to do with me. I don't really have to worry about it, do I?

He didn't reply. He seemed to be waiting for her to do – or say – something.

There was one question she could put to Rose, if she wanted to be nosey. The violence of Evangeline's death was frightening. Suppose Fritz had been mistaken about Jack? It would be terrible if she'd pointed the police in the direction of an innocent man.

She went through to the kitchen. 'Rose, does someone called Jack clean our windows?'

'He used to, years ago, but Miss Quicke got rid of him, said he gave her the creeps. Someone the gardener recommended does it now. Is there a problem?'

'Absolutely not. That lamb smells delicious! And here comes Thomas, back in good time to eat with us.'

Perhaps they'd go out into the country that afternoon for a walk. Or what about a visit to Kew Gardens? Yes, why not? Life was not all tears and tension, was it?

Sunday night

The night was rendered hideous by Midge, who gave up sentry duty in favour of headbutting the dining-room door.

Boom! Boom!

Screams of terror from the little cat.

Boom!

Eleven o'clock. Boom! Half past. Boom!

Thomas got out of bed, went downstairs, picked Midge up, thrust him into the kitchen and shut the door on him.

Bang! Bang! Midnight.

Midge wasn't giving up. Rose tottered out of her room. 'What's the matter? Is it a burglar?'

Mia joined her. Thomas returned, collected Midge and carried him up the stairs to join Ellie in their bedroom. Midge hissed out a complaint, but in a few minutes decided that he must have won, because the intruder was downstairs and he was ensconced on a chair in the master bedroom. Besides which, he knew he could always get out of the window if he wished to do so. Tomorrow, oh tomorrow, he'd drive that little rat out of his territory!

Peace at last.

Ellie stared at the ceiling. She liked jigsaw puzzles, but this one was rather too hard for her. She reminded herself that she was going to have a busy today tomorrow, which didn't help. At one o'clock she was still awake.

Why had Ears been so, well, almost secretive about the reading of the will? He'd implied . . . She didn't know what he'd been thinking, but it was almost as if he thought she knew something about it. But she didn't.

Suddenly, she remembered the two unopened letters in her study. She slipped out of bed, careful not to disturb either Midge or Thomas, and crept down the stairs to her office. She closed the door and put on the light.

Yes, both letters were from solicitors.

She opened the one from Gunnar, her own solicitor, first. He reported that until he'd seen the contract Diana had signed with Denis at the start of their business venture, he could not be expected to give an opinion. But his first thoughts were that if Denis wanted to sue Diana, Diana could in turn threaten to sue him for breaking the terms of their agreement by no longer being available. If both parties to the agreement decided to sue, then the agreement might be considered null and void. Diana could then change the name of the agency and continue in practice.

Ellie smiled. Now that was an interesting way out of the dilemma, wasn't it? But it didn't solve the problem of how to deal with a daughter who kept on wanting more money and more attention and was never satisfied with what she'd got. And who had tried to k— . . . Ellie made herself complete the sentence. A daughter who had tried to kill her mother. All right, it had been a momentary impulse. But if Thomas hadn't come in at that point . . . It didn't bear thinking about, but Ellie knew that some time she would have to face up to what had happened.

Blood is thicker than water, etcetera. Even if Diana was the most unloving of daughters, she was still Ellie's responsibility. Till death do us part. Surely that was the Christian way of looking at things?

The other envelope was from a solicitor Ellie didn't know. It was much larger and contained a letter on thick, expensive paper and another envelope. A writ from Diana?

No. Very far from it.

Ellie sank down into her chair. The covering letter was from a solicitor called Greenbody. Now that rang a bell, didn't it? Yes; he – or possibly they – were Mrs Pryce's solicitors. Edwina Pryce had mentioned them.

Ellie scanned the letter. Apparently, Mrs Pryce had left Ellie a legacy. How very pleasant. And unexpected. After all, Ellie had only met Mrs Pryce once, although she thought they might have been good friends if they'd met more often.

Mr Greenbody requested that Mrs Quicke contact him soonest to discuss the terms of the will. Fine. Ellie would do that. A few thousand would be nice, to offset the cost of redoing the bathroom and the holiday in Paris.

There was an envelope addressed to Ellie alongside the covering letter:

> Dear Mrs Quicke,
>
> Your aunt told me a great deal about you, and I have made further enquiries since her death. I understand that you administer a considerable estate for charitable purposes with common sense and mercy, while at the same time supporting various members of your family and friends through their trials and tribulations. I sympathize, as I have over the years tried to do likewise. I have always lived by the maxim that money doesn't bring happiness but can sometimes ease people's path through life and I believe you work on the same principle.
>
> My dear husband disliked the way his children had turned out, and made me promise not to give them any

large sums of money, but to ensure they were never short of the basics. For a long time I was at a loss how to arrange for this to be done after I pass on, until I heard about you.

Apart from the immediate family, I have grown fond of several people who have made my life so much brighter in recent years, and whom I shall miss when I move away. They work hard, and suitable injections of cash might make their lives easier.

I intend to spend my last years in the best retirement home I can find, trusting that my money doesn't give out before I do. But just in case I keel over with a stroke tomorrow, or die in a motorway pile-up, I have decided to make a will as follows:

Five thousand pounds each to my stepson Edgar, to my stepdaughter Edwina, to her daughter Evangeline, and to my step-great-nephew Terry.

One thousand pounds each to my gardener, Fritz; to my window cleaner John; and to my faithful cleaners, Vera and Pet.

I have appointed you, Ellie Quicke, and another trustworthy old friend to be my executors, for which you will each receive the sum of ten thousand pounds. The residue of my estate – including the house – goes to you, Ellie Quicke, to be disbursed at your discretion, either to any of the above who may be in need from time to time, or for any other suitable charitable purpose that comes to your attention. I place no restrictions on you about the house; do with it as you think best.

I wish we could have met more than once. I think we would have enjoyed one another's company, as I enjoyed that of your aunt. I am aware that I am placing a heavy burden on your shoulders. Blame Drusilla for misleading me about her circumstances all those years ago.

Flavia Pryce.

The pieces of the jigsaw whirled round and round in Ellie's head. She put the letter down on her desk and said, 'Dear me.'

She read it all through again.

It explained much that had been puzzling her.

Oh, those silly creatures, rushing around in a panic . . . Why couldn't they have waited?

Ellie read the letter a third time and sighed. She wished she'd known Mrs Pryce better. Perhaps one day Ellie would be able to deal with Diana with the same firmness which Mrs Pryce had exercised over her family.

Meanwhile . . . there were a couple more pieces of the puzzle to put into place, but she couldn't deal with them till the morning.

Monday morning

Everyone looked jaded next morning except Midge, who ate his breakfast noisily and with relish while keeping an eye on the door to the hall.

'You're staying in the kitchen this morning, Midge,' said Rose. 'Just till we can get your little friend back to where she belongs.'

Midge sent her a look of contempt, backed away from his dish, and elongated to double his length. He stretched out first one leg behind him, and then the other, strolled to the cat flap in the kitchen door, and made his exit.

Mia, stacking plates in the dishwasher, was anxious. 'He can't get into the dining room from outside, can he?' She gave a little scream, looking at her watch. 'I'll be late. Rose, can you finish up here for me? There's a board meeting at ten, and I said I'd get there early.'

'You're enjoying getting back to work?' asked Ellie. 'Is everything going well . . . At the printing works, I mean?'

'Oh, yes.' Mia was distracted, picking up her handbag, checking to see if her keys and mobile phone were in it. 'We have more work coming in now I've made them appoint a proper salesman, and I'm pushing them to consider new technology, but dragging them into the twenty-first century is like pulling teeth. Rose, can you manage without me all day today? I've got a driving lesson this afternoon. It's about time I got myself some wheels, and a friend promised to give me some practice in his car this evening.'

Good news all round.

'Bless you, of course I can manage,' said Rose. 'Off you go, and I'll have a nice hotpot waiting for you when you get back this evening. Meanwhile, I'd better make sure all the windows in the dining room are shut and locked, and our little guest hasn't done any further damage.'

Ellie looked in the fridge. Had they enough food in the house, and would she have to go to the shops to get some more? Mm. Well stocked for once.

Rose returned to the kitchen with the kitten on her shoulder. 'She was ever so pleased to see me. Hasn't she got a big purr for her size?'

Thomas wandered in and, seeing the little cat, held out his arms. 'She's a pretty little thing. I'll have her in with me in my study this morning, if you like. Midge can't open that door.'

'And I'll ring the Cats Protection League, find out where she belongs.' Ellie yawned. She hadn't slept well. One part of her wanted to drag Thomas into her office and show him the solicitor's letter, so that they could have a nice comfortable discussion about whether she should accept or not. Ten thousand pounds sounded a lot if you said it quickly, but Ellie had a feeling that accepting the legacy would cost her far more than that in terms of time and energy. It would be best if she read it all over again, quietly, by herself.

She rang the Cats Protection League, only to discover they knew nothing of a half-grown brindled cat without a collar. If Ellie had found a stray, would it be possible for her to foster it for a while? They'd get someone to call in to see her about it when they had time.

Oh. Maybe Vera would know something about the cat.

She disinterred Vera's mobile phone number from the stir fry on her desk. 'Vera, it's Ellie Quicke here. You're at work somewhere, I assume? Can you spare a minute to answer a couple of quick questions? Well; three, actually.'

'Sure, I can polish at the same time. Did you have a good holiday?'

'I did, thank you. Have you had a letter from Mrs Pryce's solicitor, saying she'd left you some money?'

'Wasn't that good of her? I told Mikey we'd get a holiday out of it, but it will have to be half term, since he's back at school now. I'm a bit worried because the rent's just gone up, but it's important to have a holiday, isn't it?'

'It is indeed. Next, there's a stray cat, brindled, only half grown, big ears, no collar, been wandering around the place. Didn't you say that Mrs Pryce had two cats, but they were taken by the Cats Protection League?'

'They were both black and white and went to a good home. I asked. The cat you're talking about belongs up the road – three, no four, houses up – and it's called Molly. I do them Wednesdays. They've got four little monsters under the age of six, three boys, one girl, and the girl's the worst for jumping on the cat. Their father thought they'd like a pet, but they scare the life out of her. I'm not surprised she's trying to find another home. I'll give you their phone number if you can hold on a minute . . .'

The girl must have put the phone down. Somewhere nearby a vacuum cleaner swooped and whined. 'Are you there?' Vera was back. 'I'll read it out to you, shall I?'

Ellie made a note of the number. 'Um, Vera; they haven't put up any notices asking for the return of the cat, have they? I'm just wondering how attached they are to her.'

'Tell the truth, not very. You want to turn her over to the Cats people?'

'I suppose so, in the end. But I'll ring these people first. One last question; when is Pet coming back?'

'Oh, didn't they tell you? No, of course, you've been away. She and her husband have been asked to stay on down in the Isle of Wight, help her friends run their boarding house. They've even given up their council flat in Acton. But my new mate's working out just fine. I really like her, and she loves antique furniture, knows how to bring it up a treat. We'll see you tomorrow as usual?'

'Can Pet drive?'

'Yes, of course. Most people can, can't they? It's just silly billies like me that can't. Oh, sorry. I didn't mean—' She'd remembered that Ellie didn't drive, either.

'That's all right, Vera. What about her husband? Does he drive, and do they have a car?'

'They did have but it died the death and they're doing without at the moment. Saving hard, you know?'

'That makes sense. All right, Vera. See you tomorrow.'

That filled in one more piece of the puzzle.

NINETEEN

Monday morning

Midge pushed open Ellie's office door and prowled around with murder in mind.

Ellie abandoned thoughts of a mysterious death and rang the house down the road which might have mislaid a cat. A distracted female nearly leaped down the phone with gratitude when Ellie said she'd found a kitten which might belong to them. It appeared that the eldest boy had been driving them mad trying to find it, rushing around the roads as soon as he got back from school, calling, 'Molly, Molly!' at every house. He had put up some notices, but hadn't used proper tacks so they'd all fallen down. He was in such a state as you wouldn't believe, and had Ellie got the kitten safe because it needed to go to the vets and be microchipped and so on . . .

Ellie sighed, said they would keep the kitten safe until called for, and hoped that would be as soon as possible.

A pity. Thomas adored that kitten.

She rang the police station, only to be told that Ears was out. Of course. Maybe he was, and maybe he wasn't, but she could always leave a message, couldn't she? She was going to enjoy this. 'Please tell the inspector that Mrs Quicke called. As she is now the owner of the Pryce house and its contents, she would like to be present when your expert opens the safe. Please let her know when this is to take place.'

She supposed that meant she accepted the legacy. She phoned Mrs Pryce's solicitor and was connected to Mr Greenbody's son, 'young' Mr Greenbody, who sounded efficient and impersonal.

'This is Mrs Ellie Quicke speaking. I've been away and only just opened the letter from you and the enclosure from Mrs Pryce. I shall have to think about whether I can accept the legacy because it has strings attached. May I ask who the other executor is to be, and whether or not he has accepted the job?'

His voice went from chilly to warm. 'I am the other executor. Mrs Pryce was one of my father's clients. He was a good friend of hers till his arthritis made it necessary for him to retire. She was not sure at first if I would be mature enough to work for her – as I'm only in my late forties – but eventually agreed to give me a trial. I am truly sorry to hear of her death.'

'So am I,' said Ellie, with feeling. 'May I ask whether you agreed with the way she disposed of her estate?'

A dry tone. 'I have been familiar with the family for many years, and so was my father before me.' Meaning he knew what bloodsuckers they all were and how difficult it was to be even-handed when dealing with them. 'And of course, your charity is a shining example of what can be done to help people without causing them to lose their independence. I can't think of anyone more suitable to carry out Mrs Pryce's wishes.'

Hm. Flatterer. 'Well, I'm not going to act hastily. I have to think whether or not I can manage to take on so much extra work. In the meantime, did you know that the police plan to open Mrs Pryce's safe this afternoon? Would it be appropriate for you to attend?'

'Very much so. Let me know when and I'll be there, even if it means cancelling an appointment. I look forward to meeting you, Mrs Quicke.'

Ellie went along to Thomas's study to tell him about the solicitor's letter and found him talking on the phone while operating his computer with his free hand. There was no sign of his part-time assistant. The little cat was curled up in Thomas's in tray, fast asleep.

'All right?' he mimed at her.

'Fine,' she mimed back. He was busy, and a couple of hours this way or that wouldn't hurt, would it? She looked in every room on the ground floor. The door to the dining room was open, but there was no sign of Midge. Ah, yes. He was sitting in the sun in the garden, ignoring them. Long might that last.

The doorbell rang. Diana. 'I must say, you don't look very well, Mother!'

'I had a disturbed night,' said Ellie, leading the way to the sitting room. She wondered why she wasn't frightened to be alone with her daughter. Was she overtired, or was this an answer to prayer? Or was it because Thomas was still in the house?

Diana was looking pleased with herself. 'Guess what!'

'You've been thinking about what you tried to do, are deeply ashamed, and want to talk to me about it?'

'I don't know what you mean.' She knew all right, for a tide of red swept up and over her forehead.

'Do you expect me to overlook the fact that you tried to kill me?'

A quick frown. 'Don't be ridiculous. That never happened.'

'I remember it all too well.'

Diana's colour was fast returning to normal. 'You have a vivid imagination, Mother. Let's get down to business. I have the most wonderful proposition to put to you. It's going to make you yet another fortune. How does that sound?'

'I'm all ears.' Ellie wondered if Ears had got her message yet.

'You know the Pryce place? Of course you do. Think how terrible it would be if someone developed the site unsympathetically. They could put up a block of flats that would tower over you and destroy the peace and quiet of your garden.'

'I doubt if a tower block would be allowed in this neighbourhood.'

'Money talks, and such developments have been pushed through occasionally. So, my idea is this: you buy the place, and I'll redevelop it for you with a block of low-rise flats which will be worth a mint. I'll be taking all the worry off your shoulders, and you'll have nothing to do but sit back and rake in the cash.'

Ellie laughed, and then sighed. 'Where does Evan Hooper fit into this neat little scenario?'

'Well of course you'll go through him to buy the place so he gets his cut, too.'

'You get back into Evan Hooper's good books by arranging the deal? What about your merger with his agency?'

'The merger goes through if I pull off the deal for the Pryce house. This ticks all the boxes, and everyone gets what they want.'

'One small problem, Diana. I haven't decided yet what I'm going to do about it, but I've just heard that Mrs Pryce has left her house to me on the basis that I continue dishing out support to her family and friends.'

Diana changed colour, from pasty to greenish-white. 'Oh, come now! That's ridiculous. Why would she do that?'

'She married into a family of wastrels who can't make ends meet but still expect her to keep them in style. She knew I'd been through much the same thing with you.'

Diana flushed, and then paled again. 'You're saying I'm a wastrel?'

'You've bought and sold, and inherited three properties so far, yet you say you're on the verge of bankruptcy—'

'Well, yes. Because Denis—'

'Tell him to get lost. Tell him you'll sue him if he drops out of working for the agency.'

'He's in jail, for heaven's sake. He isn't exactly dropping out of his own accord.'

'It's his own fault he's in jail. You have a good case. You may be in debt for other reasons, such as the extravagant purchase of a new car—'

'It's necessary to keep up appearances.'

'Not to that extent. Downsize, Diana. If you sell either your flat or the house I gave you, that should clear your mortgage and your debts.'

'I don't see any reason why I should when you're sitting on a pile of gold.'

'It's not your pile of gold, Diana. It's never going to be your pile of gold. All the money I've been given is for me to look after and disburse for those in need. It's called steward-ship. The money is not yours, and it's not mine. I'm merely looking after it as best I can. You've had your whack, and what have you done with it? Spent it, frittered it away. Now you want me to entrust you with yet another property? No.'

'But this is my chance to get into the big time.'

'You've had umpteen chances to get into the big time and

blown them all.' Ellie raised her hand to stop Diana bursting into speech. 'How many times in the past have you asked for capital and been given it? And still you ask for more? You say you're now in debt. Forgive me; but I'm not sure I believe you.'

'How dare you!'

'I dare,' said Ellie, tired to the point of not caring what Diana did or said, 'because that's the pattern of your life and I don't see you breaking it.'

'But I promised Denis—'

'Who conned you beautifully, didn't he? Well, he himself has broken more promises than a serial bigamist so I don't suppose it matters. No, Diana. Not a penny more. I don't know whether or not I shall accept Mrs Pryce's legacy; I haven't decided yet. And no, I don't know what will happen to it if I decline the honour. I suppose she had a back-up plan; probably to appoint a guardian of some kind to administer the estate on behalf of her family. But as far as you're concerned, enough's enough. Downsize to get rid of your debts, go to work for Mr Hooper and earn yourself an honest penny for once.'

Diana's voice rose. 'Are you saying I'm not honest?'

'You've always cut corners in the past, but Evan Hooper's a shark and he'll be right on to you if you start that with him.'

'You can't throw me to the wolves just like that.'

'He's a shark, not a wolf. Though I dare say he's been called both in the past. And that's enough for today, Diana. I had a bad night, I'm tired and I've got a lot on; not least helping the police with their enquiries, as they say.'

'That snake Thomas has been filling you up with lies about me, hasn't he? Well, I'm not going till we've thrashed this out.'

'Talking about me?' Thomas stood in the doorway, not quite smiling, with the little kitten clutched to his shoulder. How long had he been standing there, and how much had he overheard?

'She's just leaving,' said Ellie, feeling how hollow a victory it was when you had to cut one of your own family down to size. Depressing, very.

'I'll see her out.' Thomas held the door open for Diana, who said, through her teeth, 'We'll continue this another time.' And stalked out.

The phone rang, and Ellie picked it up.

'Mrs Quicke? You were supposed to come down to the police station this morning to see if you could identify your treasures. What kept you?' Ears, of course.

Ellie looked at her watch. 'I can be there in half an hour. Meanwhile, you got my message about Mrs Pryce's house? She didn't leave it to me free of strings and I'm not at all sure I'm going to accept. However, I understand you have an expert ready to open her safe today, and I think her solicitor and I should be there to protect our interests. What time shall we meet you?'

'Three. The safe expert can't be there till then.'

Ellie put the phone down, sighing. What she really wanted was time to sit down and think about this and that . . . and Diana. Meanwhile, she supposed she'd better get down to the police station and claim her property. Always supposing it was hers.

'Thomas; some good news, some bad. The kitten belongs to a house up the road and they're coming to retrieve it. Can we put her somewhere safe for the time being? And have you the time to come down to the station with me? They want us to identify our property . . .'

He went with her, and indeed the police had found her property. So that was one bright ray of sunshine on an other-wise gloomy day.

Monday afternoon

Ellie waited by the gateposts of the Pryce house for someone to let her in. There was no sign of the police as yet, but a dumpy, dark little man was sitting in a van which he'd parked by the garage doors. Was he the safe expert?

The sun had hidden itself behind clouds. Ellie shivered. Two deaths had taken place here in recent months. The house would need to be spring-cleaned of its dark memories before it could be occupied again . . . or perhaps it would be best to tear it down and build low-rise flats on the site, retaining as much of the garden as possible? Fritz could be given a contract to look after it. She found herself smiling at the thought of Fritz. She wondered whose garden he was working in that afternoon.

An ancient but well-polished car drew up in the road outside, and a tall, gaunt man bent down to help a woman out. Would this be Edgar, the stepson? Another ginger-top.

Edwina had got a new black outfit for the occasion. Of course. How was she paying for her clothes now Mrs Pryce was no more? Almost, Ellie pitied the woman, who looked as if she'd shrunk a dress size or two. The black-gloved hand that she laid on her brother's arm was shaking. Black gloves on a summer's day? She presented a picture of Grief with a capital G. As well she might. Neither brother nor sister saw Ellie.

A police car drew up, and Ears got out. Predictably, he turned his bad temper on the two Pryces. 'What are you two doing here? Don't you realize this is a crime scene?'

'Haven't we every right to be here?' demanded Edwina, touching a lace-edged hankie to her lips. 'When our solicitor told us what you were going to do today, we decided we had to be present. This was our family home, remember? Sullied for ever by the death of our dear ones.'

True, of course; if a trifle overdone.

Ears said, 'What about young Terry? Is he coming, too?'

Edwina pressed the hankie to her temples. 'It seems he's fallen out with the friend he was living with and is moving to alternative accommodation today. Mr Greenbody will keep him informed of developments.'

Mr Greenbody had been busy, hadn't he? Was it good news that Terry and his 'friend' had parted company? Probably. How badly was he into drugs and in debt? Ought he to go into a rehabilitation programme; how much would it cost, and would it work? Again, Mr Greenbody would know.

Ears scowled at Edwina. 'Well, I suppose it's all right if you stay in the background and don't interfere.'

Edwina spotted Ellie as she approached the house, and her voice rose into a shriek. 'You, here? Have you come to gloat? How you have the nerve to show your face here, I do not know! Heaven alone knows what lies you told Mummy so that she'd make this place over to you, but—'

'Hush, Edwina!' Her brother frowned, casting a quick enquiring glance at Ellie . . . to see what she was like?

Ellie didn't know what to say, so kept quiet.

Edwina tossed her head. 'You may well cringe, Mrs Quicke. I'm not one to be mealy mouthed when faced with sin. Yes, sin! I hope your conscience torments you night and day.'

Ellie was overtaken by a desire to giggle, but managed to subdue it. Now she knew exactly what to say. 'It's only natural for you to be upset. I'm sorry to say I only met your step-mother the once.'

Edgar seemed to dislike scenes, as indeed most men did. 'Calm down, Edwina. Remember that our stepmother trusted Mrs Quicke to look after you in future.'

Two more well-polished, new cars drove up behind the Pryces; one was a size larger than the other. The smaller car disgorged a woman in black, who had 'personal assistant' written all over her. She was carrying a laptop and a briefcase.

From the larger car leaped a sandy-haired, compact little man who bounced over to the brother and sister and shook their hands, uttering the usual condolences. Ah, so this was Mr Greenbody? Mm. He looked competent and clever. An excellent combination.

The sandy-haired man spotted Ellie and shook her hand. 'Greenbody, junior. Delighted to meet you. Have heard so much. Just the person to sort out this mess, yes?' He bounded up the steps at Ellie's side and produced keys to let them into the house. Had he got the keys from the estate agents? Or had Mrs Pryce let him have a set?

Ears and the DC followed him into the hall, gathering up the dumpy little safe expert on the way.

Edgar had to tug on his sister's arm in order to get her moving, and Ellie brought up the rear with Mr Greenbody's PA.

Ellie's eyes went to the stains on the floor at the foot of the stairs, and she shivered. You could never really get blood out of parquet flooring, could you?

Edwina was still playing the tragedy queen. Hand to forehead, she pointed to the stain. 'Was this where my darling
daughter . . . ?'

'Yes, yes,' said Ears, shifting from foot to foot. 'And we've
a warrant out at this very moment for the man we believe was
responsible.'

Edwina let out a piercing scream. It echoed through the
house. Was she going to have hysterics? 'Who was it? Who?
I demand to know who killed my only child! It was that ghastly
Terry, wasn't it?'

'No, madam,' said Ears, beginning to look just a trifle fraz-
zled. 'It was not. You will be informed in due course.' For
once, Ellie sympathized with Ears.

'Shush, now.' Edgar spoke mechanically, his eyes going
around the hall and up the stairs. Was he curious to see where
his niece had died? Had he been fond of her, given her presents
as a child, watched her grow up and even been proud of her?
Or was he remembering his youth in this house?

On closer inspection Ellie could see that Edgar had not aged
well; not even as well as his sister. Had he lost weight recently?
He could have done with a haircut, and his clothes hung loosely
on him. His skin was pitted with old acne scars.

'This way,' said Ears, impatient as always, indicating the
door to the television room. Ellie and Mr Greenbody followed
the others in. The panelling still hung in shattered pieces.

The safe-cracker said, 'Ah yes. Our firm installed this safe,
and we keep records, naturally. This type is not difficult to
. . . but it may take some time . . . does anyone know the birth
date of our client?'

'Twenty-fifth of September, nineteen twenty-five.' That was
Edgar.

Ellie was surprised, and then remembered Vera saying Mrs
Pryce had always remembered his birthday and he'd always
remembered hers.

'It's a long shot but sometimes clients use . . . ah. Got it.'

There was a click, and the safe door swung open. Everyone
leaned forward to look.

TWENTY

' t's all there!' cried Edwina and, turning to her brother, broke into noisy tears. DC Milburn donned plastic gloves. One by one she lifted a number of leather boxes of different shapes and sizes out of the safe. Next came a large, locked metal box and a couple of wrapped bundles which clinked. Finally, she withdrew two paintings in ornate frames encased in bubble wrap.

Edgar said, 'We always had the silver candlesticks out at Christmas. The oil paintings used to hang in the dining room; Father bought them from Sotheby's. The metal box contains financial papers. The square green leather box contains a French carriage clock. The other boxes are for the odd bits and pieces of jewellery and silver from her family and ours which she'd long since stopped using but didn't want to sell.'

Edwina reared up, her face blotchy, her hands turning into claws as she advanced on Ellie. 'They're our family's things, and you shan't have them!'

Ellie wanted to say that she didn't want them or anything to do with the Pryce family, but wasn't given the chance to speak before Edwina leaped at her. Mr Greenbody, ever on the alert, pulled Ellie back out of striking distance.

Edgar caught his sister by the shoulders and hauled her off. 'Come on, now; it's not her fault.'

'Whose fault is it, then? Did my poor Evangeline die in vain?'

'Well,' said Ellie, goaded beyond endurance, 'her death certainly saved the country the expense of a trial and prison sentence, didn't it?'

Ellie's words trickled away into silence.

Ears gaped. So did most of the others. Only Mr Greenbody looked as if he were enjoying the moment.

'How dare you!' whispered Edwina, hankie to mouth.

'I dare,' said Ellie, 'because it's no good covering it up any longer. Innocent people may fall under suspicion if you don't own up.'

'Own up to what?' Edwina flushed to her hairline.

'Causing and then failing to report an accident.'

Edwina screamed, eyes tightly shut, hands clenched by her sides.

Everyone else froze.

Edgar put his arm round his sister's shoulders. 'Mrs Quicke, I think you'd better explain yourself.'

'Yes, indeed,' said Ears, clearing his throat loudly.

'Incompetence and panic,' said Ellie. 'It gives me a head-ache, just thinking about it. I don't suppose Edwina ever meant to hurt Mrs Pryce, but when she fell down the stairs and died, Edwina panicked. Instead of phoning for an ambulance or reporting it, she went in search of her daughter.'

'No, no, no!' Edwina squeezed out some tears. And then, incredibly, stamped her foot like a small child.

'I think,' said Ears, 'that we'd better continue this conversa-tion down at the station.'

Edwina's eyes flew open. 'I'm not going anywhere, except home. Edgar, take me home. I'm in no fit state to listen to this wicked nonsense.'

Ellie said, 'I don't suppose you'll spend much time in jail, if any. They'll probably give you a suspended sentence.' And I'll have to see to it that you're supported for the rest of your wretched life.

Edwina ground out, 'You don't know anything. You can't prove anything.'

'True,' said Ellie, 'but I can tell you what I think happened. Shall we move back into the hall, because it's easier to explain in there?'

Ears turned to the safe expert. 'We won't need you any longer.'

'Ah.' The man looked as if he'd rather have stayed, but he grudgingly removed himself and his tools. He banged the front door on his way out, which made everyone jump.

The black-suited PA moved smoothly into action. 'Mr

Greenbody will be taking charge of the contents of the safe, as they form part of Mrs Pryce's estate. I will take an inventory now and let the police have a copy in due course.'

DC Milburn said, 'Sir, is it all right if I stay here and help take the inventory? That way, we get a copy straight away.'

Ears nodded. 'I suppose so.'

Mr Greenbody held the door open for them to pass back into the hall.

Edwina would have gone straight out of the house through the front door, but Ears exclaimed something sharply, and her brother barred the way. 'Best get it over with, Edwina.'

'Much you know about it.' Edwina turned back into the hall with a gesture of despair.

'You have the floor, Mrs Quicke,' said Ears. 'But make it snappy, will you?'

'I'll try. It's all a question of sorting out who had keys, who could drive, and what they did afterwards, isn't it?' Ellie looked up the stairs. 'What I think happened is that a number of people came to see Mrs Pryce on her last night in this house. The first one arrived soon after all the removal people had gone. She walked here because she didn't have a car. She had a key. She probably came with the intention of seeing what she could do to help Mrs Pryce pack up and leave, but she also came to ask for money.'

'Not me!' whispered Edwina.

Ellie shook her head and continued. 'No, not you. Mrs Pryce had sorted out and packed most of her things already: her clothes, favourite knick-knacks and books, all the personal items she was taking into her new life. She hadn't yet opened the safe, as she wanted to leave its valuable contents till last.

'Because she had trouble with her knees and was finding it difficult to carry everything down the stairs, quite a few of her things were still on the landing when her visitor arrived. This person offered to help Mrs Pryce finish loading the car, which at that point was still in the garage. Her offer was accepted.

'The visitor asked for money, and Mrs Pryce refused. They happened at that moment to be in Mrs Pryce's bedroom. There was an argument, and Mrs Pryce fell, hitting her head against the wall and staining the wallpaper. The visitor panicked, thinking she'd committed murder. She didn't dare ring for an ambulance. She was desperate for someone to help her decide what to do, so she used her mobile to phone her husband—'

Ears said, 'Oh, she's got a husband, has she?'

'He was working, had no car, but there was Mrs Pryce's car in the garage, all packed up and ready to go. The visitor seized Mrs Pryce's handbag in order to get at her car keys and drove off to collect her husband. Perhaps she was hoping he'd help her get the old lady to the hospital. Perhaps not. Do you follow so far?'

'Not me, nothing to do with me,' moaned Edwina.

'No, of course not,' said Ellie. 'Mrs Pryce wasn't dead, anyway, was she? She came to after a while, got to the bathroom, washed the blood off her face, took off her diamond earrings and changed into a housecoat. If she'd only rung for the police . . . but she didn't. She was disorientated. She'd always loved the hand-painted wallpaper in her bedroom. It had been a gift from her dead husband, and she couldn't bear to see the blood on it. In her confused state, she set to work to clean it off . . . only to be interrupted some time later by another visitor, who had also come on foot, who also had a key and who was also after money.'

'Edwina?' guessed Ears.

All eyes switched to Edwina, who give a stifled cry. 'No, not me!'

'Evangeline was pulling pints in a pub,' said Ellie, 'So, yes; it had to be you.'

'How dare you!' Shaking, Edwina pressed a handkerchief to her mouth.

Ellie continued, 'You had the only other front door key; all the others were accounted for. I think you discovered the old lady wobbling around the landing. Perhaps there was another argument, perhaps Mrs Pryce missed her step and accidentally fell; either way, she ended up at the bottom of the stairs with a broken neck.'

Edwina stifled a scream. 'No argument. What you said; she missed her step and fell.'

'Perhaps she did,' said Ellie, with compassion. 'Either way, you panicked. You realized how badly it would look for you if you rang the police, because you believed you were due to inherit a fortune when your stepmother died. You fled home to phone your daughter for help. You don't drive, so it wasn't you who took the car.'

'Not guilty, not guilty!' cried Edwina. 'I'd no idea what happened to her, had I?'

'That's true,' said Ellie. 'You hadn't. While you went off in search of Evangeline, Mrs Pryce's first visitor arrived back in the car with her husband, whom she'd managed to winkle out of his place of work. Perhaps his shift had finished or perhaps he got someone else to cover for him. The police can check that. They found Mrs Pryce lying dead at the foot of the stairs.

'More panic. How did she get there? The first visitor had left her at the top of the stairs, wearing different clothes and with a bleeding head wound. They wondered if she'd regained consciousness, only to fall down the stairs after all. Perhaps the husband shouted at his wife, accusing her of killing the goose that laid the golden eggs.

'They feared the police would say it was no longer a case of assault, but of manslaughter or even murder. What to do? They dithered. It occurred to them to gain time by making it appear that Mrs Pryce had driven off to start a new life on the following day, as planned. To do this, they removed everything she'd left out for that one last night in her home: her jewellery boxes including her diamond drop earrings, her overnight case and toiletries, her make-up, alarm clock, bedside light, and all the other bits and pieces which might prove she'd spent her last night at home, including her briefcase, with all the paper-work in it, and her laptop.

'By this time the car was piled high with Mrs Pryce's belongings, and there was no room for her body to go in as well, yet they couldn't leave any of her things behind or no one would believe she'd gone away under her own steam. They decided to stash the body somewhere until they could deal with it. While this first visitor had been piling everything into the car earlier in the evening, she'd noticed that by mistake the freezer had been left behind by the removers. That gave them an idea of how to delay discovery of the body. Between them they carried Mrs Pryce out through the kitchen and the yard, and put her in the freezer. They switched the power back on to keep the body fresh. In their haste they didn't realize they'd left a fold of her housecoat outside the freezer.

'I don't suppose they gave a second thought to the safe. In any event, they hadn't the combination so couldn't have opened it even if they'd known exactly where it was. When they'd finished clearing away all traces of Mrs Pryce, they drove off in her car, or more probably, one drove and one walked home.'

'Oh, the devils,' cried Edwina, pressing her handkerchief to her forehead. 'If only we'd known where they'd put her!'

'When Evangeline finished her shift at the pub she came back here with you, Edwina, prepared to deal with a dead body . . . which was nowhere to be found. All Mrs Pryce's things had gone, and so had the car. I suppose you concluded that she'd recovered consciousness and driven off in her own car. You must have thought she was so furious with you for causing her to fall that she wanted nothing more to do with you. So you weren't particularly surprised when she failed to make contact with you in due course. Did you think she was punishing you, by disappearing?'

'Yes, I suppose so. Of course that's what happened.'

'Unfortunately for you, it wasn't. Time passed and no news came. You became really worried. Bills were mounting up, you couldn't pay them, and you didn't know where Mrs Pryce had gone so you couldn't pass them on to her. It must have driven you mad, not knowing. And that is why you paid me that very odd visit, trying to push me into investigating Mrs Pryce's whereabouts.'

'She wouldn't have let me starve!'

'Starving wasn't an option. Perhaps you might have down-sized and started buying your clothes in Primark instead of Harrods. That would have helped. But it isn't your style, is it? Let's get back to what really happened. The husband and wife had not only taken the car – a valuable car – but they had Mrs Pryce's laptop and business papers in her briefcase . . . not to mention all her personal effects.

'To make it seem as if Mrs Pryce had driven off into the

blue of her own accord, they accessed the paperwork on Mrs Pryce's laptop and in her briefcase. They left messages on the Hooper Agency's answerphone to the effect that she'd changed her mind, was leaving early, and would the agency please close up the house for her. They phoned the retirement home, to say Mrs Pryce had decided not to go there after all. And – to keep the secret safe – they told Hoopers to take the house off the market. If the house was never sold, no one need ever find out what had happened to Mrs Pryce.

'I imagine they thought the freezer would keep the body frozen until they could get back to dispose of it. But when they did return, they found padlocks had been placed on all the doors, and they didn't dare remove them lest someone should notice and start asking questions.'

'Fritz removed two,' said Ears.

'He acted in all innocence, and he didn't touch the ones on the garage, which proves he didn't know his old employer was there.'

There was no need to mention how the electricity came to be turned on and off and on again. Protect Nirav and his runaway girlfriend if possible.

'Who was this husband and wife team?' said Ears. 'And why don't you think it was the window cleaner?'

'Because it was a woman who phoned Mrs Pryce's excuses around, and I think if it had been the window cleaner, he'd have taken everything in sight that he could sell, but have left her body there – as he did after he killed Evangeline.

'Now, I've heard someone who can imitate Mrs Pryce beautifully, and I know she was saving like mad for IVF treatment. You've probably never spoken to her. Known as Pet, she was one of the cleaners who worked for many years for Mrs Pryce. She had the keys to the house, as a member of the cleaning team, and only returned them to the office on the Monday after Mrs Pryce disappeared.

'I think she and her husband put the car in a rented garage somewhere till they thought it would be safe to sell it. And waited, and waited. Nothing happened. They began to relax, and perhaps to dispose of some of the less easily recognizable items they'd stolen: the briefcase, the laptop, the clothing, the costume jewellery and the knick-knacks. Perhaps through car boot sales or second-hand clothes shops? That's how I would have done it.

'The car and the good jewellery – including her diamond earrings and the rings she wore every day – were another matter. They'd stepped out of their comfort zone and didn't know how to dispose of these expensive items. They hadn't the contacts to get rid of diamonds or, for that matter, a top price car. The moment they tried to sell one of her diamond rings to a quality jeweller, say, they'd be asked to account for their possession of it. They might have taken some of the stuff to a backstreet pawnbroker and got a few hundreds here and there, but the police have circulated a description of the good items locally and there's been no news of them by now. I think the police may have to look further afield.

'Mrs Pryce was not missed for some weeks until her great-nephew Terry needed money and started to stir things up. As soon as they heard about this, Pet and her husband cleaned the car out, ditched it at the airport, and took a holiday down to the Isle of Wight. Shortly afterwards they announced that they were giving up their council flat here in London. I expect you'll find they've started selling Mrs Pryce's jewellery down there.'

'Right,' said Ears, breathing hard. 'We'll get on to that. So what can I charge Edwina with?'

'I think failing to report an accident is the only charge that will stick.'

'Is that all?'

Edwina gave a silent shriek. 'Isn't it enough that I've lost my daughter and have been made ill with anxiety all this time?'

'I'm sure you were anxious,' said Ellie. 'Your pot of gold has disappeared.'

'Unkind!' said Edwina. 'I really cared for Mummy, and I miss her terribly!'

Eyebrows were raised all round. Even her brother's went up.

'I shall need this Pet person's full name and address,' said Ears.

'I believe Mr Greenbody has her old address because Pet was mentioned in the will. Ironic, that.'

'Correct, dear lady,' said Mr Greenbody. 'Mrs Pryce was careful to give the current address of all her beneficiaries. Of course, this person might or might not have given a forwarding address when she left London, but I'm sure the police will be able to find her.'

Edwina wailed, 'I didn't kill her, and neither did Evangeline, so why did my daughter have to die?'

'Greed,' said Ellie. 'You went on spending even though Mrs Pryce had disappeared. Once her body was discovered and the will was read, you found that, instead of coming into a nice fortune, you were back where you'd started as a remittance woman. That's when you and Evangeline began to wonder about the safe. You say you'd forgotten the combination; I'm not sure I believe you, but Evangeline had certainly remembered it. Granny's birthday. Not hard, was it? And so she came along after work one night and ran into another villain. They argued, and he killed her. Now that was definitely murder.'

'Who! Tell me; who was it?'

Ellie looked at Ears, who looked at the floor. 'Probably – though you'd better not quote me – Mrs Pryce's window cleaner, who also came looking for the safe and its contents.'

'Why did he wait so long?'

'I think,' said Ellie, hesitantly, 'that he was either in prison – because he's done time before – or he was abroad. He's certainly not been round lately. I've noticed the windows of several houses around here need attention at the moment. I've been told he owned a timeshare in Spain, so he might have been out of the country. On his return he got a letter from the solicitors saying that Mrs Pryce had left him a thousand pounds in her will. A nice little windfall to some, but perhaps not much to a man who'd hoped to get more, had kept a key to the house in case he needed to strip it at some time . . . and who remembered talk of a safe.'

'A window cleaner killed my daughter! How appalling!'

It was a social misdemeanour to be killed by a window cleaner? Snob! thought Ellie. Serves you right.

And then: You poor thing!

'Have I got this right?' asked Mr Greenbody. 'We can't actually prove that anyone killed Mrs Pryce?'

Ears said, 'We might get this Pet person for manslaughter, I suppose. But . . . Mrs Quicke is right. Edwina's age, the murder of her daughter . . . No, we'll stick with failing to report an accident.'

Edwina screamed again. Her brother put his arms around her. 'There, there.'

She thrust him away. 'You're useless, you are! You never stood up for me when I got pregnant—'

'The lad only wanted you for your money, Edwina. As soon as Daddy told him the truth, he was off like a scalded cat!'

'If you hadn't told Daddy about the other girls he'd been seeing, it would have been all right. No, don't touch me! They say cancer's not catching, but I'm not taking any chances. My only consolation is that you'll soon be as dead as . . . as Evangeline. Someone call me a taxi this minute! And I've no money, so you can pay for it, too!'

'We'll see you get home safely,' said Ears. 'Once you've given us a statement, and signed it. Down at the station.'

'I am NOT going to be taken to the station in a police car. What would Daddy and Mummy have said?'

'You have no choice,' said Ears.

'Shall I take her?' Mr Greenbody's assistant appeared, shoving paperwork into her briefcase. 'Inventory complete. The DC has a copy and Mr Greenbody can now remove the contents of the safe. Come along now, Ms Pryce. You'll feel better when this is done.' She took Edwina's arm, and to everyone else's relief, the woman allowed herself to be guided out of the hall and into the fresh air.

'Everything's going straight to the bank,' said Mr Greenbody, his eyes as lively as ever. 'I'll see to it and lock up when the police have finished. Mrs Quicke, you will phone me to make an appointment?'

She nodded. How tiring this all was. Oh, the pity of it all. Such high hopes, such greed . . . so much stupid, selfish greed.

Edgar took one last look around him and held the front door open for Ellie. 'Mrs Quicke, may I give you a lift home?'

She shook her head, thinking he was a man unable to rise

above the good fortune he'd been born to, and crushed by life. 'I'll walk. It's not far, and it will do me good. I dare say we'll be meeting now and then, in the future.' Did that mean she was definitely going to accept Mrs Pryce's legacy?

'You won't have to bother with me for long, Mrs Quicke. Cancer of the liver. Takes no prisoners, as they say.'

She nodded. So that's what Edwina had meant? Poor man.

The sunshine made them both blink. He said, 'Mrs Quicke, you probably won't believe me, but I was fond of my step-mother. She was always very straight in her dealings with me.'

Ellie took another look at him. His eyes were steady, though his face showed signs of his illness. She remembered that although he'd lost a lot of money in a failed business, he'd found himself a job afterwards and kept it. Perhaps his life could be counted a success?

She asked, 'You're not married, are you? Do you have someone to look after you?'

He attempted a smile. 'I was married once – till the money ran out. I suppose I can't blame her.'

'Can you stay on where you've been living?'

'No, I've been forcibly retired. I'd like to have gone on a bit longer, but . . . I can see their point of view. They have to appoint someone fit and strong in my place, and they'll need to offer him my house. Not to worry, though. I've saved a bit from my salary, I have a small pension and my stepmother gave me a lump sum to rent a small place until . . . Until . . .'

'Any regrets? Things you wish you'd done?' Ellie cursed herself for acting on impulse, but the words were out.

He turned his face to the sunshine, half closing his eyes. 'A multitude of them. I wish I'd married a decent woman, had a child, stuck to my books instead of idling away my time at university, learned the elements of commerce before I plunged into a business which I didn't know how to run. But my step-mother sorted me out. "Find something you like doing, and do it with all your might." That's what she said. Good advice. It took me a while to find something I liked doing, and a lot of people think I took a step down the social scale when I became a school caretaker, but it's suited me fine, and I've enjoyed it.'

'Do you fancy a holiday?' Now where did that idea come from?

He managed a real smile this time. 'Disneyland? Swimming with dolphins? I had volunteered to go camping with some of the kids from school, but I don't think I'll be allowed to go now. Health and safety and all that. Not fit enough.' He took one last look at his old home. 'What will you do with the old place?'

'What would *you* do with it?'

'It's in good nick. My stepmother saw to that. It's an anachronism, but there's so little individuality in houses nowadays, I'd be sorry to see it go. She said once how much some old friends from the States had enjoyed staying there with her. They'd just loved the house and everything in it. Do you think it would work as a luxury hotel?'

Well, now. There's a thought.

Ellie looked up at the house. 'That might indeed be the answer. It would need a complete makeover, but American visitors would love it. Thank you, Mr Pryce. I'll take some advice, see what can be done.'

He held out his hand to her. 'Thank you, Mrs Quicke. For caring.'

She held on to his hand. 'Come to see me tomorrow morning. Do you know where I live? In the next road. We're in the phone book.'

A flash of surprise, then a remarkably sweet smile.

An idea fizzed into Ellie's head. Suppose she paid Vera to take Mikey and Edgar Pryce away to the seaside for a holiday at half term? It would do them all good. Ellie would have to check with Edgar's doctor to see if he were fit enough, but Vera would make a good carer, wouldn't she? Ellie told herself not to act impulsively but to discuss it first with Thomas.

Edgar got into his old car and drove away with much banging of the exhaust pipe.

Ellie walked home on the sunny side of the road.

TWENTY-ONE

Monday evening

Ellie found Thomas in the garden, attacking some ivy which was threatening to strangle a laburnum tree. His jacket lay on the bench, and on it, fast asleep, lay Midge.

Thomas suspended operations long enough to say, 'A young lad and his mother came for Molly, promising to look after her better in future. She recognized them, went to them without fear.'

'You'll miss her. Shall we get you a cat of your own? A heavyweight monster who can hold his own with Midge?'

He shook his head. 'I like peace and quiet at home.'

Ellie collapsed on to the seat. 'You're right, of course. Thomas, talk to me. Mrs Pryce had the care of her husband's family dumped on her and did pretty well right up to the end when the sky fell on her. Now she's passed the baton on to me. She's given me money and her house to dispose of as I think best, if I continue to look after those she cared for. They're a mixed bunch: a murderer, a junkie who's also a thief, one of our cleaners and several others who contributed to her death.'

He wrenched out a trail of ivy and threw it in the garden refuse bag. 'Ellie, you understand the meaning of stewardship better than anyone I know. Think of the number of worthwhile causes your charity supports.'

'I don't do it by myself; I have Stewart and financial advisers. They really make all the decisions for me. You can't call me a proper business woman.'

'You are the heart of the matter.' He sat down beside her. 'Look at this big house. It's not just so many rooms on so many floors, but a shelter and a home not only for us but for others as well: for Rose and Mia, Frank and Midge – and for me. It's also your office and mine, so we might as well include your secretary and my assistant.'

She looked up at the big house. Three storeys high. They'd never occupied the top floor, and now and again it worried her that the space was unused. Perhaps some time they could convert the top floor into a flat and let it . . . Perhaps have Vera and her son Mikey live there? Vera was struggling to pay the rent. If she had a flat at the top of the house, Ellie could pay her to help look after Rose. They could make a separate outside staircase and include part of the garden . . . It was something to think about. Meanwhile . . .

'Diana. You'll say I ought to forgive her, but I can't because she's not sorry for what she's done. I do faintly begin to understand what's in her mind. It was only a momentary impulse on her part to kill me, but it destroyed something inside me. In the past I hoped she'd change, but now . . . I don't see that happening.

'I've been trying to work out how she got that way. All these years I've blamed my first husband for the way she's turned out. As a child, if she didn't get her own way at once she went on and on until she did get it. I see now we taught her that aggression pays.

'Why did I let him indulge her? Well, I could say that they were both so clever, so *sharp* that I didn't know how to stand up to them. No excuses. Deep down, I knew it was wrong. The truth is, I hadn't the courage to object. So now I have to learn how to deal with the problem which I helped to create.'

Thomas wrenched out the last strand of ivy and threw it aside.

He said, 'Ellie Quicke, I believe in you.'